To Dony

Dejantopian

Blessings

Love

# FOREWORD
## By Wenda Shehata

It isn't easy to survive in a world where human beings refuse to consider the implications their lifestyle has for other species, compounded by the fact that the majority don't even care when they come face to face with the reality of their actions. Arrogant and untouchable!

Our fellow beings, who are supposed to co-exist on this planet, which we are so busy destroying in the name of progress, are being denied not only their right to life, free from fear and suffering, but their natural habitats. Mega-dairies, poultry and pig farms, so huge you could only imagine, no longer the subject of Science Fiction, have become Science Fact and marketed to the gullible masses as the way forward. Farming and Industry further encroach upon increasingly fragile eco-systems, devouring them at the rate Man does flesh; thus a few more species are forced to adapt or become extinct in the wake of our ignorance and greed.

Who are we to think that everything in this world is there for our taking? Isn't the reality of it all that we are at best barely equal to our brothers and sisters in their many forms, (though through our thoughtless, dispassionate actions prove ourselves to be less so); that every life is as valuable as the next, (yet we stand idly by raising not one finger to oppose the pointless slaughter of untold millions of farmed animals, killed to satisfy our addiction to flesh and dairy. Can we not see that as the sun shines and the rain falls to nurture us in our world, it does so in everyone else's? What will it take for us to recognise the fact that their world **is** our world. It cannot be divided. We, as a race, continue to take everything that is theirs and deny the most basic of rights to everything and everyone whom we consider our inferior.

Thankfully, many people are coming to acknowledge the horrors endured in the slaughterhouse; the abuse and suffering caused by animal testing and the cruel torment of animals and birds so callously used in the name of sport or entertainment; those who choose not to be a part of it all. These are the people who speak out on behalf of those who cannot speak for themselves; who stand between the developers and their warped idea of progress through the destruction of our landscapes, regardless of the consequences. Each of them is an example of the power of harmlessness.

> *"Not for any kingdom do I long,*
> *not for the kingdom of heaven,*
> *not even for freedom from the endless*
> *cycle of birth and death;*
> *for one and only one thing do I long –*
> *to free living beings*
> *from their agony and sorrow*
> *and to wipe away their tears."*
>
> Skandapurana 1

Wenda Shehata
Founder,
Hugletts Wood Farm Animal Sanctuary.

# Chapter 1

Daisy perked up considerably when she read the letter headed 'Wholly Cow', "Look at this! He's asking to meet me" she yelled over the whine of the blender as it homogenised the breakfast smoothie.

"Probably only because he thinks you're cute" shot back Brian.

"Hey, if it's going to save lives I'll use whatever assets I've got." Daisy shook back her capacious mane of shiny brown hair. Hair the colour of Christmas pudding: all golden glints, shot through with cherry reds and raisin purples. She never went to a hairdresser and just snipped a few inches from the ends of her hair if it got too straggly. Consequently it flowed right down her back, to well below her waist. She usually kept it off her face or piled up on her head, as it was very annoying to get it caught in doors as she breezed through, always in a hurry. Small in stature but swift of stride, her gait mimicked her thoughts which were forever racing ahead, as if in pursuit of some invisible but tantalising goal.

"Where are you going to see him then? Not at the factory, surely?" Brian quizzically raised his striking black eyebrows.

"No way, I'm not going anywhere near that death camp!" Daisy's brilliant green eyes flashed like emeralds in the morning sunlight.

J.B. Ballard had been a prime target of her activism, and she was intrigued by the short, almost pleading, letter which had arrived so very unexpectedly. Daisy had been an outspoken campaigner since she was a teenager, and had made Ballard's factory farm her special focus. Of all the cruel forms of exploitation perpetrated upon the creatures of the world, she had chosen factory farms to concentrate upon, and the dairy industry in particular. The fact that she had gone to University with Ballard's daughter Clara, had only encouraged her to set her sights upon bringing his empire of bovine enslavement down. In truth it had way too much to do with it, although she did not like to admit to such bias. Daisy and Clara had disliked one another from the very first day, when Clara had pushed in front, with her nose in the air, whilst another girl called Jean had been struggling to propel her wheelchair up the slope into the gymnasium. Clara had made a nasty comment about 'incapables' not being permitted at her old private school. Daisy was outraged, and immediately sprang to the defence not only of Jean, but on behalf of all marginalised people. "Everyone can see what your incapacity is, 'Entitlement Surfeit Disorder'" she said very loudly.

Daisy deliberately turned her back on Clara, addressing herself to Jean "Sheesh! Don't tell me that even here we'll have to deal with deluded snobs and phoney elitists, bigging themselves up........"

Daisy and Jean were firm friends from that day onwards. Not that Jean was in need of friends; she was never short of at least one, and frequently several companions, most of them male, Daisy couldn't help observing. Jean was an example of someone who turned disadvantage into an asset. She always looked happy and smiling, knew how to put people at their ease, and to draw out the best in them. She was training to be a counsellor, and never missed an opportunity to put her psychology into practise. By stark contrast, Clara seemed determined to make Daisy into her enemy. Provoking and goading her at every opportunity, but never willing to listen or debate properly. It was always Clara who scribbled the pathetic comments on any peace posters Daisy pinned to the common room notice board.

She had just posted a campaign to awaken people to the horrors going on in vivisection experiments, many of which were for cosmetics or household products and not even to further medical advances. Not that Daisy approved of the use of sentient animals for any experiments. She felt that the ends could not justify the means, and that positive good could not come from cruel, torturous experiments. Spiritually speaking, she believed that whatever humanity did to those weaker than them, either individually or collectively, came back to them multiplied. Consequently there were no real advances, but an ever deepening degradation of ethics, respect and values, and less chance for peace in the world. Clara, in contrast, seemed to think it was all a joke, and a fine opportunity to get a cheap laugh at the expense of what Daisy held dear. She had deliberately defaced the petition by writing cartoon animal names all over it, like 'Donald Duck' and 'Mickey Mouse'.

Tearing the petition from the wall, Daisy wanted to run away and not come back. Jean was passing by in her motorised wheelchair, and reaching out she touched Daisy comfortingly on the arm. Daisy realised that she had allowed herself to get totally wound up like a spring that was coiled to ping. Her brother used to wind her up like Clara was doing, and then sit back and have a laugh as she fizzled over in self-defeating rage. She had never learned how to avoid the trap with him, even though she saw it coming. She knew that she ought to be able to rise above it. Now here she was recreating it at University, where she had hoped to make a fresh, bright new life. And go on to make life fresher and brighter for all the oppressed human and non-human animals.

"Please come to the cafeteria with me, I don't like going over there by myself" Jean's soft voice reached her. Tearing herself out of the dark cloud which had enveloped her, and trying to repress her irritation at being imposed upon, Daisy forced a smile, saying, "That would be nice, I haven't explored over there myself yet, as I've always got my own food with me."

Well that sounded fake and patronising, darn it! Why couldn't she just be friendly and natural? Why was being around people such an effort for her? Glowering along in a grim fugue behind Jean's wheelchair, Daisy was preoccupied with berating herself for over-reacting, and then for showing her temper. Her usual pattern was to beat herself up in this way, but Jean was humming away as perkily as ever. Must be nice to have such a sunny temperament, Daisy wryly observed. As if it was some inbuilt gift of cheerfulness which she herself clearly lacked.

Jean seemed oblivious to the inner turmoil Daisy was going through. She chatted amiably about this and that, with distracted

Daisy barely managing to make responses. Then something Jean was saying seemed to slice through the fog bank in her head.

"Clara is obviously attention seeking from you, she's clearly not a happy person."

"What? She hates me!" Daisy retorted.

"No, look beyond the acting out, to the yearning she has. Consider it a sort of compliment. She wants something that you have and she lacks, even if she doesn't know what that is."

Shaking her head rapidly, Daisy said, "Isn't she just a bully? And isn't what I represent the opposite of what her influential father stands for?"

"That's not how it appears from here, and trust me - I notice more than people realise from this perspective." Jean had a knowing smile, and Daisy forgot about herself for a minute, to imagine what it might be like to be confined to a wheelchair all the time. Having to look up at everyone, and denied access to so much. It was too horrible to contemplate, she could not go there, and she turned away again involuntarily, and then felt guilty.

"It's OK" Jean had reached over and touched her again, "Everybody reacts like that; people feel sorry for me, then they get scared of being like me, and then turn away. Probably the same thing happens when you are trying to get people to walk in the animals' shoes, so to speak. They daren't allow themselves to identify with suffering, in case it claims them too."

"You're right Jean, I'm so sorry. I want to treat you like everybody else...........I mean." Daisy blushed as she heard how patronising that must sound.

"Don't worry, I'm not like everybody else, and neither are you. For some reason we are different. But different is not bad. I think it's great to be different, don't you? Just be real and honest, be your authentic self."

"I don't even know who I am" protested Daisy.

"Yes, you do, you just feel vulnerable and exposed. So part of you is straining to be out there, interacting and unselfconscious. And the rest of you is pulling back, in fear of rejection. I can see it because I have been forced to get over it myself, in order to have a life, since my accident."

Daisy wanted to be a voice for peace and the planet she loved so much. But nobody welcomed being preached at. Somehow she had to find common ground with people, speaking from her heart to theirs.

"This is going to be so hard" she grumbled, feeling defeated before she even gave herself a chance.

But again Jean swept that negativity away, "No, it's the easiest, most natural thing in the world! We are social creatures, primed to respond to one another. You're going to be a fantastic activist! Just relax and your passion will shine through".

Daisy was awestruck by Jean, and how wise and positive she was. Before she could find the words of gratitude to say, however, another of Jean's admirers had appeared and whisked her away. I probably shouldn't be calling them 'admirers' like that, she mused to herself. But it was striking, the ardent devotion with which they leaned towards her, with so much love and obvious joy to be with her. Nobody comes reaching out to me like that, she reflected.

'Hmm that could be because you don't invite them to', came a Jean-like voice inside her head. What? Oh, maybe she meant the habit she had of sitting apart. She did not really seek company, yet she didn't like feeling excluded either. Sometimes it felt like hitting the accelerator and brake on her life at the same time. Exhausting, frustrating, and counterproductive in equal measures.

Daisy's best friend, Brian, said that bringing something up into conscious awareness was sufficient – becoming aware of patterns and habits was all it took to allow them to release. He would say, "Breathe light into it."

Oh yes, breathe.........who needed to be reminded to do that? Why did she go into that breath holding tension..........no need, just breathe..........Daisy deliberately willed her shoulders to sink down, and away from where they had been magnetised up to her earlobes. Think tall thoughts. She took a long, slow, deep inhalation.

Ah, I remember why I hold my breath; she had a chilling flashback. Being held down, in terror, by doctors removing some silver foil from up her nose. She had struggled and screamed, but been unable to move. Someone was pressing her chest down so hard, and the panic and suffocation had left a lasting reflex action. She could only have been about two years old at the time. This fear had been reinforced by her older brother's taunting and domination over her. He enjoyed pinning her down and controlling her, when no-one was looking. She had learned to be guarded for the next inevitable attack, as a survival strategy. Except it did not stop her being repeatedly crushed, controlled and hurt.

If Brian was correct, then this realisation alone ought to stop the panic attacks she sometimes had.

'Get over yourself, Daze!' She chided herself, using his words and the inflection of his voice. Then she looked around her quickly, in case she had said it out loud, or acted oddly. Why was it that the more she tried to relax and behave naturally, the more self-conscious she became? Nobody else seemed to have these issues, just sitting in a college refectory. Maybe her brother was right, and she was really weird. He said that her obsession with animal rights was a mental disorder.

But she *did* hear their plaintive cries for help – in her head, or in the ether, she was not sure. Not aloud with her own ears - of course not. That really would be crazy. Everyone knew that only mad people heard voices that weren't there. Maybe she felt their fear, then, more than heard them? Her senses seemed to be mingled – like the mixture of smell, touch and taste messages. Most people were visually dominant, but because Daisy was short sighted and hated wearing her glasses, she had learned to rely on something else. Intuition, telepathy, sixth sense, some called it. However it happened, her empathy joined her to the animals suffering, and it became her own. There was no real separation, unless she deliberately distracted herself. Brian tried to tell her that it was projection. He did not mean that animals felt no pain or fear, for clearly they did. Having all the same bodily systems as humans did, sharing the same impulses and needs. In some ways Daisy knew the animals had way keener senses than the blunted, conditioned, shut down people around her.

'I've got to get used to this place' Daisy told herself firmly. The flight impulse was always too ready to kick in. Right here and now, she said to herself, what is going on? Her senses roamed the echoing dining hall where she was sitting. In a corner, as usual. The gunslinger's seat, Brian called it. He said that in the Wild West nobody wanted to sit with their back to the door, in case someone blasted through it with a rain of bullets. OK then, tune out the noise, and ignore the colours and passing forms. Breathe, relax, and simply be present.

Closing her eyes, she sensed a movement of emotions, flowing and swirling about. Some fresh and uplifting: an eruption of laughter over here, a smile of greetings over there. Others lingered stickily, just like the tacky residue from coffee cups and food on the table tops. There was sadness present, and struggle. If she knew how to paint, she could show these as colour and shape, dark and light. If she knew how to compose music, there would be lilting trills and sombre sustained mellow notes, strung together on a background of silence, woven and layered into a symphony. Different ways to encapsulate and express this ordinary moment.

Opening her eyes again, she sneaked her glasses onto her nose. Eugh that was a mistake! Her first impression was of the dangling objects suspended from the ceiling. Pieces of plastic cup and paper napkin, which some over energetic people had managed to launch up there, presumably with chewing gum and spittle. So that was what occasionally plopped down upon unsuspecting diners, was it? The loathsome glasses were swiftly stowed back in her shoulder bag. It annoyed her that so many of the Earth's dwindling resources were carelessly squandered on things like disposable tableware. It would be providing a permanent job for someone to wash up real crockery. She always made a point of carrying her own mug around with her, and presenting it to be filled rather than accepting plastic or polystyrene, which was in truth anything but disposable. It did not break down in landfill sites, it injured wildlife, and clogged up the sea.

She needed to get her brain, not her eyes, focussed, on what she was doing here, didn't she? Otherwise why had she made all the effort to get to University? It was not like she thought it would be. Disappointing, and not any more free than convent school had been. At first the campus had seemed huge and intimidating. But now it seemed to bear down on her. The lofty halls in their bright colours were gaudy and faded. Obviously it must be her, slipping into one of her low moods, and not this place she was in. The short winter days really didn't help. She was a sun lover, at her best during the summer months when her energy kept pace with the daylight. And she was desperately miserable in her relationship. She had jumped at the opportunity to run away from her highly dysfunctional family, and move to Manchester with her boyfriend. But he had changed with the move away from his own abusive family. Where she had dreamed of them finding freedom together, he had become ever more domineering and controlling. He had become very manipulative, and she was trapped. Too afraid to break out, too undeserving to seek help.

Bringing her awareness back into the hall, with its stale food smells and random human traffic, she felt like some sea bird perched on a cliff top, with the noise and clamour of kittiwakes, and the rhythmic murmur of waves on shingle. But at least this inner bird was in its natural environment, perfectly adapted to fit in. A marauding gull was winging into view; she could feel the draught of its wings, and the intention of its homing in on her. Reluctantly opening her eyes, and unblocking her ears, she wondered if other people had these inner fantasy worlds going on all the time, too. And then the sense impressions came to life, as her nemesis Clara plumped her large body down right in front of her, blocking out the light. She was a one woman eclipse, right there. Daisy sighed, and steeled herself for the inevitable attack.

"Bacon, mmmm," Clara said, deliberately wafting her sandwich under Daisy's nose. "Animals were put here for humans to eat, and they wouldn't taste so good if we weren't meant to eat them!"

"Humans are made of meat too, in case you hadn't noticed" shot back Daisy, her stomach lurching at the stench of burnt butt cheeks. "Why don't you eat a cat burger? At least that would be a fair return for all the birds and small creatures they kill – often without being hungry and just for the pleasure of it". Daisy was never short of a swift, sharp retort, even though she realised it brought her down to Clara's level. Sometimes it was simply too tempting to avoid the bait. Of course she did not wish cats, or any creature, ill will. She was merely trying to get Clara to see how speciesist she was, by calling one sort of animal a pet, whilst eating another, equally intelligent and sensitive creature. And Clara bred cats, pedigree ones, so Daisy knew that this was also a way to strike back.

"Did you know that pigs have the intelligence of a 3 year old child?" she asked.

Peals of mocking laughter came back to her, "Pigs are filthy and stupid, you moron! What are you - some pig liberation person now? Come on, they're just ham on legs begging to be turned into bacon. I'm with the bacon liberation front, YUM! haaa haa!"

How could she not react? And what common ground could there possibly be between herself and Clara? Once again, Daisy's blood pressure rose, her cheeks flamed and she wanted to kick herself, or Clara.........oooh where did that come from? She was a pacifist who didn't believe in violence. She knew that aggression never solved anything. Maybe I'm passive aggressive, she thought, whatever that might be.

Having scored her hit of the day, Clara trounced triumphantly away. Leaving her plate, with its smear of congealing white fat, and scent of dead fried pig, behind.

So much deliberate suffering for a mouthful of flesh. Daisy had made herself watch videos of what went on in pig farms. How she wished that everyone who thought it was OK to eat meat, could witness how it got on their plates. She did not hate Clara, or any human; they were merely unaware and conditioned. She pitied them almost as much as she pitied the poor creatures they fed upon. Feasting on trauma, terror and death, deadened people. If they really knew what they were doing, they would surely stop.

Brian had said that the ravages of war, and the torturous means people used on their own kind, hardly supported her optimism. But she believed that, when people cleared the effects of consuming brutal, dead food from their bodies and psyche, they would become gentle beings. Brian said he hoped she was right, but they had a long way to go to get there.

"No, Brian, it could happen in an instant!" and Daisy had snapped her fingers, dramatically. "People just need to wake up, and live with joined up heads and hearts. We all want peace, and we all believe love conquers all, but we're waiting to see it out there first, before we become it, in here." And she had rapped hard and audibly on her chest with her knuckles, as much to remind herself as to reinforce her belief. "'We must be the change we wish to see', Gandhi said. So it must be my fault: I'm not being love and peace strongly enough.........."

"Daisy it's not all about you, there are a few billion other humans creating this world, you know!" Brian had shaken his head, and dragged her out into the garden to enjoy the nature all around them.

Why was everyone always trying to tell her she was doing enough? Of course she wasn't! If there was some way she could instantly transform the world, she would do it. She fantasised about staging her own death, in a slaughterhouse, by taking the place of one of those poor pigs. And being filmed, killed, just as they were, with such callous inhumane violence. But who would slit her throat, who would film it, and who would show the film to the world? She would be locked up as a nutter if she tried to organise it. At other times she had fantasised about slitting her wrists, and allowing her lifeblood to pour out, deliberately, if only this might awaken and heal the world.

"You've got a messiah complex, Daisy. Even Jesus did not manage to change the ways of the world, and He was God come down specially to do that. Now for goodness sake, stop creeping me out and let's go for a bike ride."

And so she had pedalled away her pain. Pedalled away her futile fantasies. Thank God for Brian.

Daisy's best friend Brian always knew how to lift her out of her misery, even though it never completely went away. It would never leave her, because she could always sense the slaughter of millions going on around the world that never stopped. And yet she would not un-know what she was aware of, even if she could. If the animals had no choice in their fate, neither would she choose to block it out. If her own life was to have any purpose at all, it must be to do what she could for them. And speaking out for them, even though it made people uncomfortable, was one way to help them.

Beating alongside her compassionate heart were all the normal desires of a young woman. Of course she longed to have a real, mutual, loving relationship with a man. To be in love, and feel the delight she saw others having in the closeness of each other. How wonderful it would be to have a companion to walk through life with. Someone to share the joys and the sorrows. She was by no means immune to any of these things. And yet there was no way she could even consider being intimate with someone who was not vegan. How could she engage in kissing someone who had death on his lips and rotting corpses in his body? That was the reason she had got into the doomed union with Neil – because he was the first vegetarian she had met, and the first boy who had shown any interest in her. They had got together, and now were stuck.

Neil had entered her life when she was 17 and having an especially traumatic time at home. She had been only too eager to escape from the house and be whisked away on his motorbike to his flat. So many girls at school had boasted about losing their virginity that she had been feeling really ugly, unlovable and unwanted. Neil was 4 years older than her and had a job, and she felt special and privileged to have been noticed and asked out. In actual fact they had never been on a proper date or gone anywhere together. All he wanted to do was get her clothes off and ravish her in as many different ways as he could think up. His imagination was boundless and utterly devoid of shame. Daisy had been compliant and passive, both out of sheer, sickened fascination and fear of being rejected.    The truth was that she had been so starved of affection and physical contact with anyone since her brother had stopped fighting with her, that she was desperate to be touched. And the new, intense, all consuming activity had completely stopped her secret, self-harming habit. Also, Neil's dominant strength gave her the power to survive the horrors of family life. He encouraged her to dream about university, and spoke about them moving away together, far from their small insipid town, to a city with greater prospects and excitements.

The guilt she felt about abandoning her troubled Mother became cancelled out by the optimism of escape, and the hope that her departure would spur some similarly positive life changes back home. And so with all possible speed, she had left home after her last A level exam, and moved into a flat on the outskirts of Manchester, with Neil.

At first it was exhilarating, but Neil could be terrifyingly controlling, and prone to attacks of savage jealousy. Then as she tried to settle into her new life, Neil demanded that she come straight home from University and have his dinner ready. He was traditional like that.

Her new friend Jean would call him chauvinistic. Yet there was a comfort in routines, however much part of her longed to escape them. Her own Father had been a strict disciplinarian, and her Mother had performed the accustomed domestic roles. At least on the surface, whilst loudly raging against the shackles of an unhappy marriage. Daisy had been raised to help with housework, shopping and cooking, whilst her brother was granted total liberty. The injustice of this rankled her, and yet there was a wild part of herself she did not trust. This feral child would have gone dancing away if it could, and probably getting into danger. Perhaps it was safer to put up with the routines and expectations laid down by someone in charge. And so she had talked herself back around into living a miserable lie with Neal.

She comforted herself with the thought that nobody could control her dreams, fantasies and ideals. She clung to these like a talisman, carrying a flame of independence in the recesses of her mind. Hopes of freedom, dreams of an end to persecution. The oppression of nature, and of her own true nature were the same struggle. How could she be free whilst life itself was in chains? How could she allow herself to celebrate the gift of life, when it was stolen away from millions of innocent creatures every day?

# Chapter 2

"Lighten up, it might never happen!" came a cheery voice. Looking up from the cup of green tea she had been gazing into, Daisy smiled at Simon, a red haired lad from her ecology course, as he passed by. But she was wearing her customary mantle, which said 'I'm distracted / don't bother me'. The blanket she wrapped herself up in, which served to keep most people away. How could she 'lighten up' amidst such darkness? How could she allow herself to be happy when so many were subjugated, enslaved and slaughtered? The sheer hidden horror of the scale of it, stupefied her. It was a daily holocaust that nobody wanted to know or care about.

And yet, Daisy realised that if she could not present an image of joy, health and serenity, as the only vegan most people would meet, she would be failing. And she was a joyful soul, inside. Her true nature was playful and happy. There was nearly always a song in her head, and a smile on her lips, eager to share the happiness of the miracle of being alive and awake. Once she got past the sadness of what she knew, she found tremendous joy in the beauty of nature. Maybe she felt a more intensified happiness than normal people, to compensate for what she carried in her heart for the innocent ones? She thought about C.S. Lewis, when he described the intensity of his grief at the thought of losing his wife, Joy, to cancer. He had not realised how much he loved her until that point. He asked her how to cope with the anguish of it, and she had said, "The pain now is part of the joy then, that's the deal". Meaning, Daisy supposed, that if someone was afraid to embrace suffering, they were also denying themselves the heights of ecstasy which balanced this.
It did not matter whose suffering it was: their own or someone close to them, it was the courage to allow themselves to feel it which made them really alive. C.S. Lewis had written one of Daisy's favourite childhood books: "The Lion, The Witch And The

Wardrobe". A book which had brought hope and happiness to generations of children.

Even Jean, so kindly towards others, did not want to hear about what went on in factory farms and slaughterhouses. "It's the way it is Daisy, get used to it, you're not going to change the world. People think it's natural to eat meat, it's traditional, and they have a right to it. They don't like being made to feel guilty".

"But Jean, if they didn't feel at some level it was wrong, they wouldn't feel guilty. If humans were true carnivores we'd be salivating every time we saw a bird fly past. We'd not give cute fluffy animal toys to our children, and hide the truth about the dead ones on their plates. And it's not about habits or personal choice, it's about *informed* choice. I believe most people are basically kind and gentle, and wouldn't want to be supporting a system that causes such cruelty. Even *I* did not know how bad it was, until I made an effort to find out. And now that I know, it's like I can't stop speaking out about it. Its plain wrong, on all levels. It might have served humanity to act like predators for a few thousand years, but now we don't need to, it's time to give it up."

"But people enjoy eating meat. They don't want to give up that pleasure, even if it's damaging their health and the environment, like you say it is."

"It's not only about animals, Jean, the world's deserts are expanding because rain forests are being cut down to make pasture land for beef. And to grow soya and grains for export to feed the billions of factory farmed animals in the west. Meanwhile thousands of people are starving because they aren't allowed to grow food for themselves on their own land."

"We're not bad all the way through – you have to take people as you find them, Dazzle my darling. Activism isn't the be all and end all, you know. It would help you to spend time doing normal things with normal people for a bit. What have you got to lose anyway, not your virginity I'm guessing?"

Daisy's eyes came up to meet Jean's at that remark, and she wryly nodded, but declined to share the all too sordid details of what she endured behind closed doors. Every night and morning. Neil had an insatiable sex drive which he demanded she fulfil.

Jean leaned towards her with a knowing wink, "Hey, even disabled people get laid you know! In fact some guys get turned on by the thought of me not being able to run away – and boy do they get a shock when they realise it's me who's caught them!"

Jean was indeed very pretty, and disarmingly direct. The aura of vulnerability she had, due to being confined to her wheelchair, plus her effervescent personality, meant that she was never short of male company.

"In fact I have the opposite problem, can't get rid of them when they get boring!" she laughed. "I fully intend to play the field and indulge myself as much as I like, and why not? What else are men here for, but to pleasure us goddesses?"

The two women went into fits of giggles at this thought, and the images it conjured in their minds.

Just then, as if on cue, one of Jean's friends came over. He was a pleasant looking young man, with a floppy fringe of blonde hair, and a full beard which he had dyed purple. He was wearing orange bell-bottomed trousers with yellow ducks on them. He looked like a fun person to have around.

"Can I read you two beautiful ladies my latest poem?" he asked, producing a well-thumbed spiral-bound notebook from his jacket pocket.

"Of course, we'd love to hear it wouldn't we Daisy? This is Jasper, by the way."

Jasper smiled and sat down. The poem was rather long, and did not have any rhyme, or detectable rhythm to it. Modern poetry didn't need such contrivances, she supposed. The theme was interesting to her, because it was about rainforests, and had a lot of water imagery in it. And he read it with obvious passion, and clear inflection. The poem ended romantically with the clouds marrying the sea to the sky, in a blur of blue green. She liked it, and said so.

"We were just talking about the rainforests being cut down" Jean remarked.

"Those rainforests create most of the rain which makes the plants grow. And so the crops are failing" Jasper said.

"And the trees hold the water in the land, but when they're gone it floods. The topsoil washes away, and all the grazing cattle damage the fragile soil even more" Daisy added.

"If it's such a huge problem why don't we hear more about it then?" asked Jean.

"Because the massive meat and dairy industries control the governments and the information" Daisy couldn't help interjecting. "They only care about maximising profits, and cheap food."

"That's a valid point actually, I'll work that into my next poem!" Jasper said. "Got a lecture to go to, see you girls later, yea?" And he stood up, inclining his head and shoulders towards them in a bowing motion. Sweeping his notebook back into his pocket with a flourish, he strode away.

"Daisy, it's not that I don't believe you, and I respect you trying to make people change, but that's your thing, you know? The rest of us have our own special interests and causes. I think that with the posters you put up, and the leaflets you hand out, you're doing more than your share. Especially as you're vegan yourself. If we really are evolving as a species, like you say, then we'll get there in our own way." Jean had clearly heard enough dogma for one day.

"Now, why won't you ever come out with me and have a bit of fun? There's a bunch of us going out tonight, some cute guys are going to be there, like Jasper". Jean had clearly picked up on how attracted Daisy was to her flamboyant friend.

"The truth is Jean, I'm not free to go out. I'm living with someone who likes me to stay home with him."

"Oh, why ever didn't you say so before? What's he like? Why've you never mentioned him? Maybe he'd like to come and meet some of your new friends?"

"Er, it's complicated Jean. He's sort of protective."

Meeting Jean's gaze, Daisy swallowed hard, and blurted out, "Well, to be honest he's a bit paranoid and possessive....." She was really squirming now, and wishing she hadn't said anything.

"Oh, Sweetie, I'm so sorry" Jean recognised the symptoms of an oppressed woman when she saw them. "You're afraid of him, and I bet he controls the money too?"

"How did you know? I mean, he doesn't beat me up or anything, he just likes to be in charge. I was so desperate to get away from my parents fighting all the time that I jumped at the chance to leave home and come here. But since we got our own place, Neil has changed."

"Ah, now I see why you look so sad and shut yourself off. Listen, you don't have to tell me anything else if you don't want to. But I can help you to find your own place, I've got loads of contacts."

"I don't have any money – Neil took my student loan cash to buy things for the flat, he just gives me money for the bus every week. It wasn't a calculated thing, I'm sure.... I mean, because we are together I agreed it was a good idea to use the loan money to buy something we both really needed.........and Neil pays all the rent and bills out of his wages. It's not as bad as it sounds."

"Do you love him?" Jean cut in bluntly.

"He's the only boyfriend I've ever had; I suppose I was grateful that someone was interested in me. But when he said I couldn't join the University drama club, I realised he doesn't care about what I want. I went along to their first meeting and they offered me the lead role, but when I told him, he went ballistic. He grabbed the script and when he got to the part where I had to kiss the hero, he forbade me to do it. If he loved me, wouldn't he have been happy for me?"

"And your sex life? Are you allowed to say 'No'?" Jean was relentless at getting to the truth.

Daisy's down-turned face turned puce. Tears appeared at the corners of her eyes, despite her effort to contain them. She could only shake her head. She could not speak of the degrading things she was subjected to, in the name of Neil's explorations.

"Once I stood up to him, but he grabbed me, said I must have been with someone else. In his twisted logic, if I wasn't always available to him, I must be cheating on him. The more I tried to reason with him, and plead my innocence, the more angry he became. I got angry too, and said I didn't care anymore what he thought, that I wanted him to leave me alone, just for one night. That really made him mad; like he was possessed. His whole face changed, into a sneering monster. He threw me across the room, and then he put his hands round my throat and throttled me until I almost passed out. I honestly thought he was going to kill me. When I came round, choking and gasping, he looked really scared, and sad. He said he was sorry, he never meant to hurt me, he loved me; but he had to know I was his. Only his."

"I've heard enough! You've got to leave him Daisy, before he does you serious injury. I'm going to find you somewhere to move to, in secret. Don't worry about the money, we'll work it out. I know you're afraid he'll come after you, but I promise, once you break free, you'll see he has no power over you. You've been allowing this because of your own damaged childhood, Daisy. I'm not saying he's evil either, he's a victim too. But you can't help yourself or him until you get away. Trust me, I know about getting through a catastrophe. And coming out the other side."

And Jean locked eyes with Daisy, touched hearts with her, bringing her into the circle of her protection. Even though she could not put her arms around her, or squeeze her physically, she had immense strength. Daisy felt truly embraced, supported and safe. How did Jean do that? Daisy felt a flutter of inner wings, like a battery cage hen, suddenly released. A sense of being free and wild, optimistic and effervescent with life. Egg laying hens existed in metal slatted boxes stacked high, with no room to open their wings, and no dirt to scratch in. They were under artificial light for long hours to keep them laying, and subjected to enforced moulting by starvation to bring them back into lay. This morning, she had felt as hopelessly trapped as they were. Now, with Jean's help, she did not know how, but she believed she could break free.

In truth, by making that leap of faith and trust, she already was free. Free in her soul. Free like a slave who knows the day of liberty is near. Instead of her accustomed sense of dread, and the silent toleration of her subjugated private life.

"Breaking the conspiracy of silence is the hardest part, believe me, Daisy. I've counselled lots of women and helped them get their lives back. I can see you feel used and degraded, but I promise you'll get over that. Your body is yours! And it is sacred. It doesn't matter what you have gone along with out of fear, you can reclaim your body. You won't go through the rest of your life hating yourself, and blaming yourself. We will have a healing ceremony and re-sacralise your body."

Daisy was gaining strength from every word which Jean spoke. She had never dared to look beyond where she had been pinned before. Like a butterfly impaled on a pin, she had been slowly yielding up her spirit to despair. There was a sense in which she had fallen between the two spears of fear and self-loathing. The threat of pain if she did not do what Neil demanded of her. The warping of her natural desire at the heedless hands of men. She had been squashed into this space, part willingly at first, and then drawn deeper in when it was too late to escape. She had thought it was a route to freedom from repression, in mutual exploration. Neil had told her that her catholic conditioning made sex something sordid and shameful, and that what they were doing together would free her. It had appeared to be a means to break away from the guilt, so why did it sicken her? Perhaps it was too much to ask that the very thing which had stolen away her innocence and blighted her childhood could also transform into the agent of her salvation.

"Jean, how does anyone get into that depraved stuff? How do people find one another? I mean, how did Neil find me and get his hooks into me?"

"It's energy Daisy, we give out invisible signals. And especially if someone has been subjected to abuse by their parents, or authority figures, they believe they must deserve punishment on some level. A part of them seeks to act it out compulsively even when it's no longer happening. Maybe, in a twisted way, *because* it's no longer happening. Like any addiction, part of them craves what it is used to, even whilst the rest of them detests it. That's how come victims can turn into abusers when they get the chance.

In my time in hospitals, I've learned to spot the doctors and nurses who do the job because it gives them power over others. The opportunity to inflict pain, and control. A license to cause suffering under the guise of healing. Nasty stuff. But that's only a few of them. Most of them are really lovely, caring people. When I first realised I was paralysed, I felt so vulnerable and terrified. I was lucky to have great helpers who showed me how strong I am inside, where no-one can reach me. That's why I decided to dedicate my life to helping other people find their secret strength. The fruit of our personal suffering is our gift to others. Like you with your animal liberation. I respect that a lot, even though I can't join you all the way with it."

"Thanks Jean, I know I'm a pain about it, but time is running out. I get a real sense of urgency that seems to grow stronger all the time."

"OK, I think I begin to get it. Just like disability rights and indigenous people's rights, we need to stretch our care to cherish nature, before it's all gone. I've seen programmes about all the species going extinct, it's terrible. I tell you what, I'll help you with your leafleting and you can help me with my disability lobbying, how's that? A problem shared is a problem halved!"

"That's a great idea; we can have a vegan cupcake stall, and get Brian to help us make some banners. Yay!"

# Chapter 3

Fortified by friendship and inspired by being a change maker, Daisy did indeed manage to make her escape from Neil. Even though she had jumped at the chance to leave her parental home, with all of its trauma and dysfunction, it truly had been a leap from frying pan into fire. Now at last she might actually be able to have a life of her own choosing, away from the demands and conflicts of toxic relationships.

Jean had found a shared female house for her to move into. She and the disability transport van driver, Mike, had driven her to see the place, waiting outside. Feeling pathetic, like a child left at the school gates, Daisy had turned her reluctant face towards them at the steps. Inside her a plaintive voice was crying, 'Don't make me do it on my own.'

From the open van window, Mike waved encouragingly. She could not turn around now, which she knew she would have done without support. She would have crept back to the known, to Neil, and resigned herself to her fate.

Walking up the steps of the three storey Edwardian town house, Daisy could not envision herself actually living here. It was in an imposing row of stern fronted houses, and a part of her felt like a servant applying for a job, about to be curtly sent to the tradesman's entrance. 'Lack of deservability', Jean had called it. Because she had not been raised to believe in herself. Because she had been disciplined and silenced, punished and conditioned. Jean told her there was another part of herself waiting to take over, a bit like the hero in the wings, waiting just off stage, ready to leap in on cue. She had in fact been reciting quietly in her head what she was going to say, on the journey there. Affix smile, raise eyebrows animatedly, and go for it. Proper prior preparation, as her old drama teacher had said. It was funny, she had no fear of getting on stage and singing. It seemed like the most natural thing in the world, once she was pushed out there. A bit like swimming, the hardest part was getting wet.

Sooner than she could have dreamed, Daisy was walking back to the van with a little red rent book in her hands. Jean had sent her in prepared with the first month's money, and Mike was going to arrive the next morning, as soon as Neil had gone to work. He brought boxes, and helped her swiftly pack all of her things. Her books, her music, her clothes, her kitchen utensils. There was not really that much. She left behind everything which was a shared possession. She did not want any comeback from Neil, and anyway she was making a fresh start. Let him keep it all. The hardest part had been acting as normal the previous night, with him. Inside she was shaking, yet at the same time elated. This was the last time he would ever touch her again. Tomorrow she would be free. She realised that the whole relationship with him had been false; it had all been an act. Had she used him to escape from her family? No more than he had used her to fuel his own ends. She felt that it would be a long time before she could get involved with anyone else. Not too easily would she fall into another man's clutches.

The further away the van drove, the happier Daisy felt. Lighter and more free with every second, and suffused with energy. Mike kept a respectful silence, allowing her this time and space to herself. After they had carried all of her boxes up the three flights of stairs to her little attic bedroom, he declined a cup of tea, saying he had someone to collect. Leaving everything where it lay, Daisy put her new house key in her pocket and ran down the steep steps from the front door to the pavement. She had noticed a hill nearby with an old cemetery on it, dotted with green grass and trees. Unable to restrain herself, she ran up the hill, her heart uplifted and her heels winged. As if she was in a musical, an appropriate sound track was playing loudly in her head, unbidden and spontaneous. It was the song by "The Who" called 'I'm Free'.

Never in her whole life had she felt so free. Not when she had left home, for that was tinged with sadness. Not on school leaving day, because the future had not yet opened up. Here, now, atop this hill, surrounded by the bodies of those who had succumbed to death, she felt truly free. She got her breath back and sang along at the top of her voice: 'I'm free, I'm free, and freedom tastes of reality'. She could care less if anyone heard her, she had a voice and it had to come out.

She was so full of nervous energy she could not stop to savour the moment, but hurried back down the hill. Skipping between the graves, lightly touching a headstone here, an angel statue there. She sang to the dead people, she sang to the trees, she sang to the sky. She felt as free as a bird released from its cage. An impossibly wide grin stretched her face; her spirit was elated and buoyant as a hot air balloon, skimming the land beneath. Feeling empowered and benevolent, Daisy showered the world with blessings, praying for all beings to be as free as she was. The sun was warm on her shoulders, the ground rose up to support her, and all was well in the world.

Now she felt ready to go back and unpack her things. Everyone was at work, she would have the house to herself, to get used to everything. And no Neil to please, ever again: what bliss.
Approaching the house, Daisy noticed a motorbike parked outside. It looked suspiciously like Neil's. What? How had he known where to find her? In a flash she realised that he must have looked in her handbag and seen the rent book, with the address on it, the night before. What she felt then, surprised her. She did not go into fear, nor turn and run. She had just been more expanded and empowered than ever in her life, and the small complicit Daisy had been absorbed into this newly emerged, bigger Self. Even though one of the things Neil had said to her was 'If I can't have you, nobody else is going to.' Even if he hit her, cut her up, she would not go back, she would rather die. Armed with this resolution, she felt like a ball of determination, and bowled up to the steps.

Neil was slumped, head in hands, by the front door. He was not angry, he was not vengeful, he was sad. He looked like a little lost boy. He did not stand up, but he raised a tearful face and pleaded with her. It was disgusting to see. A small part of her wanted to lash out at him, to tell him that she hated him. But she couldn't do it. Against her better judgement, she felt a pang of pity for him, and said, 'I'm sorry, but I just can't do it anymore. Please leave me in peace. It's not about love, it's about freedom. I don't hate you."

Not expecting a response, she took out her key and let herself into her new home. It was only after she had shut the door behind her that the shakes came. Forcing herself to walk to the kitchen, and mechanically making herself a pot of tea, she could see and feel her hands trembling rapidly.

No turning back, no regrets, no crying. Tiptoeing to the front door, she silently lifted the flap on the letterbox. She needed to know that he had left. It felt like he had, but she needed to know.

His motorbike was gone.

She had done it.

But the elation of the morning had vanished, and the cold reality of her aloneness came to her. For all of his badness, Neil had been a huge source of strength to her as well. She realised that he did love her in his way.

Already, a part of her was missing the warmth, the familiar routines.

What was she going to do?

How was she going to fill the time?

How was she going to get on with her own, separate life?

She had not thought of these things.

She had never been on her own before. She had always had people telling her what to do. Slowly, the expanded Daisy was deflating, like an old birthday balloon. There, in that silent corridor, it felt as if all of the things she had thrown off herself were irretrievably gone.

In her zeal for freedom she had spurned family, past, the known, and such love as had ever come her way.

She was not up to the task of starting all over again.

She did not even know how.

Maybe her ideals of real love were pure fantasy.

An ache, a deep longing, and a terrible loss seemed to fill her being.

Forgetting the joy of running up the hill. Forgetting the reasons she had made a bolt for freedom. Those were the illusions. The truth was she was all alone, in a hostile world, with nothing to look forward to.

Daisy wanted to speak to her Mum. Not that it would help, but at least her Mum would sympathise, because her own life had been lived in despair, really. Depression had led her to drink, and her scarcely concealed misery had been transmitted to Daisy all along. When she had found out that she was pregnant again, when Daisy's older brother Joe was only five months old, she drank a bottle of gin and threw herself off the kitchen table. Clearly it failed to dislodge foetal Daisy, who had clung grimly to the umbilical cord, experiencing the shock waves.

Her mother had felt the need to confide this to her at a fragilely young age. The truth was that both of her parents were incessant smokers, ate nothing much besides meat, white bread, potatoes and cabbage, and white sugary puddings. They were poor, partly because Dad insisted that he needed a car in order to get to work and back, yet earned a mere pittance as a concierge in a large spa hotel. Having escaped from the coal mining roots of his own father, he had an aversion to physical work. Daisy never saw him raise a sweat, and he considered it beneath him to ever get on a bus. Consequently Mum did everything around the house, fighting a lost battle with dust and grubbiness. How she aspired to a big, beautiful home, like the one she had been thrown out of, at the tender age of two. Her birth mother had been abused by her father, run away, found work as a secretary and been offered the chance to remarry. The condition of this arrangement was the swift disposal of the girl child from her first husband.

So she had been dumped like a discarded puppy, at a large country house populated by several other children of questionable parentage. Their shared foster mother was a propertied woman, well respected in the area, with very strict rules, who set the children to hard work on gruel in the Dickensian fashion. She had no husband, and there were no men living there. Stepmama Enid was an uber matriarch, entirely unchallenged, and utterly feared. Daisy's mother had never met her father, and knew nothing about him. Children were not permitted to ask questions in those days. When she grew up, she had married a man 25 years older than her, thinking she would be protected, and have the father figure she had always craved for.

# Chapter 4

Leaving Neil had been a difficult transition for Daisy to make, and she was ever so grateful for Jean's support, without which she would not have found the courage to get away. Jean had asked her to join her team of helpers, who were paid to help her get washed and dressed, prepare food, and see to her laundry and other housework. Not only was it a privilege to be trusted like this, the work was a welcome distraction from the rawness of her feelings. Daisy felt like part of a team for the first time in her life. It was not easy or all fun of course, but it was deeply rewarding.

Unfortunately her new home left a lot to be desired. The other girls she found herself living with were presenting a few problems. Despite her polite explanation of her vegan lifestyle, and her request for them to only cook vegetables in her equipment, she had found her pots and pans left around, caked with animal fat. The kitchen stank disgustingly from the accumulated clutter, take-away cartons, and rotting meat and fish residue. Despite her valiant, lengthy clean-up operations, it was back to being filthy again within hours. It was way worse than the unpleasantness of having to clean up the greasy meat pans she remembered as a child. At least the clinging chunks of animal fat, and shards of splintered bone had not been decomposing and rancid, like they were here. And why was she bothering, when the five other members of the household clearly had no intention of following her lead? There was obviously no way her example was going to shame them into doing any cleaning. She felt like a skivvy, and realised that, far from inspiring them to keep their shared home pleasant, she was an object of derision to them. Her habit of scurrying out of sight before they came home did not help, but she avoided open conflict this way. Just as with her diet, she was completely outnumbered and outvoted. Eventually she gave up the unequal struggle, and took to eating out of packets in her little attic bedroom.

The living room was little better than the kitchen, carpeted by crumbs, discarded clothes and indecipherable detritus. A kitten had been added to the melee', which nobody had bothered to house train. Consequently, it left piles of its mess everywhere, which none of the girls accepted responsibility to clear up. It did at least appear to be fed, judging from the revolting pink stuff on a saucer which Daisy had inadvertently sent spinning and spilling across the kitchen floor. Filthy offal, rendered down remnants and pieces of dead creature declared unfit for human consumption. Yum. As if any dead creature was fit to be eaten, or deserving of having been killed in the first place. For what crime had they been beheaded? Thousands and thousands of them, electric prodded through slaughterhouses the world over, an endless parade of dismal death. Born into inescapable slavery, their babies torn from them, never to know kindness or respect from their inhumane captors, and the date of their deaths already predetermined. What planet had she landed on?

The bathroom was truly vile: a mess of tampons and clogged hair, dripped dye, and extruded epilation cream. Open bottles of every conceivable unguent were crammed on the shelves, and spilled over into the shower. There was all manner of gunk, crud, and detritus mashed into the floor, which might have been washable were it not for the fuzzy felt covering which carpeted it. She hated going in there, but stoically took her daily bath by candlelight, deliberately removing her glasses before entering.

Three weeks after she had moved in, Sadie, the nicest of the household girls, knocked on her door one evening. To tell her that another girl, named Britony, had contracted scabies, which was highly contagious. The doctor had said everyone in the house must be treated against it. No way was Daisy going to rub chemical insecticides into her skin, but she did bleach the bath out each time, before she dared to use it. Just as was her habit in public toilets, she never sat on this one anyway, having learned to hover above it. She used her bathwater to squeeze out her underwear in, after she had washed herself, and draped them over the chair in her room to dry. She had long been reduced to eating wheat germ out of the packet on a spoon, and cold baked beans out of the can, in her room. Like a squirrel, she had stashes of nuts and seeds under her bed. This reminded her uncomfortably of the time she had first gone vegan, whist living at home. Her Mother had told her in no uncertain terms that she was not allowed to make special food in 'her' kitchen. And so, during the years before she could leave home, she had subsisted on the boiled vegetables from family dinners, and canned beans. She kept a packet of wheat germ in her wardrobe and filled up on that, as it was 25% protein, and cheap. Because the family home was filled with lodgers, and there was just one bathroom, she had only been allowed to have a bath once a week, of a maximum 6 inches depth. Now here she was again, living under similarly extreme duress and restrictions.

She had found herself a Saturday job on a fruit and vegetable market stall, which helped a lot with her basic food needs. But she was using up her income on train fares to visit Brian in Sheffield more often. His household was far from pristine, but they did at least try to adhere to a few fundamental hygiene rules. He shared a big house on the outskirts of the city with four other students, whose untidiness and noisiness was somehow endearing. She was more than welcomed because she happily spent hours in the kitchen making tasty food for everyone. They loved her assortment of nut roasts, bean burgers and curried lentils. And the dips and sauces she created to accompany them. It pleased her to see them enjoying cruelty free food, even though she realised that only Brian was actually vegetarian. Every meal counts, she thought to herself, imagining that each dinner she made represented a saved life. She must have faith that someday these ordinary people would realise the unkindness of their meat eating habits. Every single creature was as individual as they were, and each desired to live as much as they themselves did. Daisy did not want to see bigger cages or better welfare introduced. These merely assuaged the consciences of consumers, and in fact encouraged them to support the death industries even more. If people could be duped into believing that meat was humanely produced, they would not move away from buying it. How could that save lives, bring about liberty, and clean up the pollution caused by the billions of eating, burping, defecating creatures raised and murdered every year?

Daisy did not want to confide in Jean about how the shared house arrangement was working out, for fear of being thought ungrateful. It was not long, however, before Jean noticed how miserable she looked, and made her talk about it. She had been imagining that Daisy just needed a new boyfriend to make her happy. Then she heard the catalogue of woes, including lights, TV and equipment permanently left turned on, and the heating turned up to a ridiculously high temperature. "But you have to pay a sixth of all those bills Daisy, even though you're not using things! And you don't even have heat in your attic bedroom? That's crazy – we'll have to find you somewhere else. Obviously I've never seen what it's like inside the house, because of all the steps."

"I know that Jean, and I'm sorry to moan about them. Aren't they friends of yours?"

"No, I just asked around for anyone with a spare room, and someone told me about their card in a newsagent's window. So I rang the number and got the address for you."

"Oh, I see. Well you'd never know to look at them, what filth they live in. They spend so much time primping themselves. They leave the house every day looking immaculately dressed and made up".

"Didn't you notice how grotty it was when you went to look round?"

"Yes, but I was so desperate to get away from Neil, and I sort of thought that I must have gone on the day before they did their weekly clean up, or something. And with it being in the middle of term I knew it would be almost impossible to find another shared female house. They're not actually students either; they work in an office somewhere".

Now that she realised the situation, being ever resourceful, and with abundant contacts, Jean wasted no time. She soon found another house, where one of the five students had dropped out of University and gone away. This left the other four struggling to cover all the rent and bills, so they were eager to let her have the vacant room. They even offered her a reduced rent because the spare room was the smallest, whereas the girls where she had been living had charged her more than they were paying. Even though her room had been a tiny, windowless attic, at the top of the house. It had only a dirty skylight in the ceiling, and there was no radiator up there. She found out what the actual rent was when she saw the rent book, which had been left in the living room, one morning as she was trying to tidy up.

The bad news was that three out of the four students in the new house were male. Daisy was afraid to share living space with men; but Jean actually knew one of them. She vouched for him, and so Daisy decided it might not be worse than where she currently was. Once again, Mike the disabled transport van driver came to her aid, and in no time she was settling in happily. Indeed it had proved to be a good decision, and overall a positive one. There would always be compromises and allowances to be made, of course, in any mixed, shared household. But these proved to be more 'character forming', as her Mother would say, rather than personality destroying.

Her new room was in the middle of the house, next to the bathroom, and she had to get used to the masculine smells, noises, humour and habits. The house was quite untidy, chaotic and dirty, but she soon managed to exert at least a modicum of cleanliness and order into it. She did not mind doing more housework than the rest of them put together. She had grown up in a large house full of lodgers, and was accustomed to helping her Mother stay on top of the chores. In fact, although she would never admit it, she was enjoying being the maternal figure of the house. Becky, the other girl, was an easy going person, but she refused to do more housework than the men did.

Everyone had sat down and talked about their personal preferences and tolerances, so that they could get along better. Daisy told them how important it was to her to have a hot bath just before she went to bed every night, but that she was very flexible on kitchen time. Jason, who had the big front room downstairs, said what was most important to him was not always being the one expected to get up and let in anyone who arrived home really late minus their keys. Apparently this was an all too frequent occurrence. Daisy said that didn't bother her at all, she slept very lightly, and rarely went out at night. She gave the others permission to tap on her window, which was at the back of the house. They used a long stick, kept in the garden especially for this purpose. Far from feeling imposed upon, playing the gate keeper in fact gave her a sense of being a worthwhile and inclusive member of the household. She was not able to join them in getting drunk, eating takeaway pizza, or talking about sport. So this, plus making vegan dinners for them quite often, was her way of fitting in. It was all working out peacefully and amicably.

University life continued much the same, including the frequent barrage of jibes and vegan-bashing she had to endure from Clara the carnist. The latest dig in the ribs from her came when Daisy was explaining to Philippa, another student, how illogical it was for humans to be drinking the milk of another species. Milk designed to build a 50lb new-born calf into a 2000lb bull within twelve months. She pointed out the truth that amongst the hundreds of varieties of milk-producing creatures, none continued to drink milk into adulthood, and none drank the milk of another species. Just as Philippa was nodding her head in thoughtful agreement, Clara leaned over and said, "How ridiculous! That's like saying blueberries are only meant for the birds to eat. Face it, we're clever enough to work out a way to get great nutrition, whilst looking after the herds at the same time."

Feeling her cheeks flaming, Daisy retorted, "That would explain why those countries with the highest dairy consumption also suffer from the most osteoporosis and heart disease then, wouldn't it! Not to mention the fate of all the boy calves shot at birth since they can't produce milk. Or their grieving mothers forced to produce 7 times the quantity of milk that one calf would need, until they collapse. And being mechanically raped every year to have a new calf and keep the lactation from drying up."

Either because she wanted to avoid getting into a conflict situation, or because she had no time left to listen, Philippa excused herself and hurried away.

"If you knew what a pain in the arse you are, and how people run away when you show up, you'd wish *you* had a cage to go and hide in." Clara sneered.

"The truth is never welcomed by those who are afraid of it. You'd probably have said the same thing a hundred years ago to people speaking out about human slavery, too. And what about rights for women, or child labour, or sex slavery?" Daisy winged back in response. This time it was she who got up and walked away from Clara.

But Clara's spiteful words had hit home. Did people hate her? Was her activism putting off more people than it reached? Swamped by self-doubt, she felt a headache coming on. As if it wasn't enough being a struggling student, recently escaped from an abusive relationship, doing an unfulfilling course. She had to add to her pile of woes by taking on the whole carnist world. Not for the first time, she asked herself why she couldn't just allow herself to be. Be what? No, not 'be' anything, just let yourself be. Brian tried to get her to meditate with him, and it really did help, for the few seconds she managed to slip in between the thought towers in her head. But there was always this pesky guilt which buzzed about like a mosquito. She should be helping the suffering. She ought to be defending the innocent. It gave her no rest. She was driven mad, living in a cruel and crazy carnival of carnivores.

Rushing outside, Daisy flung off her coat and dropped her bag where they fell, and sprinted to the river. Let someone steal her stuff, let someone take her life, right now she didn't care. In fact they might be doing her a favour if they turned her upside down and shook everything out. Then perhaps she could start again, from nothing.

As she ran, she thought about the lives of destitute people in third world countries. Maybe if your whole existence was compressed to the daily task of finding enough to eat, the mountain of other people's problems might look smaller? Or if you were a bag lady on the street, shuffling between the soup kitchen and your cardboard box under a bridge, would you have time to care about other things? Hmmm, what if the day stretched interminably and all you *did* have was time to think about all the dreadful stuff? At least Daisy got some respite from her compulsive thoughts when she was in a lecture, or writing an essay, weighing out potatoes, or counting out change. Was this as good as it got? Counting the ways her life might be worse? Just getting by?

What had happened to the golden opportunities she had envisaged for herself, whilst hunched over the kitchen table doing hours of stupid homework when she was young? Did that mean she was not young anymore? For sure she felt old, tired and disillusioned. But hey, at least she had legs and could run! She pushed herself to run even faster, until her temples pounded, and she felt the taste of blood in the back of her throat.

Seriously out of breath beside the flowing river, she sat down. Although her legs were quivering and she could hear her heart thumping, she felt a lot better. Running was definitely a good outlet when she got really stressed. Perhaps she should start jogging seriously. She had noticed several regular runners on the campus, but she was not fit enough to keep up with them. Maybe if she practised, built up her stamina, she might even get good enough to run for charity. Suddenly remembering her things so carelessly discarded, she reluctantly hauled herself to her feet and walked back to retrieve them. The loneliness of the long distance runner suddenly had a romantic appeal to her, and she resolved to begin training.

# Chapter 5

"Jean, don't you ever get sick of your course?" Daisy said in an exasperated voice, sitting down with her lunch box next to her friend.

No, I'm grateful every day to be here, but then I remember how depressed I used to get when I was younger. Maybe I feel I'm on borrowed time, so every day is precious. When you've nearly died, it makes you value more what you have left. Have you thought about changing courses if you think yours isn't right for you?"

"No, it's probably just me being miserable. I had a Clara clash earlier, and got wound up. Then I ran to the river and said a prayer of thanks for having legs to run on. You must see the rest of us as pretty selfish, ungrateful sods."

"Being able to step outside of ourselves, and put our own issues in perspective, isn't easy. It does help to have big, grand ideals, like you do. I can't imagine you without your banners and your causes, Daisy! You must never let Clara put you down. Use her pokes as fuel to burn even brighter!" Jean mimed herself poking a fire, blowing on it and then sitting back to warm herself with a satisfied sigh. It was amazing how expressive she could be with what tiny movements she was able to make with her body.

"You know what Jean, you have more life in your little finger than most people have in their whole bodies."

"All of my closest friends tell me that actually" Jean said, with a suggestive wink. "It's not what you've got but how you use it that matters".

They both laughed at the images that conjured up.

"Seriously, be glad that you have a visible enemy to grapple with. Our real battles are inside us".

"I suppose Clara's in my face to keep me motivated and to help me overcome my fears of speaking out.... I just wish she'd give me a break once in a while" Daisy remarked with a rueful smile.

"It's probably mutual, Daisy – I mean you are against everything she says she stands for."

"That's not the way I see it; I'm *for* the animals, I'm *for* equality, and *for* peace. That doesn't have to make me 'anti' anything, does it? I mean, I don't go on anti-war marches, or anti-government campaigns. It seems much more important to be positively, pro-actively, FOR something good."

"You can't have one without the other Daisy – it's the way reality works – polarities are what hold this 3D world in place......."

"Some say we're going to move into a 5th dimensional realm, which means we'll transcend the dualism. No more duelling: swords into ploughshares: forks over knives – yay!! Bring it on!" Daisy was visibly warming to her passionate vision.

"Ah" Jean continued, responding to her theme, "That reminds me of the Buddhist teaching, where it explains that any system of thought and knowledge, regardless of whether it's scientific or religious or political, traps you in the conceptual dream state. 'Mesmerised by the shadow puppets of the mind'."

"Oh Brian talks about that; how all boxes of conceptualisation are, in truth, prisons. Yeah, sometimes I do manage in meditation to escape for a blissful while from the endless, monkey mind chattering. Then, inevitably, the twin pulls of attraction and aversion drag me back to separation from the whole. I wake up, and there's the endless struggle of oppression, everywhere around me, again".

"Sweetie, I can't subscribe to that view of life! For me the most important thing is to live as deeply and fully as I can in each moment, without being bound by my past, or worrying about the future. How else do you think I could have survived the loss of my freedom to walk or run? If I focussed on what I couldn't do, on my limitations, I'd be a really miserable person. But I have a wonderful life, in all departments" and here Jean winked suggestively again, "Got to get my aerobic workout somehow!"

"Oh how I wish I could be as light and buoyant as you are Jean! But we're each the product of our experiences, I guess.
I am just really glad to have met you, and very grateful for your friendship, I can't tell you.........."

"No, I'm no more special than anyone else here, we're each unique and beautiful. Perhaps if you decide only to see the point of compassion and love in everyone you see, you'll get along easier."

"You know Jean, I really do try. My Dad says 'love the sinner and loathe the sin.' He's a devout Christian and he says we have to see the spark of Jesus that is in everyone, just waiting to be noticed."

Yes, that was it: address the Divine in them, and expect that it will respond. Daisy began musing upon the good things about her family, now that she had put some much needed space between herself and them. She made up her mind to approach everybody as merely a pre-vegan person who hadn't woken up yet.

"What's that you're eating today Daisy? You certainly come up with some interesting looking things to eat."

"It's flax, hemp and chia seed crackers with sprouted lentil and walnut pate; I'm trying out some raw food recipes at the moment. Here, have some." Daisy took a piece of crispy lettuce, put a spoonful of pate in it, and rolled it up.

"Hah what a neat idea, like a wrap! Wow that's really tasty Daisy, has it got something spicy in it?"

"Yes, I like cayenne pepper at the moment, and I mashed a few olives into it as well. You can pretty much put what you fancy in and it comes out nice, as long as you have a mixture of salty, sweet and sour ingredients, they somehow blend" Daisy was explaining.

"Appearances are important too, so when you first showed me your lunch it looked a bit boring. Perhaps if you added some red tomatoes and yellow peppers it would brighten it up?" Jean suggested.

"I do decorate food more when other people are going to eat it, but for myself I usually can't be bothered" Daisy admitted.

"The way we appear to others matters too, and if you don't mind me saying so, the way you dress doesn't help." Was Jean saying something a bit personal here? How funny, that they had been talking about really deep stuff, but the minute she was brought back to the presence of her body........ sitting opposite Jean's, it made her very self-conscious again. Glancing down at her clothes, Daisy tried to see herself as a stranger might view her: first impressions, and all that. She was in the habit of choosing baggy, long clothes that concealed her shape. "I have issues with being looked at. By men...." she replied quietly.

"That's OK Angel, we all have issues of one kind or another. Sorry I said anything, you wear what you feel comfortable in. It's not easy facing the world some days is it?" Jean's warm understanding smile was so very healing to receive, it was like a sunbeam shining out from her loving heart straight into yours, thought Daisy.

Wow what an awesome counsellor Jean already was! Imagining the countless people whose crippled emotional lives Jean would touch and transform, made Daisy feel intensely humbled. For a moment it helped her to put her own life path into perspective. It wasn't all down to her to save all the animals, to rescue the struggling environment, to feed the starving. She wasn't all alone holding back the floods. And she wasn't the only one who cared and wanted to make a change. Brian had told her more than once that she had a messiah complex. And a chip on her shoulder, whatever that was supposed to mean. It was a sign that friends cared when they made constructive comments, and encouraged you, wasn't it.

Just then, Jean was scooped up into the loving embrace of one of her many admiring suitors. Daisy observed that merely to be in her presence, was like a delightful spa bath of whirling pleasure. Those who drew close to her were captivated by her radiantly infectious joy. She turned and blew a kiss as she was whisked away, and Daisy caught and held it in her outstretched palm for a moment. Then the words of one of her favourite poems, by William Blake, came to her:

'To grasp unto oneself a joy
doth the winged life destroy,
but to touch the joy as it flies,
is to live in eternity's sunrise.'

She quickly opened her hand, releasing the kiss. Freeing it to alight upon some other nearby needy brow. Ah, how beautiful, and so true. To live in the moment fully, and stop dragging the past along behind. To be fully present, and not distracted, or worrying about things which might never happen. Easier said than done of course, but so very good to be reminded of it. She had to make an extra effort to find things to like about people, discover places where they had things in common. Seek points of communal care, rather than focussing on criticising their lack of compassion. Daisy had to remember, that before she had her own realisation and stopped eating meat, she too had been an unwitting consumer of violent death. She remembered how painful it had been for her, how agonising it in truth still was, to be so open and empathic towards the animals plight. She really wouldn't be doing the best she could to help them by being miserable. She resolved to try and emulate Jean's good example, and be the joyful spirit which called forth the same in others.

Daisy shuddered to think that people might actually avoid her because she laid a guilt trip on them. How could she turn that around? Trying to save lives, and plead for mercy on behalf of voiceless victims wasn't easy to make into a joyful activity. But she had to find a way to redouble her determination to 'be the change she wanted to see', as Gandhi had said.

Back at home she laid out her clothes, and saw how drab and sad they must look, even though she felt comfortable in them. How could she brighten them up? She had no spare money, like almost all students, so she would have to be creative with colour. She was already in the habit of visiting charity shops to look for sensible, cosy clothes. She could still have practical, comfortable things to wear, she just needed to dress them up a bit. Scarves, that might do the trick.

The next day she asked Jean to help her revamp her wardrobe. Jean was only too happy to spend a morning with her, going round the charity shops in town. In search of bright colours and bold patterns, interesting fabrics and adaptable shapes. It was a lot of fun, too. Daisy was not in the habit of focussing on her outward appearance, or spending time over getting dressed. But with Jean's perceptive eye, and way with artfully combining and layering items, she soon had a transformed wardrobe at very little cost. Jean had contributed a large bag full of her own discarded clothes, and told her how to cut and stitch things cleverly to make fresh new outfits. Daisy tried to protest that she could not sew, but Jean would have none of her excuses, "Look, if you can thread a needle, and pin two pieces of material together, all you have to do is weave the cotton in and out. Using as tiny a stitch as you can manage, in as straight a line as possible, and that is it! It doesn't have to last forever, in fact it would make it easier to alter when you feel like it if it isn't too tightly sewn together. And while you're at it, you could really wake your face up with a little bit of make-up, you know."

Oh what, was there no end to Jean's designs on her? Daisy did not wear make-up. It was part of not wanting to draw attention to herself, she supposed.

"It's about accentuating your assets!" Jean reminded her of how pale and recessive her own features looked when her make-up came off. It really did make a difference, didn't it? Jean was blessed with naturally delicate features, so it did not take much to make the most of them. Just a bit of colour in her cheeks, some mascara to bring out her warm brown eyes, a hint of eye shadow, and some bright, glossy lipstick.

"You have a lovely symmetrical face Daisy, and no bad features to hide at all, you're actually very lucky if you did but realise it."

So, to humour Jean, Daisy obediently let herself be talked through the actions of applying some make-up. Even though she knew she would never get around to doing it herself. It looked false, like the models in the magazines she refused to buy. She wanted to stay natural, she wanted to accept herself as she was. She strove to be authentic and real, not to hide behind some mask. If truth be told, the only way she could bear to look at herself in the mirror whilst putting on the make-up was to imagine she was someone else. Reading her mind, Jean began talking about mirror work, as a therapy. The more embarrassing it felt to gaze at your reflection, whilst telling yourself how much you loved yourself, the more important it was to do it.

"It will feel ridiculous and you won't believe it, but just force yourself to meet your own gaze, and keep saying nice things about yourself. Trust me, it gets easier. One therapist made me do it after my accident, and eventually I felt the difference that positive affirmations makes. After all, if we don't think we're worth it, who else will?"

It was only because she cared so much for her friend that Daisy was tolerating all of this. In truth she found it excruciating, and intrusive, and she couldn't wait to get away. Squirming uncomfortably and grumbling away to herself, suddenly she was taken aback.

"Oh!" When she stopped criticising for a second to actually look into the mirror in front of her, Daisy had to admit she was impressed. And secretly pleased with how she had managed to make herself look. For Daisy was like any other young woman. She wanted to be told she was beautiful, loved and important.

Jean explained to her that she did not wear make-up for her own benefit.

"After all I'm not the one who has to look at me all day, am I?" she reasoned. No, she put make-up on in order to beautify what others looked upon when they saw her. There was a difference between covering up perceived personal flaws, and accentuating one's natural attributes. Daisy decided that if the cosmetics were cruelty free, it might be confidence building. Just a little, once in a while, used discreetly.

In truth it had been Neil her ex-boyfriend who had forbidden her to wear any make-up. So maybe she ought to use some to show that she was a free woman now. Even though it would take more than escaping from Neil, and a bit of make-up, to make her feel genuinely free.

"We're all a work in progress, Daisy Dreamboat!" Jean spread her fingers out and made as large a sweeping gesture as her disabled hands allowed her.

"Life is what happens whilst we're busy making other plans!" quipped Daisy as she smiled across the ever diminishing gap between them.

True to her word, Jean had been doing a lot to help Daisy to heal her damaged self-image. They had done a powerful cleansing and re-sacralising ceremony together. Using incense and crystals to focus their intention, they had made an altar on the coffee table. Daisy sprinkled herself with some Holy Water which her aunt Patricia had brought back from Lourdes. Jean led her through some positive affirmations, about her body being a sacred temple, and surrounded by angelic protection. Following this, Daisy really did feel clean and pure. Perhaps, now that she had reclaimed her body, she could come to love herself.

Afterwards they had a meal of root vegetables stewed in coconut milk and turmeric, with red rice and saffron, and some steamed broccoli. Then they had cashew and raspberry cheesecake, which Jean was ecstatic about. Daisy beamed with pleasure, as it had turned out exceptionally well. Some favourite foods were difficult to duplicate without animal ingredients, but she enjoyed the challenge of trying different things to achieve the same texture and flavour. She had learned that flax and chia seeds, when mixed with water, swelled up to produce a glutinous mixture which had a similar binding texture as eggs in cakes. And they were very high in the essential Omega 3 fatty acids, with none of the mercury with which fish was contaminated.

Being replete and relaxed, she felt ready to tell Jean about the traumatic events of her early childhood. The things which had caused her to feel so very self-conscious, and to hate being looked at by men. Things she had never told anyone else about, ever. The words would not come out, though. It was as if her tongue had a knot of silence tied in it. Jean asked her to write it down, as if she was telling a story about someone else. This was a technique to allow sufficient distance from the shock and fear, and begin to release the locked down stasis. She instructed her to write it in the present tense, and went to fetch some paper and a pen.

Daisy sneaked her glasses out and looked around her, in an effort to distract herself from the confrontation she had been dreading and postponing for so long.

Jean's flat was lovely. There were enormous orange flowers painted onto the living room walls, on a bluey-green background. Surprisingly it looked both spacious and jungley at the same time. Jean's artist friend Derik had clearly been busy and bold, with shapes and colours. There were bright yellow blinds at the window, which Jean could operate herself. The whole place was adapted to make it easier for her wheelchair to get everywhere, and a hoist for her carers to help her in and out of the bath, and her bed. The carers came three times a day, and the disability van man, Mike, took her and her motorised wheelchair wherever she needed to go.

When Jean came back, she asked if Daisy would mind helping her empty her catheter bag, which had got a bit full. It was a very simple task, yet rather intimate. The urine bag was strapped to Jean's lower leg, and there was a velcro strap which needed to be undone, then the bag could be lifted up to the toilet, and the valve at the end of it twisted to allow the contents to flow out. Whilst Daisy was busy about this, Jean chatted on as easily as anything, which made Daisy feel relaxed about it too. The urine smelt highly concentrated and acrid, but it did not bother Daisy, who had grown up cleaning out horse stalls and rabbit cages. In fact, this simple but essential activity strengthened the bond of trust between the two women. Daisy felt privileged to be considered part of Jean's extended family of caring people. Replacing the velcro strap, and rolling Jean's trouser leg back down over the bag, she felt calmer than before.

She can do this writing. She needs to do this writing. It is time for the story to be told.

Jean is reading a book, she is comfortable, and nobody will disturb them for the next hour. Sitting very quietly in the corner of Jean's flat, Daisy picks up the biro, and starts to write.

## Chapter 6

We are watching Daisy, aged 4, with her brother Joe and neighbouring friend Kevin, both aged 5. They are playing cowboys and Indians. Daisy is a squaw, sitting in the metal cone climbing frame. In the school playground, which is close to their house.

Joe says, "We need a blanket to make it a tepee."

Daisy says, "I'm staying here to make the dinner."

"I'm going to ask Mummy for a blanket" says Joe.

Kevin goes off with Joe to fetch the blanket.

Daisy is singing, as she usually is; a magical, wonder-filled, beautiful child. Only she doesn't know that. She just is. Who and what she is are impressions being graven into her with every experience. She is already conditioned by her parents in the ways they absorbed and emulated from their parents. There is precious little space for reflection, unless they can be brought to realise that everything is a reflection.

A moped drives into the playground. Daisy looks up. The moped stops and a man gets off. He glances around, then looks at her and says, "Are you all alone?"

"I'm making food for my brother, he's getting a blanket."

Daisy is shy, unused to strangers, but has been taught to speak when she is spoken to.

"Do you want to play with me?" the man asks.

Without waiting for a response, he reaches for her hand, and leads her to the corner of the playground, into the toilets. He kneels down, letting go of her hand. Before she has time to wonder what the game is they are going to play, a huge willy is pushed into her face. In that fraction of a second her mind, her vision and her senses are all filled with this startling image. Every blue vein, the tight, shiny pink cap, the yellowing curled under bit behind that, the hardness, and the smell of it.

Shock! Indelible. An image that will never leave her. Branded to the back of her eyeball.

But it is not to be the last thing she ever sees. An invisible lady's voice tells her "Run, Dear Heart, RUN!"

And before she can think about sending the message to her legs, they are already pumping. Pumping, faster than she has ever run, faster than any gazelle escaping a lion. There is only the running, the primal instinct........run for home! Run to Mummy! Run to safety! Run for your life! Run, run RUN!

For the rest of her life, Daisy's default setting is 'RUN'

Run, and never look back.

By the time she has crossed the playground, rounded the corner of the school, and is racing for home, where she sees her Mother in the garden, a scream has started. A terrible, terrified, piercingly high scream. It finds its way up and out of her, renting the air with its expression of horror. A scream of impossible, air searing, ear shattering fear. With eyes as big as mill wheels Daisy is screaming and approaching, fleeing and reaching, escaping and imploring. Her twin goals being to get away from the man and to get back to her Mother. These strain in opposite directions, and in between is a small, impossibly stretched, out of breath child. Somehow the child cries out, with her last gasp "Mummy" as she falls into the outstretched arms.

SLAP! Her Mother hits her, hard, across the face, grabs her roughly by her shoulders, shaking her, "What, WHAT? Stop screaming and tell me!" She yells into her face. She is horrified and must break Daisy's hysteria to find out what is wrong.

Daisy is dazed, spent, and utterly exhausted. Her world demolished right then and there by her Mother's physical, mental, verbal and emotional blows. She chokes on her sobs, clamps down her eyes, and quivers. This is not a safe place to be, either. Where can I go and hide? I am dying....there is nowhere..........and Daisy is back in the hospital, being held down by countless heavy hands, her head locked back and pressed down. She cannot breathe, she must be dying........terror overcomes her and she ceases the pointless struggle, turns limp and rigid all at once, whilst the doctor inserts forceps up her nose, pushes them up, and removes the "shiny." Then they release her, give her back to her Mother, where she clings and cries and trembles. She is 2 years old, and her brother has pushed some silver chocolate wrapper up her nose.

Shaken roughly some more, Daisy is brought back into the garden, trying to tell her Mummy about the man, the willy, the willyman...........

It only gets worse from there on. Mummy panicking, and neighbours appearing, and the police are coming.

"Daisy you have to tell the policemen everything that happened".

Daisy is afraid.

The police only come when you've done something really bad, she knows that.

So she has done something very bad.

Daisy is embarrassed. She knows that 'willy' is not the right word, but she does not know the right word to use. She asks her Mother, "Mummy, why was it not like Joe's willy? Why was it all big and hard and........"

"It was not a real one Daisy, it was a plastic one."

Oh.

 It was a plastic one?

 It wasn't a real one?

 Oh, then it *was* just a game..........

Except why are the police coming if it was only playing?

 She does not understand, cannot understand.

 She finds Joe, she tells him she is going to hide, and not to tell. Somehow she manages to climb onto the roof of the shed, and clings to the ivy. Her ears are both straining to detect any sound and shooshing deafeningly with the sound of her racing heart. There is a pit of dread opening up as if she is stuck in a bog and being sucked down, down, down into pitchy blackness. Her mind cannot grasp onto anything and her hands are clamped tightly to the top of her head. If only she could disappear, become invisible, or fly away like Mister Stamford's pigeons next door.

Scarcely breathing, she hides.

Flattening herself as tightly as possible against the scratchy roofing felt.

Joe tells.

The police come.

They find her.

There are three of them, and they are all men. In dark navy blue uniforms and shiny, heavy, black shoes. Daisy cannot look at their faces, but she feels them staring at her. So many pairs of eyes, boring into her. The only lady in the room is Mummy, sitting next to her on the sofa. The cold, brown, leather sofa she is trying to burrow into and disappear. Mummy squeezes her hand, a bit too hard, and then the questions start coming at her.

So many questions.

And she doesn't know, she cannot remember.

What colour was his hair?

His eyes?

How tall was he?

Taller than Daddy?

Did she know who the man was?

Did he tell her his name?

How old was he?

What did his moped look like?

What colour were his clothes?

Had she ever seen him before?

Questions questions questions. She tries to be brave, she tries to answer, but all she can really remember, in explicit detail, is what his willy was like, what it looked like, felt like, smelt like.........but they did not ask her those questions.

The policemen must have gone away at some point, and Daisy must have relaxed a bit, sat down to tea, and life must have gone on, clearly.

But not for her, not inside.

Little Daisy got left behind.

Little, magical, perfect, innocent and beautiful Daisy was stuck, pinned up against the toilet wall by a giant willy.

Legs already racing,

endlessly running,

never ceasing to escape,

never able to get away;

not caught
but not saved either.
Stuck.
Inside, a part of her was always reliving that.
Like a loop tape, everlastingly playing, over and over again.

Daisy finished this first part of her story, and looked up. Jean had fallen asleep, her delicate blonde head leaning against the neck support on her wheelchair. She was breathing a bit noisily, and Daisy wondered if she should risk waking her by putting a small pillow under her chin to lift it up. Suddenly she was overwhelmed by tenderness and love for her friend, so small and vulnerable in sleep, yet so strong and vibrant when awake. Listening to the swift, shallow breathing, Daisy realised who it was that Jean had always reminded her of. With a sharp pang of remembrance, she was looking not at Jean but at her beloved friend Felicity, who was in the bed next to hers in hospital. A crack opened in her heart, and there was so much sadness exposed, and leaking out, that she could not suppress her tears.

Felicity disappeared one night, from her hospital bed.
Daisy thought she saw her being taken up to heaven, by a beautiful, mysterious Lady.
The Lady was dressed in deep blue, down to her perfect, shoeless feet, and her dark hair flowed over her shoulders and down her back.

Jean was awakened from her slumber by the sobbing. Assuming it was due to the reliving of the childhood trauma she had suggested Daisy write, she smiled sympathetically, and said, "It is healing to cry, please don't feel embarrassed. Have you managed to get it out of your head and onto the paper?"
Daisy nodded, but said "Well, the first part, anyway. But actually in some ways what happened next was worse."
"Are you up to writing that down too? It would be good to keep going now that you've opened the box........I have an essay to finish, and the carers won't be here for another hour. Why don't you make a cup of tea, and carry on?"

"If you're sure I'm not in your way" Daisy responded, blowing her nose, and going to the kitchen.

The friends enjoyed a well-earned mug of tea, then each turned resolutely to their tasks.

Picking up her pen, Daisy took a big, deep gulp of air, and continued with her story. She was surprised at how easy it was to write about the things she had never felt capable of speaking out loud.

Then a shiver of fear arose – what if Jean made her read it out? She would die of shame. For a moment she could sense the doors closing down around her past once again, trapping her back there.

No, Jean told me this was a safe way to get through what has been holding me back. I trust her, and I trust myself.

I will do this.

And on she went, one arm reaching back through time to rescue her inner child, the other firmly grounded in Jean's bright, comfortable flat. Resolutely taking up her pen once again, Daisy started scribbling, in a fast and scrawled style because her hand could not keep pace with the story pouring out.


Daisy has started school, and is happy and excited. The school is right next door to home, but the toilets are none other than the very same place where she had been accosted, and she cannot make herself go back in there.

So, she wets her pants.

The teacher takes her round the corner to Mummy, posts her through the railings, and Mummy helps her into dry pants.

The teacher takes her back to class.

But Daisy has also become too afraid to get out of bed in the dark at night when she needs the toilet, and she starts wetting the bed too.

Nobody thinks to link the incontinence with her trauma; instead they send her to the hospital in case she has a problem "down there."

Mummy makes her swallow a big bitter pill from the doctor, and they get on a bus, something she has never done before.

Daisy begins to feel sick, and then really green, and has a low tummy ache.

She is terrified of the hospital, but like a good girl does not make a fuss.

The doctor takes her away from Mummy and puts her on a high, hard table, where very heavy metal plates are laid on her tummy.

Massive, impossibly heavy weights loaded on, and strapped down till she feels she must surely be crushed dead as an ant beneath a stone.

Daisy tells them she needs the toilet, but they ignore her.

They stick an injection into her right arm, inside her elbow, and tell her she will feel a bit hot.

Suddenly she feels as if she is on fire!

Burning hot fluid races round her body, bursts into her temples, and her face explodes like a firework had gone off inside it.

The need to go becomes a desperate urge, "I've got to do a poo!"

Still they do not listen, and Daisy gasps in shame and horror as her grip upon her sphincter is failing: she could not have clung on more tightly to the edge of a precipice than she has been clamping shut her bottom cheeks........

but the weights pushing down on her,

the effect of the tablets,

plus the radio-active injection to highlight her kidneys,

all conspire to deprive her of control over her bowels.

All over the table.


Joe and Daisy, like most close siblings, often fight. But Joe being the older one, and being male, has the advantage. He has invented a hundred ways of tormenting her, of goading her, of making her lose her temper and wrestle with him.

"It will end in tears" Mummy says, and it does. Even if those tears come about because she has chased one or other, and usually both of them, with her slipper in her hand and smacked them soundly with it. But Daddy's wrath is far more terrifying to incur than Mummy's. He is not above cracking them round the side of their head, sending them spinning into an infinity of bursting stars. Once Daddy had walked to the cupboard door, opened it, taken out the studded dog's collar and whacked Daisy round the back of her thighs with it, three times, whilst she huddled in the corner screaming.

And just because she had been trying to whistle like Joe could.

Daddy had told her to stop.

But she just had to do one last, tiny, miniscule whistle.

Just one.

And it wasn't even a proper whistle.


She never did learn how to whistle.


The kidney x ray comes back clear.

The bed wetting continues, in spite of the nasty tablets she is given twice a day.

She hides them in the side of her mouth and spits them out in the garden, but Mummy sees, and stands over her until she swallows them properly.

They are taking her into hospital for more tests.

And this is where she first meets the Lady.

The nurses are very strict, they do not talk to Daisy or smile at her.

They take her clothes off and put a nighty on her, and make her go to bed, even though it is only morning time.

There are lots of other children in the ward, but none of them are playing.

They are all in bed, tucked in very tightly and very neatly, and it is very quiet.

A nurse brings her some food on a tray.

It tastes funny, but she eats it like a good girl.

She has promised her Mummy she will be good and not make a fuss.

There is a small girl in the bed next to her, who smiles and shyly waves.

Daisy waves back, and smiles too.

The girl whispers that her name is Felicity.

She has almost translucent skin and a doll like face, surrounded by a golden halo of curls. Then the nurse comes and thumps Felicity on her back as she is lying face down, her head hanging over the side of the bed next to Daisy.

Thump thump thump!

And Felicity's chest is very thin, and hollow.

The nurse does not stop until Felicity has coughed a lot into a metal bowl.

After that Felicity is too exhausted to speak, and too sad to smile.

The nurses will not let Daisy get out of bed, or go to the toilet.

She has to ask, and to use a bedpan.

Every time she does, the nurse writes something on the chart at the end of her bed.

When Daisy looks around at the other beds, she thinks that the children must be very ill, as many of them are lying down all the time.

Sometimes one of them is lifted onto a trolley and wheeled out of the ward.

When they come back later on, they are all asleep, and they have a black dummy stuck in their mouths.

Sometimes they don't wake up for hours.

This makes Daisy feel very frightened.

She wonders if it is going to happen to her, and what it means.

When the children wake up they are usually very sick, into a bowl.

Like Daisy was after her kidney x-ray.

The next morning in hospital she realises she must have fallen asleep, because she gets a horrible shock as the light goes on, really blaringly brightly, over her head, when it had been almost dark just before.

Felicity whispers to her that they just wake you up really, really early in hospital, to make sure everything is clean and tidy before the doctors come to look at you.

They bring horrible smelling, nasty tasting medicine round.

Some of it is sickly thick stuff you have to swallow.

And some of it is tablets that get stuck halfway down your throat.

Better not make a fuss though!
Poor, sweet Felicity,
with the cough,
in the bed next door,
has the nurse come along and whack her, hard, all over her back again,
as she is hanging over the bed.
Her face all purple and pained,
her eyes screwed up in misery.
To make her cough up stuff into a bowl that the nurse takes away.
Every morning and every night this happens, leaving Felicity weeping softly and lying pale and exhausted,
unable to speak, and incapable of smiling.
How dreadful, thinks Daisy;
maybe even worse than just having being cut open and stitched up again, like Janice in the bed on the other side of her.
Because Janice's cut is healing, whereas Felicity has to suffer the same back beating, twice, every single day of her life.
She knows it is going to happen, and there is nothing she can do about it.

After lunch, as Daisy is feeling less terrified of the nurses and of what might happen next, she whispers to Felicity, and tries to make her laugh by pulling faces and making animal noises which she is very good at.
Felicity wants to know how she learned them all, and Daisy enjoys talking about the dogs and guinea pigs, the cat and the chickens they have at home. And about Uncle Sam's magical farm with Belinda the donkey, Della the pony, and the adorable, funny pigs.
She is missing them all terribly.
"What are the pigs names?" Felicity wants to know.
"They don't have names, but I make up names for them when I'm there."
She tells Felicity how wonderful it is to ride on the back of a pony, like flying.
Felicity is not allowed pets because of her cystic fibrosis.

"How do you stand it, all that thumping?" Daisy asks.

"It's not so bad now", the faint voice replies, "I have the Lady who comes and sits on my bed and talks to me. Haven't you seen her?"

"No" says Daisy "What is she like?"

"Oh, she is the most beautiful person I ever saw, and she always says the loveliest things. She makes my bed warm and soft; like a big, mossy nest. So I imagine I'm a little bird, and very soon I'll be small and light enough to just fly, way up into the sky.

The Lady tells me wonderful stories about where she comes from.

She promises me she's coming to take me back there, with her.

She says there is no hurting, ever; imagine that!

I'll be able to breathe, and dance, and skip about!

I've almost forgotten what that feels like............"

Felicity's eyes drift sideways as with a wistful look she falls asleep again.

Her face does not relax, though;

it always looks pinched,

and her chest stays high and fluttery.

Very much like a little bird, in fact.


Daisy cannot wait to see the Lady, and she makes up her mind to stay awake on purpose to watch her come.

But she does not manage to, a bit like waiting for Santa.

She does dream about her, though.

At least it seems like a dream.

The Lady is standing behind Felicity with her arms around her shoulders and one hand on her forehead, helping her rise to her feet.

Shining softly in the darkness, the Lady has a goldey-violet light all around her, and she has the most beautiful face Daisy has ever seen.

Her eyes are a brighter sparklier blue than her clothes, which reach right down to the ground, and she isn't wearing any shoes because her feet are showing.

The violet light coming out of her seems to be shining straight through Felicity's frail body, which is rising up with joy.

A wonderful smile sweeps up from her lips to her cheeks, and she looks weightless as her eyelids close.

Daisy feels as if she herself is being gently tilted, feet over head and upside down, floating on a cloud of sweetness, so she can't tell which way up is down.

It does not matter anyway,

nothing whatever matters,

she is cocooned and utterly safe,

wrapped in the embrace of the Lady.

Her eyes close by themselves, and she sleeps.


The next morning she wakes up, and the curtains are drawn around Felicity's bed. It is quiet, and the back thumping doesn't happen.

Maybe she is all better?

Maybe she has gone home?

Daisy can't stand it any longer, so even though she knows she'll be told off, and probably punished, she just has to slip out of bed.

It is very high up and the floor is further away than she thought, and cold and hard under her bare feet.

Just as she is about to push her head under the curtain, to see Felicity, someone comes from behind her.

She is slapped very hard on the bottom, grabbed roughly, and flung back on her bed.

The look of fury on Sister's face causes her to gasp and gulp, cradling her tummy with both hands, shrinking back to the metal bars behind her.

She begins to pray.

Praying, praying, harder than she has ever prayed before :

"Oh please please Lady of the Light, please let me see my friend. Please let Felicity be well, and be my best friend forever and ever, please, please.............."

Rocking now, backwards and forwards, humming as quietly as she can, praying more strongly than she thought she could, her eyes riveted on the curtain hiding her friend,

"I won't eat or sleep ever again until I see my friend..........

I don't care if you slap me".
She wants to be so very brave; to shout out these words.
But they remain stuck tight inside her mouth, and she realises she has clamped her jaw shut. Every muscle is squeezed tighter than tight, except for her eyes which are stretched wide. Fixed on the green curtain;
willing it to open,
so she can see Felicity.


The operation trolley is squeaking its way into the ward.
It is making its way down between the rows of beds, coming ever closer.
Even though it is in extra slow motion, still it is coming way too fast
rumble
squeak
rumble
squeak
rumble
squeak
She can hear it above the beating of her heart which is almost in her throat in panic,
but still Daisy will not move her gaze from the green curtain.
The operation trolley stops right there,
 by the bed next to hers.
Felicity's bed.
It disappears behind the curtain.
There is a swish as the curtain is pulled back closed, and she hears a bit of sheet rustling, and a low mumbling of two or three different voices.
Daisy stops breathing on purpose, to hear what the voices are saying.
Straining her ears to listen for Felicity's gentle, soft murmur.
But she can't make it out.
Then, there is another curtain swish,
and the trolley rumbles out, and swiftly away.

Down between the beds,
rumblesqueak
rumblesqueak
rumblesqueak
rumblesqueak
and out through the vile, green, twin doors that swing back afterwards.
There was a very small lump on the trolley,
much too small a lump to be Felicity!
Phew,
breathing again and releasing her grip on herself,
she realises that her tummy is hurting.
She hasn't even felt it, all that time the trolley had rumble-squeaked its way up,
and rumble-squeaked its way back.
The curtain stays shut for the rest of the morning,
but no matter how hard she listens, she cannot hear anything.
Not the usual rasped, quick, laboured breathing that Felicity has to do,
where every breath is a struggle.

Breakfast gets served up as normal,
and medications.
And the washing bowls for top and tailing.
The bedpans and accustomed routines,
and the children in the other beds,
seeming not to notice the silence.
The Big Silence
that comes from behind the green curtain.
Daisy hates that curtain,
it has scary faces on it with no eyes, that look across at her.
She tries to ignore them but her gaze keeps being drawn back to them.
Joe would have told her that they were watching and waiting for her to fall asleep.

Then they would climb out of the curtain and steal her eyes for themselves.

Then someone comes and changes the sheets on Felicity's bed,
 the curtains are drawn open at last,
 but Felicity is not there!
 Felicity has disappeared!
Where could she have gone?
Did her parents come and take her away in the middle of the night?
Why won't the nurses tell her where her friend is?

The day is a fuzzy blur.
Daisy feels numb and cold all over,
and her inside is hard and tight,
 like a knotted up hankie.
She does not want to eat,
 but the nurse makes her stuff it down.
Whatever it is, it tastes of nothing.
The inside of her mouth is like cotton wool,
dry and numb,
and unable to taste anything.
 Luckily, swallowing happens all by itself,
and so does drinking and weeing.
And so she keeps breathing automatically too,
with no answer to the burning question that dominates her entire mind.
*Where is Felicity?*
'Did she go to have an operation when I wasn't looking?'
'Shouldn't she be coming back soon, then?'
Daisy makes up her mind to stay awake and watch for her friend,
all night long if necessary. She will not turn over onto her left side,
but stays stubbornly and uncomfortably facing Felicity's bed.
At least the curtains are open –
she had hated not being able to see behind them.
And the eyeless people can't see her now...

well only one or two who have managed to squeeze themselves into the folds
but they can't get you whilst you're awake.
Now she would know straight away when Felicity has come back and been tucked into her high, hard bed.
Hard and cold and starchy it may be,
but there had been some comfort in knowing that Felicity, too, was in the same cold, high place,
right next door.
Tightly strapped in with stiffly starched sheets.
Why do they bind you up so tightly that you can't turn over, and your toes are squished?
Maybe to stop you falling off
when the beds move around in the night, on their wheels
crashing into one another
Daisy is careful to keep her fingers away from the sides of the bed like in a dodgem car
in case they get crushed
The boy opposite Felicity's bed has a broken arm
and a bandaged head
maybe that's how it happened

Daisy wonders if the Lady will come looking for Felicity.
Then a startling, hopeful thought comes to her –
maybe the Lady knows where she is!
Maybe the Lady is with her there!
That relieves her feelings a bit,
and softens the knot of anxiety in her tummy.
The Lady is so very beautiful,
and Felicity absolutely trusts her.
So she has to be like the best granny you could ever imagine,
or the best fairy godmother even!
'I wish the Lady would come and visit me,' she thinks, as her eyes grow droopy.
'Maybe not to sit on my bed though;
 that might be a bit scary,

but I really do want to see her again.........'

All of a sudden it is morning again,
or is it just an everlastingly long, endless day?
Why hasn't Mummy come to see her?
The bed pans are passed out
and the medication tray comes round again
Still no Felicity.
Still no news of Felicity.
Daisy begins to wonder if the Lady has kept her promise, and she has flown away somehow. Up, out, and away to paradise, where everyone was always laughing,
and nobody ever cried.
How wonderful, to get out of here.
It seems so very long and lonely a day, even though she is happy for Felicity that she is not going to get her usual back-pounding torture.

The doctors are making their ward rounds
They stop at the bottom of Daisy's bed.
There are 5 of them,
all men,
in white coats.
They do not look at her face,
or speak to her,
but they place something on the wheeled table next to her bed.
It is a glass jar with yellow liquid in it and different length threads sticking out of the top.
She wonders what is going to happen.
The nurse pulls down the straight, crisp sheet of her bed,
lifts up her nightie,
pushing her down flat on her back.
Then one of the men bends over,
prises her legs apart
and starts poking something into her.
She tries to sit up to see what they are doing,

feeling very scared,
but another of the doctors presses her chest back, hard, into the
bed.
She cannot stand it,
feeling so small and violated,
and she feels herself rising up
between their fingers
and out of her body,
up she rises,
coming to a stop on the ceiling.

Rolling over,
she can see the doctors bent over,
doing their poking thing with her body,
but she cannot feel anything.

She is not going back in there until they all go away!
She's staying up here where they can't reach her.
She thinks she glimpses the Lady,
out of the corner of her eye,
smiling the sweetest, most encouraging smile.
But when she turns her head,
there is only the wall,
and Felicity was not with her.
There was no pain,
no anything,
and for a while Daisy stays suspended up there,
wondering if she might be dying.
She is unable to feel anything, or move.....
....but wait!
If she thinks hard enough about it, there is a way to roll over and
look about.........
she could even float over and peep out of the window, which is
frosted up to halfway up. She watches as cars drive along the busy
street outside, and there are people walking by.
She had forgotten there was a world outside of this prison.

What if she can make herself be the other side of this window?
Then she could fly away home!
But her gaze feels drawn down to the hospital bed,
where she can see her body, lying still as a statue,
it is the weirdest sensation.
But before she can think about it
 WHOOSH
she has fallen back
and is once more gazing out of her own eyes,
up at the ceiling.

Jean's carers had arrived, and were busy about their tasks. Making dinner, running a bath. Jean told them that Daisy was staying to eat, and was doing an important piece of work so must not be disturbed. Daisy wasn't fully present anyway, and merely nodded distractedly to them as she bent over her notebook, scribbling furiously. This felt like the most vital thing to be giving her attention to, and something she had put off confronting for much too long. Soul retrieval, Jean had called it. And truly it did feel as if she was rediscovering some long lost parts of her vital essence. Even as she wrote, she found a level of understanding coming to her. For years she had downplayed the trauma, telling herself that nothing really awful had happened. She had not been raped by the willy man, she had not been operated on, or hurt by the doctors. But it was now clear that a real violation had happened to her. She had indeed been abused, and her private places had been harmed. Her integrity had been breached, and her will had been disrespected, at the very least.

Jean had explained that perceived trauma was a highly individual response. Some sensitive people could be indelibly scarred by an experience which might be comparatively mild to others. Post traumatic stress didn't only happen to soldiers who had confronted hideous atrocities. Attempting to deny or repress the psycho-emotional effects of extreme shock and dis-empowerment only drove them deeper. And the earlier in life the trauma started the more pervasive it became.

Daisy felt she had come to the end of what she needed to offload. She put down her pen, and saw that the table had been set and the food was being laid out. It was a perfect way to gently come back into the present moment and have her mind taken off herself. Jean looked so pretty in her cerise dressing gown, with her fine golden hair like a halo around her.

Jean's disability was such that she even needed help to eat. She had only minimal use of her right hand, sufficient to operate the controls of her wheelchair. She could manage to write using a special pen, and moving the notebook into place with her chin, but the large arm muscles did not work. Neither did she have any control over, or movement in the left arm, or her legs. She could not raise her hand up to brush her hair or clean her teeth. Daisy had never asked her any personal questions, sensing that Jean did not want to talk about her situation. If Jean wanted her to know anything, it would emerge naturally at the right time. It was obvious that she had come to a place of acceptance and peace with how she was, which consequently allowed her friends to do so too. In secret, Daisy often prayed for a miracle to happen, for Jean to be totally fit and well. Whilst giving thanks for the many gifts which clearly sustained her, and endeared her to others.

After dinner, Daisy cleared up, and helped Jean into bed. Then she leaned over and kissed her softly and gently on her forehead before leaving. Jean said searchingly, "You alright in there? You want me to read your story tonight?"
Daisy shook her head, and raised her thumb in reassurance. She was too choked up with emotion to say anything, and hoped that her heartfelt kiss would convey the depth of her love and appreciation.

Travelling home, she felt as if she had shed a skin. Sloughing off a restriction might be beneficial, but the raw nakedness made her wince. She was not entirely sure that hypersensitivity was preferable to numbness. Not given the way the world closed around like a pack of predators. She felt very exposed, but somehow she made it through the next few days to the weekend when Brian was coming to see her.

"Consider it a biological adaptation to survival, like an upgrade: super sensitivity for super heroes" was Brian's unhelpful suggestion. "Enjoy it, you might not get another one this side of 40!"

That earned him a cushion to the back of the head. As usual, this escalated into a rough and tumble between them, which only ended when Daisy smelt the buckwheat pancakes burning on the stove. Brian was supposed to have been slicing up nectarines and bananas to go with them.

"Where's the fwoott?" she demanded in an exaggeratedly petulant voice, her lips pursing up.

Brian's penitent face and low slung stance betrayed his negligence. He hobbled sideways like Quasimodo, grabbing an enormous carving knife and brandishing it skywards triumphantly. With her best 'Attenborough' voice-over, Daisy said: "And so the hominid grasps the concept of club wielding, thereby ensuring the downfall of the entire planet."

As they ate their breakfast, Daisy asked whether Brian really thought humanity was evolving.

"Which way are we going, really? I'm so sick of the arrogant entitlement of people."

"Maybe we'll live to see the post hominid era, when the naked ape lays down his club."

"Oh how wonderful Brian! I love that image, thank you!" Daisy made the motion of peering through a lens and clicking the camera. "And the animals reclaim their right to roam the land."

"Free, noble citizens, equal, and valued for their store of wisdom."

"And there was no more killing on the holy mountain. Every lake a sacred swimming place, and all the water safe to drink."

"Let's pretend we're already there, Brian. Witnessing the emergence of Homo Lucidus, the dawn of humane beings. Some things have to be believed in to be seen".

And so they lay on their backs, next to one another, with their eyes closed.

"I see a healing chamber, made of crystal, open on three sides. It's on the flank of a hill, surrounded by purple heather and bright berry bushes. The sun filters through from above, and a pure stream bubbles up from beneath the earth.

Under the chamber is a vast network of caves, whose walls glisten with deep green moss, and delicate ferns. Deeper in, there are carpets of fungi between the rocks, and limpid pools of mineral-rich water. In the centre there is a hot spring surrounded by smooth rocks which pillow your head so you can drift off to sleep, and awaken refreshed. All the vegetation is delicious to taste, and restores imbalances." Daisy begins.

"And it somehow knows when to grow where people most need it" was Brian's contribution. "There is music, sweet and high, very gentle like tinkling wind chimes or the laughter of fairies, in the air. And from within the ground comes a very deep reverberating noise, which vibrates through the rock."

"The warm, somehow yielding rock that makes you feel welcome, like an old sofa." Daisy stretches and sighs.

Together, the friends weave a colourful multi-dimensional tableau with their minds and imagination. Yet it feels more like a memory of some long lost paradise. What if time was in truth not linear at all, but circular, or spiralling? Brian introduced her to the fascinating concept that the apparent future was in fact informing and shaping the present, which implied that time was fluid. So they might be having memories of long distant past civilisations, or indeed of future experiences, from their current viewpoint. She felt this gave weight to her 'instantaneous awakenment' theory, wherein it need not take aeons for society to evolve or transform, it could actually spontaneously occur. For certain she hoped it would. Paradigm shifting was a reassuring thought.

## Chapter 7

Jean was having a bit of an emotional crisis.

"I'm such a burden on people, aren't I?"

"No, you're not! Jean, you help the world go round for so many of us – just by giving your carers a job, counselling screwed up people like me, and shining your beautiful light on us! I would still be under Neil's thumb if it weren't for you. You are more than worth your weight in gold."

"Daisy I have to tell you something. I wanted to tell you before but the time never seemed right." Jean really was upset. How to make her feel better, now that was the question. It was probably inevitable that she should occasionally doubt herself, just as everyone had to sometimes. Daisy had thought more than once about herself, in bleak times, that she did not deserve to breathe the air and stay alive. And then there were the even darker days when she did not want the burden of carrying on breathing, consuming, staying alive. What had she achieved anyway except to make people feel uncomfortable by guilt tripping them? She had gone fruitarian for several weeks, so that she need not bear the guilt of killing any plants, because they too, had feelings. They had no central nervous system of course, and therefore couldn't feel pain like animals could. She wondered, as so many times in the past, whether Jean felt any pain in her immobile, almost lifeless body. She hoped not. Even so, it was impossible to place herself in Jean's stricken form, with her total dependency, and her curtailed prospects.

"Let's go out Jean, let's go to the river and watch some clouds, you'll feel better then".

But Jean shook her head, "No, I've started and I must finish. Please don't be upset by this, it's really not about you at all, it's just that......" Jean drew in her breath, and then blurted out: "I've been having sex with Neil".

Daisy's mind and stomach turned over, and she felt as if a bucket of ice water had just been thrown over her.

"You know how you always said he was insatiable; well I think I've helped him to find a positive outlet for that: he comes and facilitates me with the Para's. He's so uninhibited and creative, and he gives so much pleasure to them. Please don't hate me, or him, Daisy........."

But Daisy had already grabbed her coat and bag, and was out of the door before Jean could finish her sentence.

Betrayal, shock, disgust, but mainly betrayal was coursing through her. She wanted to scream so loudly. She wondered what else Jean hadn't told her, if Neil and she had talked about her, made fun of her prudishness, her leaky bladder, and everything else about her. She could not bear to think about them together, and with a sharp stab of realisation she suddenly saw how Jean had been trying to entice her to join the group sex sessions that went on, by insinuation, enticement and subterfuge. She was so angry and hurt, she knew it would never be the same between them.

How could she ever look Jean in the face again? She had loved her and looked up to her, confided in her and cried over her. And all this time she had been deceived. Daisy was running recklessly fast, across traffic and through dimly lit streets, pumping her fists and driving her legs on with merciless iron spurs. Her thinly constructed life was dissolving from under her, and it felt like drowning.

Somehow she reached her room, managing to not bump into anybody on the way. Feeling too upset to do anything, she flung herself on her bed, and cried herself to sleep.

Daisy woke up the next morning and impulsively walked to the nearest hairdresser, asking them to cut off her hair. The hairdresser's eyes widened in a mixture of glee and concern. "Are you sure? You've obviously been growing your hair for years!"

"I've never had short hair in my life, but I suddenly feel I want a complete change, to be free from the weight of all this hair. I've never had a fringe either. So I'd like a neat, short bob, please."

She was surprisingly calm as the hairdresser took up her scissors. She could hear the sound of them snipping all around her head. It took a long time. The hairdresser explained that a precise cut of straight hair like Daisy's was the most difficult to get right, "You're never going to forget this haircut, so it has to be perfect!" And perfect it was.

Daisy gasped in delight when she was finally allowed to see her hair, all blow dried and gleaming, "Wow, I love it!" she said. Just like the shampoo advertisements, when she shook her head every hair fell immaculately back into place, and flowed like a slick wave, glossy and shining. The back of her head was a bit of a shock, as the bob stopped short of her neck, and the tapered under layers were ultra-short. It felt very strange beneath her fingers as she stroked it.

The hairdresser was saying, "You'll need to have it cut every six weeks to hold the shape like this".

Six weeks? Crikey, no wonder women spent so much time and money at the hairdressers! No way was Daisy going to do that. She couldn't afford it anyway. She had to suppress an urge to skip out of there and dance her way down the street. Every shop window she came to she sought her reflection to check her hair. What a difference, would anyone even recognise her? She could feel the wind on the back of her newly exposed neck, and thought she would need to start using some of those lovely scarves she had bought from the charity shops on impulse, during her shopping expedition with Jean. She had not got the knack of how to wear a scarf convincingly, in the way some confident women did.

What was Jean going to say about her new hairstyle? She had already decided to forgive her. After all, she no longer wanted anything to do with her old boyfriend, and she had never found it in herself to hate him. What was it to her if his obsession could be turned to good use and not harm anybody? It all felt unreal to her now anyway, and she was well into creating a new, happier life away from him. She would find Jasper, and take him up on his offer of joining the drama and singing group. She was going to make much more effort to be sociable, and not hide herself behind books so much.

How would Brian react? She was very excited and happy with her hair, and suddenly felt herself to be properly adult. Which was weird because as a child she had felt very ancient inside; 'an old soul' someone had once remarked about her to her mother.

Most people's reaction upon seeing Daisy's newly cut hair was positive. A few asked if she missed her long hair, and if she was going to let it grow back again. Jean was aghast; her mouth fell open and she tilted back her head in amazement, making little twirly motions with her moveable finger. Daisy obligingly spun round, danced about, and threw her head coquettishly over her shoulder like a catwalk model.

"Stunning! Gorgeous! I mean it Daisy, I'd never have thought of suggesting it, but you look fabulous! Full of confidence and up for anything". And they fell about laughing.

"About last night...." Jean began.

"I don't ever want to talk about it, but I suppose it's good that I know now, and I think I'm OK with it. Just promise me I'll never have to see him, and you'll never mention him, ever again."

Jean nodded, and Daisy smiled reassuringly. Forgiveness was a beautiful gift, both to yourself and the one you felt harmed by. Daisy realised that Jean had only kept quiet out of the need to protect her. And it was none of her business anyway, what other people got up to in the privacy of their own homes. As long as she didn't have to come face to face with Neil, or ever see him again, she thought she could cope with it. She had long ago developed a knack of walling off and compartmentalising painful events, which enabled her to keep functioning.

Strangely, Clara's reaction to the hair cut was the most odd of all, "Oh, what have you done?" she said in a sorrowful wail, with a look of undisguised horror on her face. "How could you do that? You had such beautiful hair, your crowning glory, and now it's gone."

She even looked as if she was going to cry, but turned and hurried away quickly.

"What was that about? What's it to her anyway?" Daisy shook her head in genuine bewilderment.

"Don't let Clara's negativity upset you" Jean was saying.

But Clara had indeed burst the pretty bubble, and caused Daisy's hand to fly up in search of her reassuring curtain of hair, now missing. She looked about the hall, her eyes scanning the heads in search of long hair. Nobody had lustrous, poker straight, shining hair like hers had been. It would take years to grow it like that again, if she ever did. And now her hair was like everyone else's: ordinary and cropped.

That weekend at Brian's, over a delicious meal of smoked seitan and pinenut bake with spring greens and roasted vegetables, he observed, "How we wear our hair is quite a personal statement actually, isn't it?  Think how bold and empowered the women's suffragettes must have felt when they cut their hair. It was a symbol of their stance against oppression at the hands of men. In those days women had no socially acceptable choice but to have long hair, worn up, so their ultra-short bobs were a brave show of determination. And you're demonstrating your new found freedom too. It's very appropriate, and perfect timing. Personally I'm looking forward to your next phase, which hopefully will include various forms of body art and piercing". Brian lunged at her, wiggling a pointed index finger in a provocatively suggestive way. She might have been angry at this, but for the grotesquely overdone, lascivious grin which accompanied the gesture. As it was, she could not suppress a girlish scream, and furious hand flapping to fend him off. They both ended up out of breath, and laughing.

Ah, Beloved Brian! He always said the right thing, bless him. When they had first met, Brian's dark hair was long and unkempt looking, and sometimes he wore a full bush of ginger-tinged beard. Aside from the habit of dragging his fingers through this, the beard clearly received neither trimming nor combing. She half expected it to harbour a family of resident mice. Today, though, his hair was mid-length but very clean and groomed, and he had a neat moustache. Funnily enough, he would become quite upset if Daisy failed to notice his changes of facial hairstyle. In truth she was not a visually dominated person, being much more orientated towards sound and intuition as her primary sense impressions of the world. Consequently, Brian would erroneously feel that she did not bother to look at him when they met up, every week or two. Whereas in fact she was busy reading his energy signature in more subtle ways, albeit less than fully consciously. She had an understanding that not just animals, who were lucky enough to be less removed from their natural surroundings, but also companion and domesticated animals, were capable of perception beyond the 5 sensory human capacities. She hoped and trusted that humans were gradually reacquiring their innate sixth sense.

Chapter 8

There was a desperately attractive man whom Daisy couldn't help noticing at Uni. He was so heart stoppingly handsome it took her breath away. He had a gorgeous, muscular body which moved so fluently through the air, almost feline in its grace. His skin was dark, and his eyes were perfectly almond shaped. She fantasised about finding out that he was vegan, and as drawn to her as she was to him. His hair was thick and curly in a way which made her long to push her fingers through it, and explore the shape of his head, whilst drawing his face closer to hers. So close that she could smell him; so close that she could feel his breath on her cheek; so close that she could hear the quickening beat of his heart.......... But he never even noticed her. He seemed to be a bit of a loner like she was, not surrounded by friends.

Just then, in the midst of her reverie, Jean appeared beside her as she was trying not to stare across at him. The ever perceptive Jean had noticed her look, "Hey Daisy there's a predator inside of you after all!" She teased. "I suppose it's got to come out somewhere, and better to target a human more than capable of defending himself than an innocent creature."

Daisy had to laugh at the analogy. It was true: she did harbour a powerful interest in pursuing and catching this gorgeous hunk of male kind. She confessed then to Jean that she had been thinking about this Adonis for a long time. A good day was when she caught a glimpse of him somewhere on campus, even though it meant a painful pang of loneliness and left her wanting so much more.......

"Why don't you follow him and find out what department he's in? Come on, let's pretend we're leaving at the same time and trail after him!"

But Daisy was mortified, and blushed deeply at the mere thought. "No! Please don't draw attention to us, I couldn't bear it. He'd never look at me, and anyway he's probably a corpse muncher."

"Oh the excuses you make to avoid intimacy Dreamboat, for crying out loud! Give him a chance. Give yourself a chance. I didn't help to get you out of prison only to watch you waste your sweetness on the empty air, you know."

"Sometimes it's better to yearn for something than to get it and be disappointed, don't you think?" Daisy asked, suddenly sombre.

"No, definitely not! Go for it, girl!"

Just then, Clara hove into view. Sitting down uninvited, she began to boast about her hunting exploits on her family estate. When Daisy looked less than impressed, she said, "Don't force your cowardly beliefs on me, just because you haven't got the guts to kill an animal yourself. I've been killing and gutting animals all my life and I'm proud of it! It's my natural heritage".

Daisy groaned inwardly at this display of neo-neanderthalism. 'Once more unto the breach', she thought to herself, and pointed out that the pheasants and grouse which Clara and her family enjoyed shooting were not wild birds with a fair chance of escape. They had all been captive bred in pens in the woods, and fed by humans they had learned to trust. And they were only released when the wealthy hunters came for their parties, and had never learned to fly before. It was a massacre. And hunting was not a sport, because in sport both sides know the game and consent to play it. Even so, she could not get as upset by this as she did by the horrors of factory farming, where millions of pigs, chickens and cows were raised indoors without ever seeing the sun, or eating fresh, natural food. Predictably Clara scoffed at this, saying that the animals didn't know any different because they had been born indoors. Daisy could not get her to think about the thwarted instincts of these poor creatures who had no way of expressing their needs to roam, forage, scratch and bathe in the dust, build nests, or find mates.

"Nah, they're lucky, they get food, water and shelter. Anyway, we have to eat them or they'd take over the planet."

If only she could hear how astoundingly ignorant that was. When animals had lived in balanced ecosystems for millions of years, before man proliferated and took over.

"Natural creatures do not destroy their environment. It takes the spectacularly arrogant short-sightedness of humans to mess it all up. Animals are intelligent and sensitive, and have obvious desire to enjoy their lives. If they weren't imprisoned in cages, barns and fields they would run away, so they're all being held against their will."

In a scoffing voice, Clara retorted, "Animals don't have wills, or souls, or any concept of the future, so it doesn't matter what happens to them. My Dad says they wouldn't eat and grow so fast if they weren't happy".

"Look" shot back Daisy, "Food is the only stimulation they get, so of course they're going to eat it, when there's nothing else to do".

"You really are some bunny loving freak, aren't you? Must be fun for you being the only one this side of the cage, seeing all your bunny tribe in their little bunny prisons!"

Right then, Daisy thought that she had never seen a more ugly, despicable face in her whole life. Clara's puffy round face, pinched into a retarded concentricity, and tapering down to chinlessness. Her brassy, strawlike, fake yellow hair, and her sneering curled lip were almost too much to bear. Her left eye did not match the right one, and it was at least an inch lower. Thankfully, having had sufficient pleasure from the exchange, Clara hauled her clumsy, lumpen body up from the chair which made a screeching protest. Away she lumbered, swaying and dragging her splayed flat feet, in those ridiculous shiny shoes, with her enormous ankles flowing over the sides.

Predictably, Daisy was to share this sensation, shuddering as she recounted every detail to her long suffering friend. Over a gargantuan Sunday brunch with Brian, Daisy was asking him, "How can I counter Clara when she dismisses as sentimentality whatever reasoning I bring up? She's always calling me stupid and deluded, and yet she comes out with the most pathetic reasons to defend what she does."

Reaching out for another scoop of scrambled tofu, Brian responded sympathetically, "Give yourself credit for single handedly trying to overthrow the powers that be, who of course will fight against changing what they think are their 'rights'. There's nothing like a spark of opposition, the lifeblood of politics".

"Brian, for me they are the powers that *were:* the 'Power Over', old paradigm that is crumbling. And please don't take that as an invitation to go on a rant over the class system. I'm not going to get side-tracked into that dead end. There are too many activists out there using animal rights as a way of stabbing at the system. I'm keeping my focus firmly on the animals."

"But you just said yourself it has to topple."

"It's dying because it's time is up. People are taking back their ability to think for themselves. I'm into evolution, not revolution."

"I know you want it to be bloodless and sweet, Daisy Dreamer. I love that you wave that Peace banner. I truly hope it happens that way. In the meantime, other people are using whatever they've got, to break through. Can I finish the mushrooms, they're delicious!"

Daisy enjoyed keeping up the tradition of a large cooked breakfast on Sundays. Brian liked her tempeh rashers, made from fermented soya beans, marinated in shoyu and fried crisply to resemble the bacon they had grown up eating. She also made sausages from ground nuts and cereals, with herbs and a little spice. There were the obligatory baked beans of course, and grilled tomatoes. He was much less fond of her usual breakfast, which was a litre of healthy green smoothie, made from handfuls of sunflower greens she grew herself in trays in the courtyard, half a cucumber, lots of fruit, and big scoops of hemp and brown rice protein powder. He would knock back a small glass of this as if it was medicine, because she told him it was good for him. How could she drink a litre of the stuff? It was the same with her enormous salads, all that chewing and watery stuff. Left to himself he would rarely eat fruit or greens, being a bread and potatoes man at heart, which is why she indulged him with her big brunch. Even the bread and cakes she made were weird; she used strange grains he'd never heard of, like amaranth and teff, sorghum and millet, and buckwheat. He realised that people learned to like the foods they were raised on, and most were resistant to trying anything different. It could actually be exciting being around Daisy, because she was always coming up with new ideas and food combinations to surprise him with. Some of them tasted wonderful, others might take a bit longer to get used to. Like her kale chips, made from kale massaged with tahini, tamari and chilli, dried out overnight in the bottom of a warm oven. These were oddly addictive. There was something more-ish about the cigar shaped seaweed creations she made too, by wrapping sprouted sunflower seeds, nutritional yeast and herbs in nori sheets and drying them out. Brian called them green torpedoes. Food was certainly never boring with Daisy around! In fact he thought that she had probably never made the exact same meal twice in the whole time he had known her.

Replete and satisfied, the pair sprawled in the warm clutter of Brian's house, with the Sunday papers spread out. Occasionally reading out particularly interesting snippets, or passing pictures to one another. Daisy preferred The Times, whilst Brian favoured The Guardian. Because neither of them had a television, they stayed in touch with current news this way. Even whilst criticising the newspapers for being selective, and for spectacularising events. And bemoaning the fact that so few positive, uplifting happenings made their way into the national press, whilst even fewer got through the filters of the world news. Brian said that the media was all stitched up and controlled by the controlling elite anyway, and that politicians were puppet figureheads. Even though she disliked political talk, Daisy had learned the truth of this by researching the way the meat, egg and dairy industries were hugely subsidised and supported by governments. The amount of money these death industries spent on advertising was staggering. No wonder people believed the lies about animal foods being good for health. Even though those countries like Norway and Switzerland which consumed the most dairy also had the highest rates of osteoporosis. And those countries with the highest meat consumption like the USA had the greatest heart disease and cancer rates. Furthermore, the advertising tactics these purveyors of incarceration and death used were blatant lies! Happy meat, dancing cows, chirpy chickens: all cartoon characters that mocked the true hideous facts and fate of precious beings who yearned to live out their natural purpose, unthreatened by heartless human greed.

As on countless other occasions, Daisy had ranted herself into such a clench of misery over the whole thing, that Brian had to literally drag her into the fresh air and compel her to pour her sorrow into a jog. At first unwilling, resentful, and angry with him for stemming her flow of rhetoric, by the time they had got to the park she was shaking off the shackles which bound her to her sedentary activism. Half an hour later she was just getting warmed up and raring to open up into a fast run.

"Blimey Daze, you're getting fit! Whoo hooo check out those calf muscles! I can't keep up with you."

This pleased her no end, and she realised that the quiet purposive runs she had been putting in by herself at night were indeed paying dividends. Her singing voice had improved too, as she could hold and control her breath so much better. And her body had become firm, slender and agile, though she still kept it well concealed. For she had not succeeded in overcoming the hypercritical, cruel comments that her brother Joe used to make when she was adolescent. He had taunted her, and called her fat and ugly so often that she still believed it. Even though she was wise enough to realise he had been controlling her, and displaying his own feelings of inadequacy. Those early beliefs and negative self-images might never be completely erased.

Jean had told her that bullies were themselves the product of bullies. Joe had never ever mentioned having been bullied himself by anyone.

"They don't, Sweetheart, they have to preserve their outer image as being strong, or they think they will dissolve completely. That's what makes bullying so insidious and reinforces the abuse, do you see?" It was a very dark and entangled mess, to be sure.

Chapter 9

Brian was reading politics and philosophy, at Sheffield University, some 36 miles away from Manchester, where Daisy had elected to study ecology. It had taken her a while to decide, and eventually she picked that subject because it had the broadest spectrum there was, embracing sociological, geographical, and geological studies as well as biological sciences. She wanted to give herself the best possible opportunities to be in an authoritative position to improve the lives of the animals and environment she loved so much. She really hated arguing though, and did not derive pleasure from it the way Clara clearly did. For Daisy, her main motivation was to end the suffering, of human or non-human animals. She could not understand why other people did not immediately want to change their eating habits, once they realised that it was not necessary to kill anything in order to stay alive yourself. Why continue to live on death, carnage and bloodshed? Could they not see the link between predatory eating behaviour and preying upon one another? How did they justify the mass slaughter of 56 billion animals, across the globe every year, by humans? When they could live healthier, gentler lives as happy herbivores, friendly fruitarians, and gleeful grain eaters!

Daisy had really wanted to study permaculture and biodynamics: the deep spiritual ecology, but there were no such courses attracting student loan or grant status. Her primary concern upon finishing her A levels was escaping from her highly dysfunctional family situation.

Her parents had finally argued themselves into separation, sometime during her GCSE finals. Dad had left, and Mum had started drinking in earnest then, leaving Daisy to bear the brunt of the work required to run the guest house. Shopping, cooking and cleaning for 15 people whilst studying had not been easy, plus working every Saturday in a local shop for pocket money. She had sided more with her Mother though, because her Father never bothered to explain or defend himself. In fact he had never shared any of his childhood or past with her at all, and was a mystery as well as a tyrant to her. He had not permitted her to stay out with her friends after 10 o'clock at night, even though they were allowed to stay out until midnight. He obviously did not trust her, which wounded her deeply.

Somehow life ground on inexorably, sheets got washed and meals got made. Daisy retreated inside her head, and wrote her misery into songs which she sang whenever she left the house. The tension and despair at home was a miasmic fog bank, bearable only with diligent work, focussing attention on the minutiae of meticulous crevace cleaning, dusting, polishing and hoovering. Her daily reward and escape came by virtue of her walking the dogs ritual, which she relished and clung to regardless of weather. Dogs and Daisy both watched the clock and the leads on the back door with mounting intensity, awaiting their daily moment of freedom. The dogs leaped up and sprang into their collars as Daisy heaved herself out from beneath her yoke, and away they would go. Across the fields, through the woods, around the park, it didn't matter so much where they went. The vital thing was to get out of that oppressively stultifying house.

Daisy took a special pride in grooming the dogs to perfection, which as they had the thick double coats of collies, was indeed a labour of love. There was the densely soft, woolly under layer, which she used to prise from the combs and brushes and keep in carrier bags for eventual spinning into knitting wool. Her Mum had once said she wanted a cardigan made from her own dog's wool, and always seeking for ways to lift her Mother's spirits, this became a long term goal. She had accumulated 15 carrier bags full, which she kept in the shed, but as it compressed down such a lot she imagined she would need at least 50 bags to make sufficient skeins to complete the whole garment.

One very special day in her life, Daisy had met Brian coming home on the bus from her Saturday job. He sat down on the seat across from her and asked "Do you remember sitting next to me a few weeks ago on this bus?" Startled, and more than a little suspiciously, she leaned back whilst gripping the rail in front of her. She peered round at the source of this pleasant sounding voice, and tried to bring him into focus by squinting her eyes.

"Sorry, but I'm short sighted and live in my own little world most of the time" she apologised.

Forcing himself to continue the speech he had been practising, Brian said as casually as he could, "I've noticed you on the bus before and I think we live near to each other. Do you think we could go for a walk sometime?"

"What's your name?" she heard herself asking, even whilst wondering what he wanted and why he would be bothering to speak to her. Nobody had ever interrupted her thought bubble on a bus before, and it was both very alarming and welcome.

"My name's Brian, I go to Grizzly Grammar and I live in Brambley Close" he blurted out, careful not to move closer in case she sprang up and ran away like a deer. She was so very much like a wild creature, and smelled like a barely contained force of nature. His heart was almost jumping out of his chest, but he forced himself to sit still and casually relaxed. He had reached the end of his introductory speeches, and was desperately trying not to wring his hands.

Don't stare!

Look out of the window.

Whistle.

Act like it doesn't matter.

Be cool.

There was an interminable pause, which he simply couldn't resist breaking by saying "I heard you singing, you have a very beautiful voice, what music do you like listening to?"

"I love singing, and music makes like worth living doesn't it!" She had decided that he was safe, and bestowed one of her smiles on him. The first of the many millions he had fantasised about basking in, ever since he had first seen her.

Their friendship moved imperceptibly and seamlessly into deep water after that. They met up frequently for dog walks and bike rides. He seemed to understand exactly what she was going through, and she was able to confide in him those things she had not felt able to tell any of her school friends. Brian's family, too, was deeply wounded, and he bore both visible and invisible scars from it.

Neither of them invited the other back to their homes. There was an unspoken sense of keeping themselves sacrosanct and separate. And anyway, Brian's family did not welcome strangers, and were socially inept, according to him. This made Daisy laugh, as her home was always full of random strangers, brought together in tersely distant company under the one roof.

Then, one horrendous day, she returned home from school to find her brother Joe there, saying he had found their Mother with her head in the gas oven. This attempted suicide almost fractured Daisy's already fragile mental state, causing her to pour caustic blame upon herself. She believed that she must be a part of the cause of her Mum's agony, by simply existing, regardless of how endlessly she struggled to make things right. Her Mother had always warned her not to make the same mistakes she had. When she tentatively took a meal to her Mothers room it was flung away, and she heard the words, "Never get married, and never have kids. This is a shit world, why didn't Joe just let me die?"
Covering up for her Mother's frequent bouts of afternoon "sickness" was a well-practised habit. But this descent into the realms of death wish enactment was like a jagged tear in the fabric of her life, which she found almost impossible to conceal.

Amazingly, her Mother still managed to be up before everybody else each morning, cooking a full breakfast, and putting on her landlady face. It was as if there were two people cohabiting within her. Not to mention the conspiracy of silence that she, Joe and Daisy colluded in. The lodgers and the animals had to be fed, that was the overriding priority. Just as the homework must be completed, no matter how late into the night Daisy had to sit hunched over the kitchen table.
And then leave it scrubbed and laid ready for breakfast. Marmalade pots topped up, knives and forks placed just so. Kettle filled ready to switch on.

Brian said that she could maybe better help her Mother by ceasing to keep the rotten ship afloat. If she wasn't there, maybe her Mum would move to a small, easy to manage house, and sort herself out. She was clearly so very miserable struggling to run the guest house, and had no time or energy for anything else. The pair had talked about their hopes of going on to university. Nobody in Brian's family had ever done that. Daisy loathed the strictures and prim narrowness of convent school, and longed to be released, body and mind, into the lofty halls of knowledge and freedom. Somehow she managed to get through another year, but her Mother refused to take her seriously when she said she was intending to go away to university.

Meanwhile Daisy had become increasingly involved in animal and environmental concerns, and found it ever more disgusting to be having to prepare, serve, and clean up after all of the carcasses of murdered beings that disgraced the daily dinner table. She thought about how wonderful it was going to be to never have to touch dead creatures ever again. She dreamed of waking up not to the stench of sizzling bacon and sulphurous eggs, but to colourful bowls of tantalising fruit, warm fluffy pancakes drizzled with amber maple syrup, and exciting muesli mixtures drenched in almond milk. The best she could manage at home was wheat germ sprinkled on her porridge.

As time went by, Daisy began to realise that people had a deep disconnection between what they said they believed in, and how they actually acted. So, apart from Clara, none of her other fellow students could admit that they would cheerfully and deliberately kill an animal. Especially when she asked them if they could do it with their bare hands and puny teeth, assuming they were capable of having chased and caught it. Did they seriously believe that humans were natural predators, despite having neither claws nor powerful jaws? She really did not want to be antagonistic to everyone around her, constantly pushing her agenda. Yet it seemed that, because she had so forcefully put her position across from the first day, she had no option but to keep on being the agent of change. Hoping always for breakthrough of the compassion she knew lay within their hearts.

Daisy assumed that she was the only vegan in the university, and the two vegetarians on her course were not interested in activism. They saw their vegetarianism as a personal food choice. It did not rule their lives, as her veganism was doing to her. They felt they were doing their bit to minimise harm – way more than most other folks did, anyway. Consequently, Daisy felt even more that it was all down to her. It went way beyond personal eating preference, it was a way of living which touched every aspect of her life, including what she wore, supported and promoted.

Deciding to be proactive, she had put up a notice asking for anyone interested in animal rights or veganism to come to a meeting. She planned to suggest that they get together over tea and cakes she would make, and write to supermarkets asking them to stock more healthy plant ingredients and to veganise their foods. Most veggie things contained eggs or milk, but if would be very simple to replace these. It would benefit those people with dairy allergies too. They could ask for a separate section for the veggie foods, as she found it upsetting to see them lying side by side with the shrink-wrapped corpses. Maybe some people might even feel brave enough to campaign with her. Arriving early, she had laid out leaflets and note pads, some muffins and chocolate cake, but nobody turned up. No takers at all.

Feeling crushed and disappointed, she went back home feeling thoroughly disillusioned. It was not enough to be the only vegan in Uni. For her, veganism was actually the least anyone should be doing, the baseline from which humanity ought to be sharing and caring for the one planet all living things had to live on. Not for the first time, she drifted off on the bus home into a reverie of how she imagined the world could be when there was no more killing or fighting, and no creature lived in fear. It was a place so idyllically perfect and exquisitely beautiful she almost fainted. Each butterfly and bird was not merely going about its business, but somehow responsive to her noticing them. With its harmony of symbiosis and togetherness, living magical colours and liquid sounds, nature vibrated all around her.

This was the Peaceable Kingdom she so desperately longed to see manifested. This was why she had been born: to lead others back to the Paradise Garden of her visions. Restored to original innocence, far from ego, and self-conscious struggle.

Here, in this alternate reality she retreated to, humans had not used their genius to create weapons of war. There was awesome technology, yes, but none of it harmed the natural world. There were crystal cities, and aerial orchards on rooftops. Nature was neither destroyed nor suppressed, but worked with harmoniously, to benefit all of life. Following the natural world in its model of perfection, forest gardens proliferated in every walkway. Although many plants were cultivated for their inherent beauty, most of the shrubs, climbers and trees bore edible fruits and flowers. There was no monoculture of grain fields, but instead the land outside the living cities was a stunning patchwork of very intricately entwined plant species. Making the most of the sunlight and rich, fertile soil.

And not only the plants lived companionably here. People lived honest, translucent lives. Perspicacious, open, and genuinely sharing with each other. Nobody would dream of stealing, or of deceiving another, and defensiveness was not needed because there was no concept of attack. If there ever arose any conflict of ideas, these were always settled in a loving, mutually supportive way. It would not serve the peace and delightful array of differences to have any one predominate. So people would gravitate to the areas which best reflected their own interests and talents.

Telepathy was a given here, and people delighted in showing their unique, true colours, much like the bright plumage of the winged creatures. Unlike on old 3D earth where people, including Daisy, felt they had to shout loud and long to be listened to. In this 'terra' there was song, yes; but equally there was sweet, serene silence also. Music arose, either spontaneously or by deliberately practised skill, and always appropriately, sensitively and purposefully. *Vegantopia*, she called it: the Nirvanah, Eden, Shangri La, or Paradise described by most earthly religions and mythologies.

"Away with the fairies again Dazzle?" Brian's gentle voice interrupted her reverie, piercing the bubble of the inner sanctum into which she retreated when life hurt her too deeply.

Calmer, but still subdued and disappointed, Daisy cried on Brian's shoulder. He was, of course, his usual sympathetic self. He knew what she was like, so did not waste time trying to deflect her attention in other directions. She was simply obsessed and passionate about her cause, and the best he could do was console her when she was reduced to depression and tears.

"It's not that you're the only one who gives a damn Daisy, it's just that they have so much else in their heads, you know?"

"Yeah? Well so do I! I'd love to be doing more theatre, and singing, travelling and cycling, you know. Do you think I want to be spending so much time speaking up for the animals? But if I don't, they won't have anyone on their side." With a display of passion verging on melodrama, Daisy threw herself on the carpet and drummed in frustration.

"Let it out, Daze! A good dose of displacement activity really helps! Wanna wrestle?" and here Brian dropped to the floor near her, posturing in classic warrior mode. Complete with animalistic grunts, chest beating and ridiculous facial expressions. He bobbed and swayed around her, nudging her with his shoulder and grabbing at her with his long gorilla-like arms.

It was no good, she couldn't stay sombre when he acted like that, despite the seriousness of her feelings. Her inner tigress emerged, and she hissed, arching her back and tensing every muscle in warning. The gorilla whooped and leapt up into the air, imaginary club raised.

The tigress gave one menacing growl, then launched herself, hoping to use the force of her spring to knock the gorilla down. This was playing directly into his hands, if she did but know it. This frustrated gorilla had his own agenda, and encouraging the suppressed passion of a tigress might just get him laid. For a while they wrestled and fought, panted and shrieked, until Daisy was laughing so much that her bladder failed. Pushing Brian away, she ran to the bathroom.

Emerging crestfallen, she asked to borrow a pair of jogging pants, whilst she hung up her damp jeans to dry. She was glad that Brian understood about her lack of bladder control. The way she dealt with it was by restricting her fluid intake whenever she went anywhere, otherwise she was always searching for the loo. At least she did not have to feel embarrassed in front of Brian.

Quieter now, but inevitably returning to where she had left off in their conversation, she remarked, "I just have to hope that my example will eventually rub off, and people will hear the truth".

Brian was a vegetarian, but his interests lay in philosophy and politics. He would always help Daisy with any of her projects indirectly, by helping her to make posters or carrying leaflets around and so on, he just made it clear that it was not his thing to be an activist himself. Of course she respected that, and was really grateful for his empathy and friendship. She occasionally did reflect, once in a while, that she must be actually quite a nuisance to have as a friend, because of her relentless single mindedness. If they went anywhere, like to a concert, she could never resist bringing animal rights into it in some way. So she made a point of always asking what 'cruelty free' foods they had at festivals, even though she had no intention of buying anything. She thought that at least the caterers could no longer claim, "Nobody has ever asked for veggie burgers before" after her visit. Except of course they always did claim that, which made her annoyed. She was sowing seeds and letting them know there was a demand, but it still took a long time before vegan options even began to appear on menus. If nothing else, it was an exercise in patient persistence, Brian used to say.

"Nothing transformative like awakening and radically changing society ever came easily, you know" he reminded her. "Margaret

Mead said, 'Never doubt that a small group of thoughtful people can change the world. Indeed it's the only thing that ever has.'"

Back at University, Jean was more direct with her advice. She had a golden way of pointing out suboptimal behaviours without making anyone feel wrong, or bad, or foolish. What a gift that was.

"You always rise to Clara's bait, instead of keeping your calm centre," she observed astutely. Clara had just chewed her out over the fact that the pen she was writing with probably had animal products in it like so many other everyday things.

"Hey that's probably squid ink from some poor squished squid right there, oozing out! What are you doing about his family waiting in vain for him to bring their supper home, eh?"

Of course people around the table laughed along with her. Looked at from that perspective yes, modern society made it impossible to live entirely harmlessly. But surely the point was to minimise what harm one's daily life caused, as far as reasonably possible? It did not make her a failure, or a hypocrite, just because she had to live in a society that routinely exploited one another, the planet, and all other species, did it? Society had been built and structured upon the enslavement of others, and not from idealistic concepts; for quick profit not sustainability, sadly.

"Anyway" Clara had seized the attention of the group, "How can animals have rights? That's just ridiculous! What, you want them to have mortgages and be able to vote, to stamp their muddy hoof prints on a voting form?"

"Politics and possessions are human constructs, Clara. All beings have inalienable birth rights: the right to live free from oppression, and to pursue their natural, instinctual needs. It is a wicked arrogance of humanity to deprive them of these by inflicting confinement and institutionalised violence upon them".

"Don't you think that we need to secure rights for ourselves first? 'Always fit your own oxygen mask first before assisting children or others with theirs'" Clara trilled, and again everyone laughed.

"It isn't merely the plight of the animals which troubles me, even though you accuse me of not caring about humans. How many everyday items are the product of slavery, sweat shops and child labour, for instance? Yet how caring are you about what you spend your generous unearned allowance on?"

No sooner were the words out of her mouth than she regretted that last dig. The others would think she was jealous of Clara's wealthy background. Rushing ahead with the next point she wanted to ram home, and cutting into a comment which Simon was starting to make, Daisy realised she was starting to shout, "And what about starvation in third world countries directly caused by western meat eating? Forcing countries that were impoverished by us to grow soya and cereals for export to rich nations, just to be fed to all the intensively reared animals. When the people should have been eating their own crops directly."

"I thought you weren't political, Daisy" Simon interjected. "Its way more complicated than that".

Attempting to not get sidetracked, Daisy continued with her thread, "It's extremely wasteful to 'cycle' food this way, second hand through animals, not to mention all the transport, processing and refrigeration costs. 12 kilos of grain only yields 1 kilo of cow flesh, for example, and 3 acres of land can support 12 vegans but only one meat eater."

But it was clear that she had lost the attention of the others, who were already turned away and having their own conversations. She had done her research and memorised the facts to back up her assertions, but who wanted to listen to her spouting?

"They're young, carefree people, out to enjoy life and have exciting experiences" Brian was attempting to console Daisy during their next meeting, as she sat glumly deflated on the carpet.

"Yea, who wants to be depressed by Daisy downers every day, eh?" she grabbed hungrily at the bowl of walnuts and cranberries in front of her.

"You mustn't bring yourself down Daze, it's incredibly difficult to be called upon to be the bearer of uncomfortable truth, you know."

"Yea, well they treat me as though I'm just scoring points in a debate, instead of trying to save lives. I mean, why would I deliberately antagonise people and alienate myself if not for a very good reason? I like to think that I'd give someone the benefit of a listen, instead of jumping into defensive or deflective cross talk. Quite often there's half a dozen or more people sitting around all firing ideas over mine, and nobody backing me up."

"Well my darling, that's because you're directly challenging their daily habits. And because they are only human."

Brian was very loyal and dedicated to his friend, but even he secretly wished she could lighten up more. On the plus side she was bright and funny, generous and intense, and they had a lot of fun together. They went on long hikes, and camping expeditions, and cycled about exploring. He loved listening to her beautiful voice, so high and clear, strong and expressive. Daisy always made sure to take food supplies, or what she called 'marching biscuits'. Things she had made herself like fruit and nut bars, vegan sausage rolls, and seaweed crisps and flapjacks. And she never went anywhere without her trusty flask of green tea, and a bottle of filtered water.

Daisy always attracted wildlife whenever they were outdoors, and they had a level of responsiveness to her presence which no ordinary person could evoke. Even the domesticated animals they met, noticed her, and invariably came over in response to her obvious love for them. It was rare for her to be able to pass a field of cows without feeling compelled to climb over the fence and mingle with them. She had a disconcerting compulsion to lie down amongst them, keeping completely still with her eyes shut, and awaiting their inevitable curiosity. Only when she felt herself completely surrounded would she gently open her eyes and speak softly to them, laughing in delight as they licked her with their large, rasping tongues. She was as fearless and trusting with them, as they were with her. She said it might be the only time in their entire lives that they had been shown love by a human, and that in her way she felt a connection had been made.

Daisy was trying to explain to Brian that she felt she might help them to cope with the inevitable fear when their time came to be slaughtered, by somehow being there with them and reassuring them that it would be over very soon, and that they would be happy on the other side of the rainbow bridge. He did not quite understand how this could happen but she said she held them in her heart and prayed. She totally believed their spirits lived on after their bodies died, every bit as much as humans did, and she regularly 'saw' spirits.      Brian knew that she believed these things, and he knew she was sincere. And why would she not be gifted with the ability to see spirits? Brian had read that people noticed what they expected to see; that life was more a function of one's perception of it than it was an objective 'reality' out there, passively awaiting notice.

So, even though their philosophical outlook might be different, the two friends had a depth of mutual respect and acceptance they might seek but fail to find in any other. Yet there was some force which prevented them from becoming more physically intimate; Daisy said it was as if they had been siblings in a former life, and hence it felt inappropriate. Brian did not share this feeling, and never gave up hope of a full blossoming of love between them. Yet he knew better than to bring the subject up, because her past rejections of him still rang in his ears:

"I love you Brian, but not in *that* way."

"You're my best friend Brian, but you feel more like a brother. It wouldn't be right."

"Brian, you know I'm all screwed up about sex, and it would ruin our friendship. I refuse to talk about it."

# Chapter 10

Jean was telling Daisy about a condition called Tourette's syndrome, the symptoms of which included an inability to suppress repetitive noises, odd mannerisms, tics or behaviours. The classic case led to uncontrollable exhortations of profanity and swearing, which could erupt at the most inappropriate times. It often was covered up by obsessive compulsive habits which the sufferer had developed in their effort to control themselves. These could become quite elaborate, intricate and convoluted. Then it became obvious to someone who knew them, that they were not freely expressing themselves, but stereotypically acting out. Jean was reassuring when Daisy, with a flash of self-awareness, linked this syndrome to her own funny habits. She was somewhat given to grimaces and gesticulations, odd noises and mimicry, after all.

"You do not have Tourette's, Daisy Darling! You are one of the most spontaneously free beings I have ever met. Tourette's people have no choice in their behaviours, whereas you can creatively decide from an endlessly expanding repertoire how to put out there what is in here" Jean leaned over and touched Daisy on her chest, at heart level. "Me, I channel a lot of my feelings into fantasy, because I am not able to move my body like you are."

"Jean, one of the first things I noticed about you was your vocal dexterity. I love how you can use your voice so expressively. You have a special signature sound for everyone, don't you? And you can project that sound right across a noisy, crowded campus and the person hears you. It's awesome, cuts through everything! 'Laser Lung Lana' is one of my secret names for you, actually."

"Why Lana?" Jean's face was quizzical.

"It just came to me, I don't mean to be rude, but 'Jean' doesn't have much of a ring to it. Although I do like the fact that nobody can say it without smiling" She exaggerated the effect by putting her little fingers into the upturned corners of her mouth. "Photographers should get people to say 'Jean!' instead of 'cheese!'" They both laughed.

"Especially if they're at a vegan convention" Jean quipped.

"It's true! I hate the word 'cheese' for what it represents anyway – it's a product of the systematic incarceration, rape, enforced lactation and infanticide of grieving mothers."

"Wow, it must be so hard for you to live in the world the way it is, if you think like that" Jean's face was suddenly sombre.

"Yes, it is. But how can I un-know the truth of how cows are treated?"

"I do get what you say about it being weird for humans to drink the milk of bovines, actually Daisy. I've been thinking about it quite a lot. But I really don't want to go there with you, you know? I mean, my life is already restricted enough as it is, without adding a whole bunch of forbidden foods to it."

"I see where you're coming from Jean, but how about you turn that upside down, and view veganism as a liberating decision? Honestly, it opens up a wonderful array of exciting taste sensations which are closed to people who plan their meals around something dead, you know?"

Seeing that Jean really was interested, Daisy thought that she might at last be ready and receptive to sharing the truths she herself had discovered through her own path.

"Eating fresh, colourful, living foods, and creatively combining the subtle tastes and textures of plants, actually gives you more choice, not less."

Jean still looked puzzled. "But I can eat all the fruits and seeds and plants I want, as well as the meat and dairy, already" she argued.

"Ah, you might think you can, but meat and cheese are such predominant substances, they deaden your taste buds. Also, people usually use strong crude unctions to anoint their meal of death; smothering it in mustard, ketchup, gravy and spices." Daisy paused as she saw that Jean was thinking hard. "And most people in practise tend to have the same dozen or so recipes repetitively, which is really quite restrictive, especially as its centred around the meat item, with potatoes, rice or pasta and one or two others veggies next to it."

"Hmm I see what you're saying, and it's true that most people have the same familiar meal choices, over and over. It's been great since you joined my carers' team cos you have such exciting ideas." Jean was as adventurous when it came to food as she was about life in general.

"Food is not just a social or a survival thing; eating is a spiritual act." Daisy went on.

"Sounds like what I tell the Para's about sex" Jean commented. She had a special interest in helping other disabled people to awaken and fulfil their sexuality, especially fellow paraplegics.

Elevating eating to the conscious level, this Daisy could 'get'. But due to her bad experiences in early life, she had walled off her sexual side to a large extent.

"Tell you what, Daze, I'll come to your 'Compassionate Eating' group if you come to my 'Celebrating Sexuality' group. How's that for a deal?"

Daisy groaned, her heart dropping like a stone kicked into a pond. The most she could do was say "Maybe one day" through pursed lips and with a sad, sideways, half smile. Jean had a habit of hitting on her hidden buttons, which left her feeling very exposed and uncomfortable. She so could not go there. Certainly not here and now. She was genuinely happy that Jean was uninhibited and passionate enough to share joy and intimacy, especially with those stigmatised by disabilities. There was no judgement about it, just her own, damaged, inner self.

Their respective University courses continued, and Daisy often managed to work the vegan message into her essays and dissertations in some subtle way, even though it was frustratingly difficult, and she was sad to realise that she was not going to automatically open doors for the animals just because she was a graduate. Her course work was suffering because of this realisation, but she determined to see it through, because she felt that people would listen to her more if she had a degree. Several times she had been marked down because she had strayed from the question set, in her zeal to score a point for animal liberation. In truth she longed for a break from enforced academic study, because there were always so many important books she didn't have time to read as they didn't fit into her subject. She was determined to catch up on these works as soon as she graduated, and to write her own books someday. Sitting quietly in a corner of the college with her big bowl of sprouted lentils and coleslaw, topped with pecans and cherry tomatoes, her thoughts were shattered by the sudden appearance of Clara, blocking her field of vision.

"What's that rabbit food you're eating Hazie? No wonder you're so pale, you need to eat like a lion does! What kind of an idiot would rather be a rabbit than a lion? You're letting the side down: humans are the top of the food chain Dazey". And smirking, she flounced off.

I refuse to let her upset me, said Daisy to herself. But who was she kidding, Clara always got to her; and what's more, she knew it. Why can't she live and let live?

"Because, my darling you are an affront to her, that's why." Brian tried to explain for the umpteenth time. "You're giving her more influence than she really has. You know that you have the moral high ground and don't need to prove anything to her, but she feels she needs to undermine you all the time, to negate your influence."

Daisy wrote on her notebook, 'Don't fear your power, or you give power to your fears', and 'Love is power' to try to remind herself to trust in the rightness and purpose of her cause. 'Intention and focus over force and power' her doodling continued, written as an equation.

It was obvious that humanity had used their ability to think ahead and plan things out in order to exert control over beings far more physically powerful than they were. Elephants and cattle were subjugated from birth by the use of restraints and force, in order to convince them that they were powerless to resist. Horses were relentlessly harnessed and trained to submit and obey enforced commands.

On a positive day, she felt optimistic for the future. But only on a positive day. And Clara seemed to be able to eclipse what started out to be a positive day, no matter how Daisy tried to bolster herself up.

"My Dad says you've got an eating disorder, and you need to be force fed like a goose! He says weirdos like you used to be put in institutions for the good of normal people. You're not getting enough protein – when's the last time you had a proper meal anyway?"

On and on, she always had some cutting comment to make, which left Daisy feeling angry, or upset, and usually both. She began to get palpitations, and her day would cloud over with the expectation of Clara's next attack. And sure enough here it came, "No wonder you never get invited to parties, who'd want you nosing into their fridge, trying to make them feel guilty? I bet you're out liberating mink and stuff at nights, aren't you? That's what extremists like you do. Pretty soon you'll be put in jail as a terrorist. My Dad says they're bringing in laws to stop you lot poking your cameras into his business. There he is employing people to feed the nation, and bleeding heart softies like you get in the way. You're a menace to society, DayZee Doolittle".

"Something has to shift inside of you my darling, in order for Clara to stop bullying you. When did you first feel like a victim of someone else's persecution?" Daisy had confided in Jean about just how much it had been hurting her to have Clara's incessant onslaught. She had shared her childhood wound of being goaded into fighting with her brother, who had taunted and ridiculed her mercilessly about her appearance, her size, and her comparative physical weakness. Why did he do that? Just because she was alive, and in his way? Or because she had been born a year after him and taken their Mother's attention? At least Clara didn't abuse her physically like he had done. For Joe had turned the practise of subtle torture into an art form, creating pain that left no trace. One of the worst was the 'donkey bite' on the inner thigh, caused by rapidly grasping the flesh there between the heel and fingers of his hand, and sharply compressing them to crush, but not bruise, the soft tissues.

There was the thumb knuckle jab between the ribs, swift and deadly, that left her incapable of breathing deeply afterwards.

Another of Joe's well practised and invisible inflictions was the 'head rap': a hard rap to the top of the head by hammer blows of his knuckles, so very disorienting.

What about the 'dead leg' he could induce by precisely kicking her in one spot on her leg; and the way he could make her collapse to the ground by a karate chop at the back of her knee. He really enjoyed flicking her ears in passing, with a swift deft flick of his middle finger, which could really sting and smart for a surprisingly long time, particularly when repeated in exactly the same spot a few times.

And always, these tortures were accompanied by the sound of his mocking laughter, at his skill and at her misery. Often, when he had grabbed and thrown her to the ground and had her pinned beneath his knees, immobilising her shoulders with his hands and superior body weight, he would cough up a big glob of spittle and drool it into her face, aiming to get it to fall into her eyes. Her long hair when braided was a favourite target of course, and he delighting in yanking her ponytail backwards, making her head jerk back painfully.

Sometimes, when he was feeling benevolent, he insisted that she choose her method of torture for herself, and she always chose Chinese burns to her wrists, because this only stung, and stopped hurting immediately he finished inflicting it.

The wet tea towel, flicked expertly to the back of her legs, was another favourite of his, striking as she stood with her back to the kitchen, doing the washing up. That really stung, but at least it didn't ache for hours, and sometimes days afterwards, like the elbow dug and ground into her shoulder blade, with his full body weight behind it, as she was held face down on the ground.

Joe also had a range of painful pinches, deep punches, and swift kicks in his arsenal. Worse still, in their way, were the psychological torments, like the night terrorising, creeping into her room in the dark. And putting horrible things in her bed, or hanging her dolls by their necks inside her wardrobe, so that their gouged eyes were on her eye level when she opened it.

Outdoors, Joe kept hidden a range of dangerous items he had acquired, such as his catapult and whipping switches. Mum had confiscated his gat gun though, after he had inadvertently shot her in the back of her leg with a pellet as she had been hanging out washing. He had 'only intended to wing it past her ear to wake her up a bit', he claimed. He had a knife collection of which he was very proud, and his stated reason for throwing them perilously close to her in the garden was because the soil they embedded themselves in on landing was the best polish for the metal that there was. He aimed for between her feet, and said that if she kept still she would be safe, as he had been practising his skill. Once he had pinned her shoe to the lawn with her foot still in it, and sat laughing like a drain as she struggled to remove it. Even when she showed him the blood where it had grazed her toe, he mocked that it was only a scratch and she was over-reacting, as usual, like the weedy girl she was.

"Does it still happen now, with your brother?" Jean was asking.

"Well he still teases me a lot, mocks me and belittles me, but he stopped the wrestling stuff when I made the mistake of growing stronger, and then one time I was suddenly able to throw him on his back and pin him down for a change."

"Wow! That must have felt awesome!" Jean dinged the bell on her wheelchair rapidly to reinforce her exclamation, imagining the thrill of overthrowing the tyrant.

"No, it was horrible! The look on his face was so betrayed, like I had broken some unwritten rule........I jumped off him straight away and apologised, but he turned his back on me, and never touched me again."

"I don't understand, wasn't that good?" Jean's puzzled expression had the faintest shadow of her brother Joe's incredulous face that day. In fact she saw Joe's face superimposed upon Jean's face, in exact detail, and once again felt the pang in her heart.

"It broke my heart. I knew that I had committed the unforgivable sin, by overpowering him. Even though I was young, I sensed he was cruel to me because he loved me really, but could not show it in a nice way. That sounds really messed up doesn't it? All I know is he never touched me again – ever, not even a hug."

"Aaaah" Jean received a bolt of insight then, which was to help her unravel future cases of sibling abuse in families. The conspiracy of silence that operated to mute them. The victim-hood of both abuser and those they abused. The cycle of acquiescence which could lead abused children to find life partners who would treat them similarly badly. She could see how desperately Daisy missed the contact with her brother, and how some vulnerable people became drawn into escalating downward spirals of masochism.

Daisy had already shared with her how she had taken to self-harming following this pivotal incident with her brother. To replace the lost feeling of being alive which his physical punishment had given her, she had started cutting herself. It was somehow a calming influence that reduced the anxiety which otherwise arose and intensified. She learned this when she began shaving her legs and underarms and accidentally caused little, richly bleeding, nicks. Soon it was becoming a daily habit, and she would cut herself accidentally-on-purpose whilst peeling potatoes, or chopping cabbage for the family dinner. Her Mother thought that she was going through a clumsy phase, and it became normal for her to appear with several sticking plasters showing. She especially felt compelled to cut the corners of her eyes and mouth, she didn't know why, and it became frustrating to only permit herself to dig lines there with her fingernails, for fear of arousing attention. Cutting where it did not show did not feel nearly as satisfying. On the hands felt most rewarding, but she knew that she couldn't get away with doing that too many times a week.

At least when Neil had come into her life she had stopped cutting, because he provided more than ample, strong physical stimulation, and bucketful's of distraction.

"Have you not realised, precious animal defender and fearless environmental warrior, that your strength to stand up and speak now has come precisely from that oppression and vulnerability?" Jean's words, in the exact inflection of her voice, kept reverberating in Daisy's head. Causing a jolt of purest clarity to sweep through her troubled mind. Her eyes closed involuntarily as she swooned, in the sunlight by the river, reflecting. Jean's insight was like a tsunami of Truth, sweeping away the clinging cloud of inadequacy, failure and sorrow which had hung over her for so interminably long a time. Another piece of childhood soul reclaimed, back from the isolation and separation it had remained marooned in. In a totally real way, little Daisy had been continuously reliving, re-experiencing her torture at the hands of her brother, who should have been her best friend and defender, playmate and confidante.

For lost children, and for animals, there was no passage of time, there was only the tormented moment which could not be erased. With this insight piercing her childhood prison, she had become enabled to reach back in, and retrieve her inner child. It felt literally like becoming more whole and alive than ever before. Empowered, at peace, and safe. As the reclaimed child melted back into her, she found herself in a beautiful fertile valley of exquisite life and colour, where everything was a hundred times more alive and beautiful than anything she had ever seen, felt, or heard.

Heard? Oh, there was a perfect sound, like a gong tone, resonating through, and with, and around her. So loud and low, yet so high and soft, it was almost invisible to her ears. Yet all her senses were picking it up. All her senses were exchanging with one another – not just senses; she was 'theeling' in a total body-mind way. She was able to see all around her without turning her head, and she felt what lay over the horizon as if she knew this place intimately. The meditation cave up there in the mountainside, for instance........the mere thought of which would transport her there effortlessly.

She knew this place! The clear light bathing her, so pure and sweet. She had been here before, it was intimately familiar to her.

"Where did you just go?" Jean's angelic face smiled at her with such kindness that it lifted her heart. Like a thousand butterflies all taking off at once, from a single point of restfulness.

"VEGANTOPIA!" replied Daisy with a beatific smile, as tears of joy came unbidden from the corners of her eyes. The two embraced then, with an unselfconsciousness and mutuality, as if nobody else existed to see them. As if nobody else was there. As if nothing bad could ever come near them again. Daisy slowly came to, hearing herself humming and toning in the strangest way, with several notes coming out of her simultaneously. Jean was making similar humming, toning sounds, in exact harmony with her. What? Had they been spiked with some drug or something?

"No drug" said Jean as if she had telepathically caught the thought from Daisy's mind. "And no illusion either, this is the way we're meant to live, Sweet Angel. This is how we used to live, in Eden. And this is how we shall live again, as we return to The Garden."

Jean's face had morphed again, this time into the most stunningly glorious face anyone could ever gaze upon – The Lady! But this time she appeared not just as the face of the quintessential Mother, whom Daisy had first encountered when she had been in hospital. She revealed herself as vast, yet intimate; universal, yet personal. Surrounded by her bluest of blue cloaks, under which she was sheltering all her children. And these children included all of the creatures, in safety and shared Oneness, together. She was the Mother of All Life! Giving safety to all the innocents of the world. The blue was so intense, it reminded her of the bluebell wood she loved to visit every May time. Where she would lie down amongst the flowers, inhaling their intoxicating scent, and sensing the awake presence of the living landscape. And the blue was reminiscent of the vivid blue of Daisy's Father's eyes. She remembered, with a sudden rapturous gasp, gazing into them as a new-born baby, held safely in his arms, in wrapped bliss. And the blue was like the sparkling ocean where she had once porpoised about, diving into its welcoming embrace. Discovering in self-forgetfulness an unimagined freedom and joy. Losing herself completely, for a long lovely while.

Then, reliving this peak experience by herself, in her memory or living fantasy, as gently as could be, the surf rocked her back upon the shore. She stretched out her fingers and toes and found herself once more returning to the familiar refectory. With its everyday noises, and mundane mumblings, incoming like the language of bees.

As if to break the bubble, Clara hove into view, too quickly for Daisy to put up her shields.

"How many vegans does it take to change a light bulb, Bedazzlement?"

Daisy couldn't help but laugh, and responded, "I don't know Clarity, how many vegans will it take to change you?"

"None, because vegans will never change anything!" Clara completed her joke.

But a glance had passed between them, in that unguarded moment, and Daisy felt a heart's pang that was not hers, piercing bitter sweetly. In the next moment it was gone, and Clara was moving away. There was an inexplicable weightiness about her which Daisy had never noticed before, worn like a cloak of sorrow about her shoulders.

As suddenly as the reverie had come upon her, it had passed. She had somehow got up and appeared at her next class, courtesy of her legs, which thankfully knew how, all by themselves. And her hands had written 'THE RAPTURE IS REAL' in the middle of the blank page in front of her. And then gone on to doodle flowers, and magical creatures, and cloudscapes, and music notes all around it. 'The Rapture is Real' she said over and over again, as she rode on the bus home. It was her new mantra, even though she was not sure what it meant. The world looked different to her somehow, less hostile, and more secure. She tried sharing as best she could with Brian, over the delicious meal which he had prepared.

"Brian, you made this food with love, didn't you? I can taste it! Why do people not feel the huge difference between foods thrown together in a factory, and food carefully prepared by hand?"

"They do, Daisy Dreamer!" he laughed a bit shyly, "That's why people cling to Momma's meals, a home cooked dinner they remember from childhood."

"Ah, of course!" Daisy suddenly got it: why people found it so difficult when their eating habits were challenged. Familiar family food was sacrosanct, primal and pre-rational.

Oooh, so she would have to find some way of ever so gently showing this to people, and replacing the feeling they were seeking to recreate. Not with counterfeit pieces of mock roast chicken, or fake steak pie, but with the actual feeling they were hungry to fill themselves with. A sense of belonging and comfort, a sense of forgetting all of the scrapes and falls, the disappointments and the squabbles, for that special time that they were all sitting down together, sharing the same meal.

Daisy's usual personal preference was for simple food, as near to natural as possible. But today Brian had made one of her favourite comfort dinners, which was jacket potato with hummus, salad, and baked beans. He had even made some coleslaw with her special tahini mayonnaise. They took it in turns to make a communal meal in the shared household of five students. Even though the others were not vegetarians, they were considerate enough to make at least some of the food suitable for Daisy. She never tried to force her vegan views on them, and delighted in seeing their faces when they tasted, and enjoyed, some new recipe of hers. She hoped that she was slowly converting them, but appreciated that to be lasting, change had to come from within themselves. So she never complained, even if the meal was white pasta, which she thoroughly disliked. And she did not point out the higher cost of the meals she made with red, wild and brown rice, cashew nuts, and soft shelled hemp seeds.

She was grateful for the mixed group of folks who had got together to share this funny old house. It was a typical, dilapidated but cheap, student dwelling. Their landlord, Will, was friendly and understanding, and did not mind them decorating the place. The only time he got annoyed was when James and Becky had decided they were a couple, and knocked a hole through the wall between their rooms. He did not find out for a long while, because they had hung a huge, multi-coloured spread over one side, and pushed a wardrobe in front of the hole on the other side. They enjoyed pretending it was their portal to a different reality; some sort of personal fantasy they had going on. Will, perhaps reminiscing about his own rather wild student days, now long gone, had relented and been generous enough to let them keep it, on condition that they bricked the hole back up properly at the end of their tenancy.

Every couple of weeks, Daisy caught the train from Manchester to Sheffield, where Brian was studying, then cycled the three miles to his rented home. Although there was no garden at his shared house, they did have a cobbled yard surrounded by a high wall where their bikes were safely kept. Brian had constructed a lean-to roof under which he could work on the bikes, which were constantly in need of attention. He enjoyed being out there, tinkering and inventing ways to keep them running. He much preferred doing this than the housework it got him out of doing. He was adept at spotting and bringing back odd pieces of broken, abandoned bicycle to his shed, from skips on his way home. Many of the students in his University had benefited from his sharp-eyed acquisitions, and he was famous for the speed with which he could resurrect deceased bone shakers. He had a dream of cycling around the world, carrying all of his provisions in panniers strapped onto his trusty, handmade bike. Daisy preferred walking, and envisaged long, barefoot pilgrimages, for her future.

Together, during the holidays, they had completed many camping and touring expeditions, both on foot and with their bikes. They had accumulated and adapted whatever equipment they could find, much of it leaky and inadequate. Far too many rides had been marred because of sweating then chilling beneath voluminous capes, hand-me-down jumpers and taped up cagoules. Their shared ambition was to be able to afford the lightest, most breathable, and waterproof clothing possible. Daisy teased Brian that she was going to find him some discarded, skin-tight, lurid, lycra garment in a charity shop and make him wear it. Considering his well-toned, muscle-defined body and the astonishingly over-endowed assets of his 'family jewels', he was overly modest. Since loftiness and willowy limbs seemed to be highly prized attributes in the social attraction stakes, and he, like she, was of less than average height, maybe this explained his shyness. In fact, she felt that being petite, small and agile was an advantage and an attribute.

Whilst managing at last to relax and settle in at University, Daisy still felt that she had to make big efforts to be an example of rationality and loving kindness as she interacted with others. It was as if she was the representative for all vegans, and it was her responsibility to be a model of benevolent gentleness. Needless to say, she was often failing to keep up the impossibly high standards she expected from herself. She had started leafleting at Animal Charity events, which meant lots of people stopped and talked to her. More than once she had been complimented on the non-aggressive, sympathetic way she listened. And on her willingness to compromise with those not ready to give up meat and dairy completely. There must be some dogmatic, inflexible activists out there, she realised. One young man told her that he had been sneeringly called, "Murderer" when he admitted to enjoying a "nice steak", even though he had bothered to stop and sign petitions at another stall. A couple who stayed and chatted for quite a long time, then returned later with cake and tea for her, shared that they had met very belligerent, pushy activists in the past, and it had put them off.

Secretly, to herself, Daisy sympathised with those angry activists. She remembered how difficult it had been for her to not express the rage she felt – it went way beyond anger, following her compulsion to watch appalling, undercover videos. There was a lot of graphic footage of the atrocities which had been secretly filmed, in many an animal breeding facility or slaughter house.

Forcing herself to bear witness, without turning away, because the animals had no option but to endure it. Only to feel helpless despair when people refused to hear about it, or dismissed it as isolated incidents, or even as faked propaganda. Talk about denial!

People were so focussed on keeping their fingers in their ears and not hearing the cries of the innocent victims of the world's inhumanity. She wondered how they could simply walk away, having been informed about such appalling things. Especially as some factory farm and slaughterhouse workers had been caught deliberately abusing the animals. This was a sure sign that they, too, were suffering in their own way, from the sheer horror of the job they were doing.

What bright young man wakes up one morning and decides that his life's purpose is to dismember still living, gasping, throat-slitted pigs as they whizzed past on a conveyor belt, dangling from one hind leg?

What happened to the life's dreams of some young woman who spends her days hooking chickens up by their feet, as fast as her hands can move, only to watch them pass by in their journey to the electric bath. The water was supposed to stun them into unconsciousness before they reached the throat cutting blades. But it inevitably happened too many times in every day that some individuals would be craning their necks up at that crucial moment, and therefore miss being stunned. And then some of these would similarly avoid the blade, and end up being plunged into the scalding tank. The boiling water tank designed to loosen their feathers from their skin, and these little beings still fully awake, aware and heinously tortured.

'The way humanity treats animals is a reflection of the way they treat one another, for all things are connected'. This she knew in her heart. Yet she also knew that people reacted to anger and judgement by shutting down, not opening up, their awareness. Her Mum used to say, 'You catch more wasps with honey than with vinegar'. And for certain, in order to awaken compassion in others, many different approaches were needed.

Logic and proof were only a small part of the process, because humans did not live entirely from their rational minds. It felt essential to be coming from a place of love and respect, and not simply pushing her beliefs upon anybody. Appealing to the innate kindness and sensitivity she sought to elicit from them. It irked her tremendously, however, when she heard the response, "I respect your choice to eat plants, and I expect you to respect my choice to eat animals." Because, of course, there was a third party in this so called 'personal choice', who's life and feelings were being completely disregarded: the individual being deprived of her very life.

Perhaps there was a key to every person's heart, and very sensitive skills required to find and turn that key. This was part of what Daisy was learning and practising with every interaction. It was completely obvious to her that others were operating from limited forms of consciousness, which enabled them to maintain a tragic and fatal distancing from all around them. This alone could account for the history of horrors which humanity had become accustomed to inflict without any awareness of the suffering it caused.

# Chapter 11

Daisy went along to a pagan group she had seen advertised on the Uni noticeboard, imagining that worship of the Goddess must be inspired by an awestruck adoration of the glorious life She carried on her back. Surely, reverence for the feminine archetype must include a reverence for the dignity and purpose of the astonishing array of beautiful beings adorning Her mantle.

She agreed with them that the patriarchal religions were somewhat to blame for the objectivisation and subjectivisation of beings deemed lesser than humans, because it taught that man was above them. Yet she could not help observing the same old speciesism at work here too, the unquestioned second rate citizenship afforded to the types of animal which humans had best learned to dominate. These pagans were as blatantly carnist as everyone else, yet when she attempted to point out the discrepancy between their beliefs and their practises, all she got was piffle about it being natural for them to eat meat. It was the same mindset as her father had given her, that 'animals are here for our use.'

So, they thought they were honouring Mother Nature, whilst contributing to Her degradation and downfall? This seemed to be a highly selective, human centred viewpoint. Even though these pagans said they rejected the patriarchal belief system, there was still clearly a homo-centric core, and the sensing and shaping of nature from that supremacist, speciesist perspective. Daisy was deeply saddened, because she liked the notion of gathering in the sacred groves of trees, working with the elements as forms of consciousness, and getting in touch with pre-domesticated, wild states of being, in community with others. It just seemed false when it was not underpinned by, and reflected within, their basic lifestyle.

Connecting with a lady who was wearing fur, Daisy said "How do you balance out the fact that the fur you are wearing came from one of nature's beautiful beings whose life was stolen so that you could wear it?"

"This fur came to me by power animal magic. The animals seek to help us to connect with Gaia by giving us their energy."

"Oh, so the former owner of this skin actually walked out of the woods and lay down asking you to kill her then, did it?"

"It knew its purpose was to be woven back into the web of life. Life is inseparable from death, and it is being honoured and respected every time I put it on."

"Was it a male or female fox? Did they have a family? How old were they? You didn't bother to enquire, so how respectful was that? No, it's the skin of a dead fox, murdered by anal electrocution, after a life of utter depravation of all their natural instincts, having been kept in a metal cage."

The fur wearing lady had lost her genial countenance, "You obviously don't resonate with the higher purpose of nature, and the web of life" she said condescendingly.

"What I see is a way for you to get away with wearing fur that your conscience can live with, because you want to. Frankly, I think its worse when people make excuses to do what they wish to do, by dressing it up as something noble or spiritual."

Daisy tuned on her heel and left the meeting before she could be thrown out.

She genuinely had not gone there to antagonise anyone, but in search of like-hearted company. Was life always going to be such a compromise? Did she really need to 'live and let live' with other peoples choices and values, even though they demonstrably were not 'letting live' other beings, in their own pursuit of pleasure?

Sowing seeds, questioning assumptions, speaking out from the animals perspective, that's what she was called to do, that was her higher purpose. It was not about being liked, or welcomed for her truth telling.

The next day, sitting with Jasper, she was relieved to see that he was wearing a very attractive belt with pouches on it made from fabric. He did have other belts made from leather, which she had remarked upon in the past. Was it wishful thinking that he had got rid of them? He had a mediaeval look about him, with an elaborately embroidered waistcoat over a billowy-sleeved, soft muslin shirt. She loved the way he dressed, in such contrast to the joyless black garb of most other students. However, he was eating a cheese sandwich. It was not really any preferable to sitting watching someone eating a dead animal. To her, it was secondly removed death; why did nobody ever think to ask about the fate of the calf whose milk it rightly was, which they had condemned to death by stealing his Mother's milk? She had pointed this out to Jasper before, about how a cow or any mammalian mother only lactated after giving birth, for up to a year in the case of cows. And how the dairy industry had no use for all the male calves that were born, and hence killed most of them, whilst their grieving mothers looked on.

Thinking that she would have another attempt to explain this to him, but in a different way, she remarked, "It is no coincidence that man had selected the most gentle and docile creatures to enslave. Do you think anyone has ever tried to confine and milk a tiger and got away with it?"

"I bet tigers milk has less saturated fat than cows!"

"Are you deliberately missing my point here, Jasper? How about caging and stealing the eggs away from an eagle, d'you think anyone's ever done that?"

"People take the easiest route to staying alive and seeing to their needs that they can, I don't think it was deliberate enslavement, more opportunistic and using their intelligence to not be hungry".

"Yes of course, thousands of years ago when the idea first occurred, fair enough. But my whole point is that now there are billions of animals bred and raised in factory farms, which is inherently evil."

"Doesn't 'evil' imply wilful, deliberate cruelty?"

"Precisely, and even more evil because it is deliberately hidden away, and not openly known about. Why doesn't anyone think it's weird that the earth is groaning under the weight of at least 3 times the number of cattle as there are humans on the planet?"

"For sure I see the way centuries of heavy, cloven feet has shaped the landscape, and are currently turning to dust the precious topsoil, without which no plants can grow." Jasper was focusing his final year at uni on environmental architecture, and was keenly interested in blending the natural with the man-made world. Daisy loved hearing him talk about bio-mimicry, green cities and incorporating vertical agriculture in designing the buildings of the future. It reminded her of the visions she and Brian shared and cherished. She used to assume that she was having some memory recall of lost civilisations like Atlantis and Lemuria, but when Julian described his designs, her heart swelled up with hope that they could actually be prescient dreams of the world to come.

There was something qualitatively and energetically different about the conversations she could have with Jasper compared to other people. Even though there were places where their views failed to agree, there was never any rancour or anger. He had some pretty weird ideas though. For example he had tried to suggest that animals were actually 'thought forms' and not individual sentient beings.

"Back in Descarte's day, whilst dissecting a dog strapped to a table, he had made the audacious claim that the howling noise it was making was merely a reflex action, and no more indicative of consciousness and ability to suffer than the clanging of a bell. And up until the 1960's, doctors used to operate on human babies without anaesthetic because it was believed that their nervous systems hadn't developed sufficiently for them to feel pain. Can't you see what a massively disconnected view that was Jasper?"

"To be honest, Daisy, I think that you over sentimentalise and project your feelings onto externalities. What if babies and animals lack the referrents you have, because they have not learned to distinguish pain and pleasure in the same way as you?"

"Consider this: what if you cogitise and disconnect from the obvious capacity of other beings to have intense sensations, possibly way more exquisitely sensitive than yours are? Don't we owe them the benefit of the doubt? My feeling is that our blunted senses and numbed capacity are a mere fraction of what they probably feel."

"But Daisy, now you're the one judging the ability to feel by outward appearance. Some old geezer in the park with his bottle of meths, apparently all shot away and incoherent. The kids on the swings off their heads on DMT, who are we to objectify their subjective experiences?"

"Meaning what, that we can never really know what anyone else is going through?"

"No, more that we shouldn't infer that their experience is the same as ours would be, were we to swap shoes and skins with them".

"Hang on, this still doesn't detract from the fact that we now know that babies feel, without having to be taught, what pain is. It has been shown that they even have awareness and consciousness pre-birth. I don't believe babies are blank slates, either. I think they bring all sorts of consciousness in with them at conception."

"You mean from past lives and stuff?" Jasper was clearly sceptical about that.

"Why not? And on a proven factual note, lest we forget, the authoritative wisdom of the 19th Century was that black people were incapable of finer feelings or higher level thought by the white supremacists who wanted to continue exploiting and keeping them as slaves."

Daisy paused as she grasped for further analogies to prove her point. "You must have seen documentaries of third world countries where 'beasts of burden' are being mercilessly driven and beaten to carry impossible loads, whilst emaciated, where ill-fitting harnesses have rubbed visible sores on their backs, and they're hobbling along lame with crippled feet". Daisy was almost in tears as she described it. "Then recall how painful it is to have just one little blister on your heel, and have to keep on walking until you can get home and find a plaster, and change your shoes."

"Are you saying its a matter of degree, or of relative comfort and discomfort? Let me put it this way. What do you make of the learned syndrome that sadomasochists get into whereby the infliction of what would be pain to the average person has been somehow re-asigned as pleasurable to them."

"How can we know what atrocities they might have endured as children to cause them to crave to recreate them later in life? Jean has a friend who is a dominatrix, and she claims that it is empowering and releasing to her clients to have their chosen 'strong discomfort' inflicted on them. But that's still a long way from the techniques used in circus animal training such as bull hooks, whips and starvation, to force them to perform unnatural tricks. Taking children to watch such things is not only demeaning, its a major instigator of the disconnection that permits and perpetuates the inequality and suffering in our societies. So we end up not even empathising with our own kind."

"I do see a connection between that and vivisection, where scientists dismiss as anthropomorphic the idea that the animals they experiment on feel fear or anxiety. Whilst at the same time testing and developing anti-anxiety and pain killing drugs on them in deliberately designed stress situations."

"Oh my God yes, Jasper. Believe it or not, I have sometimes had telepathic conversations with animals. For example, I was sitting in a field with some cows, and quieted my own chattering thoughts enough to link in with their, quite different, wavelength of consciousness. I asked them what their wishes were for their lives, if they had the choice. They said that their overriding need was to roam freely across the earth, as it is inherent in their nature to walk great distances, following the cycles of sun and seasons in annual migrations to find their ancestral grazing, mating and birthing grounds."

"Wow, that's amazing."

"What, that I could understand them, or that I could receive their message? Please understand they don't think in language, so it takes the ability to convert into words the sense impressions they conveyed to me. Every species of animal has a slightly different 'frequency' I suppose you could call it, a bit like radio waves that they share a group mind on. The 'collective unconscious' was the way Jung described out human-centric field of vibrational communication. Except that we selectively block most of it out, in order to live the distracted mechanical lives now forced upon us."

"I like that concept, it reminds me of the saying 'those who were dancing were considered mad by those incapable of hearing the music'".

"Exactly Jasper! I think that through social constructs and conformity we've been conditioned and brainwashed into narrow patterns of thought and behaviour, so much so that we're receiving a mere fraction of the inputs and perceptions that could be available to us. It is no measure of sanity to be adapted to our profoundly sick society, frankly".

"What if the masses of the people have been deliberately bred in a slightly more sophisticated way than we breed other animals, by a ruling elite who stay hidden, yet manipulate what we are exposed to. Like education, mass media and entertainment are programming how we live and behave to such an extent that we don't even think for ourselves? And vaccinations, the radiation from mobile phones and computers, fluoride and toxins in our food and water supply have calcified our pineal gland, which is where we get our ability to access expanded consciousness."

"How would we even know? And where does intelligent scepticism turn into paranoia?"

"By waking up and seeing the wiring under the board, the matrix. By noticing the shuttered minds, and shining a spotlight on them".

"It's a sobering thought, for sure" said Daisy with a shudder.

"How about the even more outlandish idea that the human race might have been genetically modified, dumbed and numbed down, cloned and corralled, for the longest time by a race of beings who syphon off our emotions as fuel? Imagine these beings have no capacity to feel for themselves, in the rich way that we do. Might not raw, psycho-emotional energy, be hugely attractive to them? Suppose they get high from watching us fight and kill each other, like people used to enjoy watching gladiators, or cock fights".

"Now you're really creeping me out! So they would deliberately incite conflict and wars. Oh wow. You don't really think that could be true do you?"

"Some people, like David Icke, say that the ruling elite are in fact reptilian aliens."

"Frankly, whether they are or not, it doesn't concern me as much as the urgent need to raise our current mass consciousness sufficiently to wake up and stop destroying the planet."

"I'm with you on that one for sure. Hey, look at the time. Phew, this has been a bit full on, hasn't it! I need a coffee to clear my head, and to get to my lecture. See you in interdimensional hyperspace, Daisy!" Jasper reluctantly grabbed his things and left, leaving Daisy's head spinning wildly.

# Chapter 12

Falling asleep in a particularly boring lecture on plant genetics and gene splicing, Daisy had been musing about epigenetics. This made much more sense to her and was exciting, not a drag down of energy. This was always her personal benchmark of truth in any subject; if it depressed her it was either a bad thing or a lie, but when it inspired and uplifted her it contained truth. Stumbling out of the lecture theatre, Daisy saw that Jean and Clara were deep in conversation on the grass. She felt a bit betrayed, as if her friend was consorting with her enemy. It ate away at her all the rest of that day, and left a very unpleasant taste in her mouth.

With a dull inevitability when Brian next came to visit, she was sounding off about this, but he cut her off in mid rant.

"Paranoia" he said with uncharacteristic bluntness. "You ever hear the saying 'Be gentle to all, for everyone is fighting a great battle'?"

"What do you mean? Do you feel sorry for Clara too? The poor little rich girl? Inheritor of her father's empire of death?" Daisy was clenching her fists in temper.

"For goodness sake, stop demonising Clara. She can't help who her father is any more than we can...."

"Yes but.........."with immense effort, Daisy managed to stop herself from saying something really nasty. Maybe she was projecting too much onto Clara, maybe she hadn't ever given her a chance. But she stubbornly did not want to. Yet she could not get rid of the picture she had seen in the refectory that time, of Clara's pained face, and the heart-stab she had felt. What *was* that all about? On the one hand she had to admit that she had discovered in her nemesis Clara a target for all her barely repressed frustration. To be fair, it was not this gawky, regressive woman who was single handedly decimating the natural world. Frankly, there was something unsavoury about her which caused a reflex of revulsion and repulsion to arise. Almost as if they were matter and anti-matter, incapable of co-existing in the same space. Daisy could not wait to finish university and be rid of the hideous woman! Everything about her was gross and ugly, from her upturned snout of a nose to the flap of her out-turned feet. She even smelt disgusting, had greasy bumpy skin and dull spiky bleached hair. It was hard not to actually vomit on the spot when she watched her stuffing her miserable pie hole, even though that action at least meant that she wasn't spouting her hunting, fishing, hanging propaganda. Truly, the other side of the planet was closer than she ever wanted to be to the vile person.

On some level Daisy recognised that she must be over-reacting, and yet she really had come to loathe the very sight of Clara. Even the Interior Design course she was doing reeked of privilege and conspicuous consumption.

"Why can't she just stay away from me, get a life, and leave me to do my thing?" she wailed. With a shudder, Daisy suddenly wondered out loud if Clara stalked her and spied on her even when she didn't know she was there. Then laughingly she imagined the impossibility of that bulky body hiding behind any bush or tree, or having the capacity to keep up with Daisy's speed and agility.

"What if she comes armed with one of her father's weapons, in stealth, lurking in camouflage clothing, her narrow eyes lining her sights mercilessly upon your heart?" Brian teased wickedly.

"Now you really are making me paranoid". Daisy leaped up and shook herself, head to toe, until her teeth rattled and she went dizzy. She had to make a huge effort to shake those misgivings from her mind. Try to ignore the wretched woman, stop even talking to her as it only seemed to encourage her. 'It takes two to fight', her mother used to say when she found Daisy crying after a painful and demeaning struggle with Joe. She was no longer a child, trapped in a house with a brother who had all day to think up evil tricks to play on her. Somehow she must be buying into, and colluding with Clara in order for their conflicts to happen. She resolved to stop anticipating, and hence attracting to herself, any more interactions. "From now on, I shall rise above her games, and simply float away. Clara has no power over me".

"That's the spirit, Daze, you can take charge, and choose to think of something wonderful instead".

"I choose to focus on something fun, like the upcoming open mike night, and what I'm going to sing." Having a versatile voice capable of singing lots of different vocal styles, gave her too much choice. She didn't want to be always singing protest songs, or only folk, or blues, and pop was most people's choice. She enjoyed surprising the gathered group with something different. Last time she had sung a sweet traditional ballad called "Garten Mothers Lullaby" which was well received, followed up by a rendition of the stunning song "Spirit" by "The Waterboys". She usually managed to add an extra verse or two written by herself, which shared a message about honouring the earth, restoring rights to indigenous people, and freeing the animal slaves.

"I want to sing something sacred and beautiful, this time, and maybe something in French" she said, hoping to squeeze an opinion out of Brian. His raised eyebrows told her he thought that might be a bit extreme. Which of course only encouraged her desire to shake up the scene a bit, as well as to inspire other singers to choose something unexpected. In the end she chose "Plaisir D'Amour", a French song made famous by Edith Piaff. Following that she spontaneously chose "Ave Maria" by Schubert, sung in the original latin.

"Why did you choose that, out of all the billions of pieces you could sing?" Brian wanted to know.

"I'm not sure, but it keeps popping into my head. I used to love singing it in the school choir. It always lifts me up to hear it, and it's so very beautiful."

"Fair enough, for sure the open mike nights have been very opened up since you started singing there! I could listen to you sing anything, but I'd really like you to sing something raunchy, just once."

"I'll think about it, but I'm not putting in any silly pouting or posturing, so don't get your hopes up. How horrible it must be, to be so driven by testosterone and condemned to thinking about sex every few minutes of your life! What about when we're running? Does your mind get a rest then?"

"Yes, when I manage to get in the zone where running is effortless, which as you know is very rare. The doorway seems to be on the far side of the wall you hit when you're out of breath and can't carry on. Like that time when I left you standing gasping, and suddenly got a huge spurt of energy from somewhere because I forced myself to keep going anyway."

"I had stitch so badly and was panting so fast I was scared I was going to kill myself" Daisy remembered with a pained expression.

"But you wouldn't have, Daze, it was amazing, like having an orgasm; I seemed to become very vast and got outside of my self-identity".

"All down your leg and no paper, eh? So it was still all about sex."

"Thanks for demoting my peak moment, Daisy. Even though I realise you're making a joke about it because any talk about sex makes you uncomfortable. You're missing so much joy, you know".

Changing the subject skilfully, Daisy said, "Do you think that wild animals live constantly in the zone? As in that secret hallowed place where athletes and artists, and even scientists only realise they've been after the event. When they've downloaded some inspirational insight or created something out of the ethers?"

"To the extent that wild animals have never been habitually entrained and conditioned like humans have, so they're free in each moment, maybe. That's an interesting thought actually. People seem to think only along the tramlines of concepts laid down for them, by deliberate indoctrination."

"Precisely, so what might be the best way to show them that they're not making free choices at all, but pre-programmed, other-directed ones?"

"Choice implies some awareness of the act of choosing, doesn't it?" Brian was grappling with this one.

"What totally pisses me off is when people trot out that line about my leaving them to choose what they eat, because they 'respect my choice not to eat meat'. I have to remind them of the 3<sup>rd</sup> party in their personal choice: the animal who isn't offered any choice at all. The animal who isn't an object but a sentient being with a strong desire to live; 'the absent referent' as Carol Adams calls it in her book: "The Sexual Politics Of Meat".

"Heck yeah, I wonder when the personhood status of animals will be honoured. Why can't these 'animal loving' meat eaters see the hypocrisy of adoring the unique character and personality of their own cat or dog, whilst denying its existence in any other species?"

"Tell me about it Brian, the other day this bloke was laughing as he called his vegetarian girlfriend a hypocrite because she admitted to feeling tempted by the bacon he was frying. I gave him my most withering look and said, 'Shame on you, you don't deserve her'".

"Maybe he was so good in bed she overlooked his ethical failings."

"There you go bringing sex into the conversation again, stop it Brian!"

"Sorry, but when love comes through the door, reason flies out of the window."

"Do you really think that? It seems a sad thing to say. I've been trying very hard to treat everyone I meet with love, as if they're already the gentle fellow Vegantopians I want them to be."

"How about breeding with this Vegantopian who's right next to you, waiting to populate the world with lovely vegan babies?" And Brian bravely leapt on her, smothering her with his ardour.

"Get off you oaf! We were just having a good intellectual conversation then!" Daisy was laughing in spite of herself. She was in the fertile period of her monthly cycle, and knew that he knew this, being the animal that he was.

"You're a woman, you can multitask, how about seeing how we could enrich our conversation whilst making love, my lovely Vetopiana?"

Pushing him away with a great effort, Daisy rolled her eyes exasperatedly, "Can't a girl keep her personal space around here?" She brushed the back of her hand across her mouth as if deliberately removing his slobber, and stood up.

"Shut up wench and make some tea! And what's for pudding?" was his infuriating reply.

Daisy threw a cushion at him on her way out to the kitchen.

"It just so happens that I have a plum crumble I made earlier, waiting to have rice milk custard poured all over it."

"Oooh you know just how to get to me, don't you!" he playfully lunged at her one last time.

"Don't get too excited, I made the crumble with wheat germ and coconut flour for extra nutrients, and of course there's no sugar in the plums, they're quite sweet enough as they are."

"I might have known, 'healthy food' again," Brian's two index fingers made quotation marks in the air.

"You don't have to partake of nature's bounty, but you know that the longer you keep pandering to your sugar addiction, the longer it will control you."

"Look, I'm doing really well: I've cut down to only 1 sugar in my drinks now. There's no way I could get going in the mornings without full bore coffee".

'Miracles take a little longer' she intoned under her breath, another of her frequent sayings. This one came from her Uncle Sam's workshop, the place of her happiest childhood memories. He had this ancient metal sign hanging up which read:

IMPOSSIBILITIES DONE IMMEDIATELY
MIRACLES TAKE A LITTLE LONGER

"I think there is some soul connection between you two antagonistic women, which will have to be resolved someday" Brian was saying.

"What's that mumbo jumbo? Are you spouting about polarities, and opposites attracting, or something new agey? Doesn't make sense to me. Sometimes having a best friend who quotes philosophy at you can be very tiring." Daisy made an elaborate swooning gesture, back of hand to her forehead.

"Yeah, well try having an animal activist for your best friend – that's really tough! Give me thought pushers over virtue police any time" Brian did a quick check of her response, in case he had gone too far. Sometimes he really pushed her buttons, then had to start running for cover. Daisy may have the name of a pretty flower, but her voice was a flame-thrower when wound up to its top volume. He wouldn't have her any other way though; he loved her passion, her energy, and her single pointed purpose. He had horrible memories of his ex-girlfriend, who used to do the opposite to Daisy: give him the silent treatment, sulk, and refuse to tell him what he was supposed to have done wrong. This and the sanctions which came with the cold war: withdrawal of privileges and attentions, freezing him to death. He could feel himself turning into a Popsicle from the outside in. Or was it the inside out? Maybe it was, because the first symptom was always a stab in the heart, followed by a spreading frigidity. Before she had dumped him, his whole torso had become an immobile, seized up, lump of muscle. Shut down, stiffened up, knotted and inflexible.

By the time he realised that their relationship was irrevocably over, his neck was so rigid that he could not turn his head sideways to check for traffic when cycling. After nearly getting wiped out on his bike, he had taken the bus, sitting lumpenly morose in a misery of self-blame. Over and over he asked himself how he could have prevented her from leaving, why he had not been good enough. Filled with remorse, bitterness and depression, with glazed eyes, numbly hanging on. For no reason except he was too afraid to die. His best friend had committed suicide when he had been only fifteen, and Brian inevitably blamed himself – he should have known, been there, done or said something. These feelings, never far below the surface, had resurrected, and joined up with this relationship failure. A dismal army which crowded around him, utterly eclipsing the light, and mocking his illusion of love.

He was in this state of misery when Daisy had entered his life. She later told him that he had been the saddest person she had ever seen.

All that he knew was that she had appeared like a bright angel, suddenly sitting beside him on the bus, on her way home from her Saturday job whist still at convent school. The nearness of her, the warmth emanating from her body, and the fragrance of a meadow came through his unwashed miasma of grief. She was like sweet rainfall upon parched earth. She was like the first ray of rosy sunlight pulling morning behind it. She was quite simply the most beautiful thing he had ever seen. And that was all in the first five seconds of their encounter. She was hope, and light, the possibility of love, and the promise of relief. A chink of purest light had poured in through the crack in his armour, and he felt..........he felt! He actually *felt* feelings flooding back into the corpse he had been.

Had he been turned to stone by some curse, and left stranded on the roadside for a thousand years? Maybe so, until this magic moment floated down; a feather from a high flying dove, and touched his frozen shoulder. And from that lightest of touches, a whisper of hope spread across his chest, stroking his heart awake. Offering escape from the prison of himself. With mounting emotion, he knew that he could not let her leave him. He would follow her off a cliff feeling only dizzy, ecstatic joy. He would devote whatever life he had left in him to making her happy.

And then, the pubescent girl who was sitting down next to him, whose name he did not know, yet whose presence was essential as oxygen......... began to sing! Oh my goodness, the voice that came out of her small frame and arced into his body was like electricity! So quiet that nobody around could hear, it was more a vibration than a sound. What, was she humming? Like the deep purring of a cat, the resonance of this sacred noise shook the seat they shared. Rising from the base of his tailbone, seeping up through his pelvis, and sweeping up his spine. Awakening him vertebra by vertebra. He literally felt, and heard, the clicks and releases as each bone popped back into perfect alignment. The wave of song stroking up his back had reached his neck, and from there it sprang out sideways, murmuring through his shoulders and cascading down his arms like molten honey. Involuntarily his hands opened, turned palm up, and he could almost see the golden healing energy as it broke through.

And then as fast as it had started, the miracle stopped. She was getting up! He was back in his own piece of skin, his bottom glued to the front seat, on the top deck of a number 28 bus. On a grey monochrome afternoon. Travelling between misery and ecstasy. Left trembling on the edge of awakenment, teetering on the brink of the abyss she had hauled him up from. No no, it could not end here! This was worse than dying.

"Legs don't fail me now" he commanded.

And yes, they obeyed him.

"Calmly now, don't pounce on her, Buzzy boy" he reined himself in with a mighty effort.

"I'll just follow at a respectful distance, yes, that's what I'll do." She was real, and she was walking along the pavement in front of him, casting colourful refractions as if she were a prism casually throwing out rainbows, from its very nature. For this was his first glimpse of the girl he had not dared to look at before. She had got up and walked away, and he had been incapable of turning his eyes towards her. He had sat there mute, as if nothing had happened between them, as if they were strangers. Whilst inside of him a voice had been screaming, "Don't leave me! Let me come with you! Please...."

Oh, she was singing out loud now! The notes fell upon his head like delightful glittering motes. They seemed to radiate off her like diamonds which wafted in an incense cloud and settled upon his head. From them he inhaled a sense of reassurance, and dropping back, he stopped straining to catch her. Perhaps his first love had been smothered by the intensity of his grasping? What if he had needed to let her go in order to have this sensation here, now, with this new object of his desire? For it was totally clear to Brian, even if he never spoke to this goddess striding before him, her hair streaming out parallel to the ground, that he loved her with every fibre of his being.

The goddess swung through the gates into the park, and turned left to follow the river which bisected the town. Brian had never even thought about it before, but he could see now how this cleaving and motion of sparkling water, trilling across the earth, had shaped and sculpted it. The insistence of the softly fluid element moulding the resistance of the clod of earth without which both were lifeless. The goddess' legs twinkled on, alongside the gleaming green grass which bordered the path. Revealing bursts of colour as flower beds sprang up in her wake. With massive self-restraint, for he was magnetised almost beyond control, he decided to follow her and find out where she went. So that he could find her again, and somehow summon up the courage to meet her.

"You should be so lucky, having me to keep you motivated – like your own personal trainer and body guard!". Brian was teasing Daisy as they were running along the canal tow path together.
"Looks like we are 'two good 'uns for a pair', as Mum would say." Daisy broke through the memory musing which Brian had been indulging in. Yes, he had succeeded in meeting her, gaining access to her inner world, but his very being cried out for a real, complete relationship with her. Thinking that by being useful and compliant, thoughtful and considerate, he might win her over. Once and only once he had made the unforgivable mistake of bringing her flowers. She had snatched them from his hands, cooing over their wilting bodies which he in his thoughtlessness had beheaded.
"Now I've got to watch them wither and die when they should have been left to smile in the sunshine" she had said as she put them reverently in a glass of water. They had remained there for months, a visible taunting reminder and reprimand, still beautiful in their desiccated state. Unlucky for him that he had retorted, "That's what they were grown for, to adorn a flower shop. I thought you liked nature".
"I adore nature Brian, and thank you for your well-meant gesture, but I think its sad to grow and sever the heads from flowers just so that we can stare at them. Not as bad as thinking we have the right to breed and murder animals so we can eat them, though".

"Do you ever get anyone when you're leafleting say, 'what about the plants, don't they have feelings?'"

"Oh heck yes, and they seem to be serious about it too. I try to keep calm and patiently remind them that plants do not have nervous systems to feel pain. And if they push it I'll say if you love plants so much then you must go vegan, because all the billions of animals and birds people eat have had to be fed on trillions of tons of plants, so you kill way more plants than you ever would by eating them directly."

Daisy was grateful for the change of topic, because in truth, although she would have denied it, the romantic gesture he had tried to make had sparked off an inner conflict within her. She had an innate fear of intimacy, and her reflex action was to instantaneously slap down any suspicious male overtures. It was obvious that she cared about him, but equally clear that she was neither available nor approachable. He was learning how to read her fluctuating moods, and had an instinctual awareness of her hormonal cycles, which allowed him to move slightly closer to her at certain times of the month. She even permitted him to kiss her, briefly, if he timed it exactly right. He was not trying to be manipulative; he genuinely wanted to make her happy, and longed to be permitted to express his devotion to her. Sometimes she tried his patience and endurance to breaking point, and at other times she deliberately seemed to toy with his feelings and behaved in a flirty or suggestive manner.

"You need to find yourself a girlfriend" was her blunt advice if he dared to broach the subject. But he didn't want anyone else. It would have been a betrayal of his love for her. He could look at other women in appreciation of their appearance, and even fantasise about them, but they were no substitute for the love of his life. He really only had eyes for Daisy, and he had long ago slipped his heart under her ribcage as he watched her sleeping, to keep her warm and safe whilst she was away from him.

Then she had met Neil, announced him as her boyfriend, and permanently shattered a fragment of Brian's heart. All without even realising it.

# Chapter 13

One of the books Daisy had read was called "Eternal Treblinka", which drew the comparison between the way humans had been treated in the death camps during the 2nd World War, and the way animals were treated in modern factory farms. She was aware that some groups of people did not appreciate the comparison, because it had been their families, millions of Jewish people, and gypsies, and other marginalised folk including Christians who had been murdered there, whilst "good people did nothing" to stop it. So how could she not keep on speaking out about what she knew to be wrong and what she considered to be evil? The industry practices developed to maximise production and minimise costs, with indifference to the suffering involved? Clara's father was responsible for just such a place, which sent a chill down Daisy's spine every time she went near it. A death factory, hidden away behind blank, high walls.

Death was not in itself evil, of course, it would come to every living being at some point. It was the mechanisation and the heartless reduction of sensate beings into things, demeaning their life into objects to be mindlessly consumed, which was wrong. Zero respect or gratitude shown for stealing their irreplaceable lives. At least in the olden days, when tribes or families kept a herd of animals, they had some relationship with them, even if it was not a very kindly one. Jasper's Ghanaian friend Melissa had talked about the captive animals in her home village. The creatures at least enjoyed a small portion of what their natural existence might have been. But factory farmed animals never saw the light of day, or stood on the earth; how could that be right? And it was entirely unsustainable, given the ever growing human population, and increasing demand for meat and dairy. The sewage from intensive units polluted rivers and land, the methane was 30 times as damaging to the atmosphere as the carbon dioxide produced by cars.

It was simply not possible to feed approaching 7 billion people with meat and dairy foods. And still, despite drawing upon sources of patience she did not know she had within her, to painstakingly share the information she had taken the trouble to accumulate, she would meet with the blank, uncaring stares of so many members of the public. Sometimes she wondered if it was only the nearly awake who bothered to come over and engage in conversation. But then she reminded herself of the times when she had literally witnessed awareness dawning in someone's face; those beautiful light bulb moments, when someone would say, "I never realised, this is plain wrong, no living thing should be treated like that."

Then she would seize the moment, and ask if they were prepared to make a commitment to cutting out meat and dairy from their daily diet, for a month. Some of them said they could easily manage that themselves, but they had to cater for their families who would be very resistant to any changes in what they were accustomed to eating. She had an answer to that too, with dozens of easy recipes and ideas for replacing favourite family foods with vegan alternatives. She would tell them the pleasure and fun of trying out new meals from cuisines around the globe, and how in truth it felt like the opposite of restriction or giving anything up, because whole new worlds of exciting taste sensations opened up.

Usually, when doing talks or outreach, Daisy would have a big batch of vegan goodies to share with people. There was a poster she had made up of the many animal free foods easily available in supermarkets and heath food shops, and a list of ways to adapt popular meals to make them compassionate. It had never been easier to make the change to plant based eating.

Daisy remembered only too well the response she had got from her Mother, when she had declared she would no longer eat meat, "You're not messing around in my kitchen, and I only do one meal, so you'll just have to have the vegetables on their own." She had been 14, yet she had managed with no mentor or support, and it was to be many years before she met another vegan. There were a few vegetarians about, but these seemed to be as blithely unaware of the cruelty in the egg and dairy industries as were meat eaters. It was a very slow process of spreading the facts.

The rosy farm image from children's picture books, with contented cows generously donating their milk, and cheerful chickens effortlessly popping out eggs in time for the farmer's breakfast every morning. And the happy pigs squealing in delight at being incarcerated in piles of their own dung. Such lies people needed to believe, and pass on to their children, whilst tucking them into bed cuddling their fluffy animal toys. A nation of animal lovers? Whilst eating pigs, wearing cows and feasting on baby lambs? Each of these species were intelligent mammals who should be having a life with their own kind, free and natural, not confined and turned into a parody of their birth right as fellow Earthlings. Humans had a lot to answer, and atone for. Because of the exploitative way they behaved to each other, yes; and because this was a direct result of thinking the way they treated animals was justifiable.

If humans really wanted to proclaim themselves as superior beings on the planet they ought to be acting as loving, guardian protectors of everything else, not ruthlessly exploiting and plundering in ever more despicable ways. Daisy was not one for quoting the bible, but one line in it sent a chill through her:

"And the fear of you and the dread of you shall be upon the hearts of every creature." Genesis 9:2

What a legacy! Truly 'superior' species would demonstrate their superiority by showing clemency and kindness, awareness and allowance, for whomever they were gifted to have as neighbours. The very least humans ought to do is leave the animals alone in peace, to allow them dedicated spaces in which to live out their gift of life. Man could not create life, nor return it once extinguished, and until he started acting with reverence for the awesome array of life which surrounded him, he remained a deadly, and a deeply unevolved, creature.

Indeed, the very definition of stupidity was to get yourself into situations you had no way of solving. She loved Einstein's words, "You cannot solve a problem at the same level of consciousness that created it". Oh how she wished that Einstein was still alive! Arguably the greatest mind ever to be born in human form, he had been a vegetarian. In addition to his paradigm breaking scientific work he had left behind the prophetic words, "Nothing will so improve the chances for life on earth as the evolution to a vegetarian diet."

He had died in 1955, so whatever would he feel about today's world, where the privileged 1% gleefully preyed upon everyone else, in very real, though heavily disguised, ways. Even the overt benevolence of many charities was covertly dis-empowerment. Instead of leaving other countries to enjoy the riches of their own lands, and helping them to conserve, share and exchange their natural bounty fairly, the wealthier nations still maintained control by insidious resource-stealing programmes, and the bestowal of dubious welfare. Meanwhile doing nothing substantial to eradicate the poverty which they were actually deliberately perpetuating.

Daisy was able to draw a parallel between this domination behaviour, and the "animal welfare" mind-set, whereby the public was duped into continuing to support the extortion and enslavement of billions of defenceless creatures. If Daisy heard another person say "I only eat humanely raised / organic / grass-fed / free range meat" she would scream! Even if there was such a thing, which there in truth was not, with approaching 7 billion humans to feed every day, what percentage could even afford the premium prices for such 'happy meat.' Why, even the word was an oxymoron! How could slaughter be happy, or killing be cruelty free? Logistically there was simply not enough land to be producing meat like that, which was one reason why factory farming had come into being.

In retrospect, Daisy had come to see that it was thanks to her old nemesis Clara's fearless, if ignorant, comments that she had become such a fluent activist. The very ludicrousness of her arguments, and the weakness of her blinkered attitudes had served to galvanise Daisy's rhetoric, and propel her into ever greater lucidity. Brian had told her about the debating which

Tibetan Buddhist monks practised amongst themselves in their formation and journey into becoming Awakened Ones; using logic and reason against itself to expose the flaws and limitations of relying upon them as effective ways to live. The rational mind was indeed a very small part of consciousness, and had to be transcended; but the delicious irony was that it could be employed against itself, to fuel sufficient propulsion to achieve escape velocity from the prison it represented.

"The intuitive mind is a sacred gift, the rational mind is a faithful servant; we have created a society that honours the servant and has forgotten the gift." Einstein had said.

So, Clara had been a worthy and worthwhile adversary after all. Certainly Daisy was at last overcoming any dislike she felt towards her. The old defensiveness, which used to drop down like a portcullis over her heart whenever Clara approached, had vanished. They would never be able to call one another friends, but she genuinely hoped that Clara would have a wonderful life, and use her inheritance wisely. It must be quite a burden being financially wealthy, and feeling the responsibility of what money had the power to do in the world. Yet Daisy had come to appreciate her own very different form of wealth, which was spiritual richness. A resource which unlike money, could not be stolen from her. Compassionate awareness was a virtue, harmlessness was a gift, and kindness was a blessing available to all. The Grace to use them could never be bought for any amount of cash.

Daisy prayed every day for the patience and humility to continue the work she felt born to achieve. She prayed for the endurance to fulfil her unfolding life's mission. And she prayed for the wisdom she so needed to descend into her, and convert her selfish and reactive nature. It was painfully obvious to her, the more she experienced, that she had a long way to go to be a consistently pure, noble, decent being. All she had to do was observe the unconditional love with which any dog expressed itself towards its carer, regardless of the treatment it got in return, to know her own shameful self-absorption. It was not about her, it was about saving lives.

"Lord, keep me out of my own way" was a regular mantra she recited.


The postman had brought a letter. It was written on heavy cream paper, in turquoise ink, beautifully scripted in a delicate filigree handwriting which she recognised instantly as Jasper's. He was in the habit of occasionally sharing his thoughts with her in good old fashioned pen, and real ink. He had copied out a speech which Charlie Chaplin, the famous silent film star, had spoken when the technology had first advanced to allow for verbal recordings:

Darling Daisy,
Did you ever listen to Charlie Chaplin in his final speech in 'The Great Dictator?' I read it and thought of you, and your quest to save the world. It reminded me of the long conversations we used to have about programmed people, and free thought. I sense that you indeed shall be a major agent in the eventual emancipation of all beings, and feel optimistic about the future with you living in it. You will be happy to know that I have succeeded in getting my wife Hannah to turn vegetarian, and that we are expecting our first baby in the Spring. I'd love for you two to meet, I think you'd get on really well. Let me know how you are, and please keep in touch, Earth Angel Daisy.
 Here is the speech:

*'I'm sorry but I don't want to be an Emperor, that's not my business. I don't want to rule or conquer anyone. I should like to help everyone if possible, Jew, gentile, black man, white. We all want to help one another, human beings are like that. We all want to live by each other's happiness, not by each other's misery. We don't want to hate and despise one another. In this world there is room for everyone and the earth is rich and can provide for everyone. The way of life can be free and beautiful. But we have*

*lost the way. Greed has poisoned men's souls, has barricaded the world with hate; has goose-stepped us into misery and bloodshed. We have developed speed but we have shut ourselves in: machinery that gives abundance has left us in want. Our knowledge has made us cynical, our cleverness hard and unkind. We think too much and feel too little: More than machinery we need humanity; More than cleverness we need kindness and gentleness. Without these qualities, life will be violent and all will be lost.*

*The aeroplane and the radio have brought us closer together. The very nature of these inventions cries out for the goodness in men, cries out for universal brotherhood for the unity of us all. Even now my voice is reaching millions throughout the world, millions of despairing men, women and little children, victims of a system that makes men torture and imprison innocent people. To those who can hear me I say "Do not despair". The misery that is now upon us is but the passing of greed, the bitterness of men who fear the way of human progress: the hate of men will pass and dictators die and the power they took from the people, will return to the people and so long as men die [now] liberty will never perish. . . Soldiers: don't give yourselves to brutes, men who despise you and enslave you, who regiment your lives, tell you what to do, what to think and what to feel, who drill you, diet you, treat you as cattle, as cannon fodder. Don't give yourselves to these unnatural men, machine men, with machine minds and machine hearts. You are not machines. You are not cattle. You are men. You have the love of humanity in your hearts. You don't hate, only the unloved hate. Only the unloved and the unnatural. Soldiers: don't fight for slavery, fight for liberty.*

*In the seventeenth chapter of Saint Luke it is written: "The kingdom of God is within man" Not one man, nor a group of men, but in all men; in you, the people. You the people have the power, the power to create machines, the power to create happiness. You the people have the power to make life free and beautiful, to make this life a wonderful adventure. Then in the name of democracy let's use that power, let us all unite. Let us fight for a new world, a decent world that will give men a chance to work, that will give you the future and old age and security. By the promise of these things, brutes have risen to power, but they lie. They do not fulfil their promise, they never will. Dictators free themselves but they enslave the people. Now let us fight to fulfil that promise. Let us fight to free the world, to do away with national barriers, do away with greed, with hate and intolerance. Let us fight for a world of reason, a world where science and progress will lead to all men's happiness.*

*Soldiers! In the name of democracy, let us all unite! . . . Look up! Look up! The clouds are lifting, the sun is breaking through. We are coming out of the darkness into the light. We are coming into a new world. A kind new world where men will rise above their hate and brutality. The soul of man has been given wings, and at last he is beginning to fly. He is flying into the rainbow, into the light of hope, into the future, that glorious future that belongs to you, to me and to all of us. Look up. Look up.'*

Wow. Daisy had to sit down as she read these powerful words, written so long ago. Words with as vital a message today as it had been then, only even more so....... for every generation believes its particular striving to overcome its problems is the epitome of an insurmountable struggle. Just as each individual person in their own way was fighting against, or for, whatever they most closely cherished as a purpose. When she heard people say they would not have children because the world was too awful to deliberately bring a baby into, her response was, "Don't you suppose that in any given time or place throughout history, people have thought and said that? And with justification. Yet here we all are, a triumph of nature over reason. Because if everyone had thought that, and nobody had given birth, none of us would be here now." On one level it was true that the more mouths there were to feed, the more rapidly the earth was being consumed. And yet, every unique person coming into being could herald the victory of hope over adversity; any one of them might hold the key to the transformation of the way things were.

Even so, for all that wonderful rhetoric about humanity coming out of the darkness and into the light, it seemed to Daisy that what humanity had done was to push its darkness underground. Hidden it in order to fool themselves that they were more free and loving than their predecessors. Because when she looked around her own culture, she saw not community spirit, but separated nuclear units in their little fortress boxes. Where both parents in a family had to work in order to fund the overtly affluent lifestyle that entrapped them. Meanwhile the children were being institutionally brainwashed and bred to consume. Even though she would be the last person to advocate couples staying together in misery, it seemed that divorce was fracturing society.

The irony of her own inner isolation did not escape her either. Some people were obviously more afraid of living than they were of dying, was that it? She thought about those words of Anais Nin, "One day the pain of remaining tight in a bud became greater than the pain of blossoming."

And she knew that her time to unfold her petals was upon her. No matter how much deflection she poured herself into, every night she had to lie down with herself, alone. Even whilst frankly announcing, "I do not share my sleep space, it is sacred and personal". Yet that dominant part of Daisy did not speak for the whole person. What about her other aspects? Why was this controlling part always in the driving seat? Was it not time for an inner democracy, where the less forceful, but equally valid, parts of herself were allowed to vote on decisions?

The more she thought about this, the more it seemed as if there was some self-appointed queen sitting in her throne room. But the queen was not in touch with her subjects, and so needed to come out and mingle more. Not a revolution or a deposition – Daisy was grateful that she had been enabled to reach her current stage of life relatively intact. She had learned enough from her reading, and from discussions with Jean and Brian, to understand how fractured the psyche could become. She did not wish to precipitate a cascade of split personality disorder or potential breakdown. It was to be hoped that an elective process, initiated by herself, would just naturally and gently produce greater health, wholeness and integration, and promote inner balance, poise and acceptance. Her reading of psychotherapeutic techniques did not give her any faith in shrinks, or encourage handing her power over to any so called expert, or guru. Perhaps ironically, she wanted to stay in control and not be manoeuvred by any proscribed agenda. No dependency upon a counsellor for her! Much as she respected Jean, Daisy felt strong in herself, with a deep certainty that she would close together in harmony the parts of her that did not yet touch.

# Chapter 14

The summer break was upon them, and Daisy decided to go off by herself with her little tent to a beautiful spot she knew. In the elbow of a bend in the river, on private land where she was confident she would not see anyone. Brian was supportive, if somewhat unsure of her motivation, and helped her to transport several gallons of water, together with her tent and bedding. It took two trips across cow pastures and through woods alongside the river, clambering over barbed wire fences, to reach the spot, and set up her little camp.

She did not need any food because she was going to fast; just plenty of water to flush out toxins from her system. She had done short fasts before, over long weekends, and once for five days, and found them wonderful for calming the mind and cleansing the body. Fasting was a time honoured spiritual practise also, and Daisy was relying on its effects to facilitate the psycho-emotional transformation she sought. Much as she wanted to bring her sketching and writing books she deliberately and determinedly left them behind.

"I don't want to have a part of me sitting aside observing and recording myself, that would defeat the object" she explained to Brian as he reluctantly took his leave of her. "All I need is lots of sunshine!" she smiled as his retreating figure shrank smaller and smaller away across the meadow. It did not take long for his body to merge into the landscape, because the other thing Daisy had left behind was her glasses. Myopic since a traumatic experience in her adolescence, she had always loathed wearing glasses. They were another form of dependency; an attempt to enforce a linear, hard edge around objects seen. When really, everything was like a watercolour painting, blending into everything else.

The only time she allowed herself to wear glasses was in order to see presentations at University, or to read the overhead signs at railway stations. She befriended the blur which closed in around her like a comfort blanket. Seeing in sharp, stark definition frightened her. And anyway, glasses had always felt uncomfortable; both on her nose, and to her eyes. It felt as if the strong lens was drawing her eyeballs out. Opticians did not understand when she asked for a lower prescription, to just allow her to pick out the minimal detail she needed. Oh no, they had to ramp it up so that the bottom line of letters was chiselled in sharp, black and white clarity. She hated that! Once she had borrowed a friend's glasses, which had a much weaker prescription, and these felt restful and complimentary to her natural vision, the aid they were meant to be, not the imposition the specialists were taught was necessary. Yet another example of un-wholistic medical intervention. Daisy stayed as far away from doctors and their drug pushing as possible.

So, here was her opportunity. Here was her safe space. She congratulated herself on the triumph of allowing this time, rather than following the myriad of distractions she could have gone off chasing. The air was warm and dry, and the first thing she did was take off all her clothes. She hated wearing clothes! So unnatural and restrictive, and one of the many insidious ways society encouraged people to conceal their true self. Gradually, her breathing became slower and deeper, and her body dropped its habitual tension, as she eased into the bliss of solitude. She wanted to return to being a nature girl, a creature of the land, not a blot upon it.

Her bare feet were soundlessly delighting in the varying textures of the many different grasses which made up this ancient water meadow. Not many of these left nowadays, she sighed, appreciating this small stretch of the river. Because it was inaccessible, and because it flooded every winter, it had never been subjected to plough or pesticide. There were wild flowers everywhere, and insects galore. Even though it was a mere mile from the nearest road, it was an oasis of nature as unspoiled as she could access by bicycle.

Sitting still beside the river, smelling its sweetness, Daisy delighted in the creatures which darted about, above and below the water. She began to loosen her grip upon consensus reality as it had been presented to her. She had long learned to challenge everything she had ever been taught, yet she realised there had to be layers and layers of conditioning of which she was yet unaware. It all had to go: if it was a fake construct, she wanted nothing to do with it. Leaving the human world and its woes resolutely behind her at home, with the promise that she would pick it back up again when she returned; gradually, the hold she usually kept upon herself was releasing.

Those parts of her which she was accustomed to relying upon to interface with the outside realm were ever so grateful for their chance to sleep. It reminded her of the special, Silent Retreat days they used to have at her convent school. Blessed retreat time: permission to be quiet. And so, the normal chattering ebbed away. The alertness to be prepared, with instant verbal responses, whenever an adult fired questions at her, dissolved. The striving for the next funny thing to say, to amuse her friends, had gone into abeyance. What a relief to set it all aside, gathering in the threads of her scatteredness. Into this precious, present, moment of awareness. Here, and now, that which did not simply dissolve like morning mist had gone into hibernation.

Aaaah............ the breathing became deeper and slower, all by itself. The coiled spring of the daily grind was unwinding. Goodbye to expectations, farewell to responses, excuses be gone. Still the monkey mind leapt about from tree to tree in her head. Recalling conversations, such as her Mother's voice saying, "What is all this 'stress' everyone has these days? We never had it in my day; there was no such thing. You just got on with life. Stress doesn't exist."
Daisy smiled, without annoyance, as the monkey swung by her knees from a branch.

Daisy remembered being at the Natural Spirit Festival, back in the summer of the previous year, with Brian. They were watching someone suspended upside down, balanced on the feet of another person, enjoying an Inversion Experience. The one giving the treat was a lady named Tilarnia. She lay on a mat with her legs straight, and at a right angle to her body, with her feet supporting the suspended one. Almost bat-like, the flown person had the soles of their feet together with knees apart, leaving their body hanging down, in a reversal of gravity. Looking incredibly relaxed, The face of the 'bat' was so ecstatic, with the top of his head hovering inches above the belly of the Tilarnia.

"You never see anyone walking around in public wearing an expression like that. Totally blissed out." Brian was saying, intrigued.

Daisy simply had to know what it felt like. "I want what he's having, how about you, you up for it?"

"No, not me, but I'd love to see you do it!" he grinned in encouragement.

Daisy stood patiently waiting, drinking in the image before her. Something very special was occurring between those two people. A profound connection, a union borne of trust, and a mutual energetic exchange. Tilarnia was rotating the Flyer's shoulders, twirling his arms sideways, and gently rotating his freely hanging torso to facilitate maximal stretch. The Flyer audibly took a very deep inhalation and released it through parted lips. Time seemed to slow down as Daisy watched this amazing fluidic dance. It was aerial and acrobatic, yet simultaneously rooted and stable. In triple slow motion, Tilarnia was placing her hands supportively under the Flyer`s shoulders, whilst ever so slowly lowering one of his hips by bending her own knee, and simultaneously lowering his opposite shoulder. This effected a visibly releasing twist through the whole spine.

"She's keeping his centre of gravity perfectly balanced over her all the time, do you see that?" Brain was keenly observing the biomechanics, as he practised many circus skills himself which involved ultra-finely poised balance. Pausing in the flow of motion, back to the neutral position, Tilarnia began to ever so precisely tap either side of the Flyer`s spine, up and down his back, with the blades of her hands. Next, she slowly and deeply massaged his neck and shoulders, then gently rotated his head.

"That looks like the best way to massage someone" Brian was commenting, "Because gravity is reversed, and all the weight is off the muscles." It was typical of Brian, to be analysing the techniques of the event, whilst Daisy was too engrossed in the feeling of it to be able to do that.

At last, the therapeutic dance between the two was coming to an end, as Tilarnia was bringing the Flyer back to awareness of where he was, and readying him to slowly lower his feet to the ground. After a pause, she instructed him to gradually stand upright once more.

Then the pair bowed in mutual respect to one another, hands in prayer position at their chests, saying "Namaste" with a bow. They smiled and hugged like old, trusted friends. It had all taken place in ultra-slow motion, unlike the customary rush which even yoga classes seemed to take. Pushed along from one pose to the next, with only scant holding of the stretches. Daisy had discovered by herself, that it was only after several minutes of stillness in maximum stretch that suddenly a release would occur, and a deeper level of stretch would become possible.

Seeing Daisy's rapt attention and obvious eagerness, Tilarnia looked up with a calm smile, "Would you like an inversion now?" she asked.

"Oh, yes please, if you're not too tired, if I'm not too heavy, don't your legs get weary?"

"Not really, because the other person is balanced over my centre of gravity, so it's really no different than what my legs do all the time, supporting my own weight. It's just in reverse, do you see?"

"Ah, I think I do" Daisy nodded.

And so, Daisy was taken through the preliminary step of turning her back to Tilarnia, who was lying on her back with her feet raised. She was instructed to sit down on the feet, reach down and grab the ankles, and then bend backwards until her shoulders felt the Base's hands supportively receiving them. Daisy was already effortlessly airborne.

"Now very slowly bring the soles of your feet together, and reach up to grab your own ankles."

"Yep, got that far" thought Daisy, who was already a bit unsure of where she was, spatially, in this unaccustomed position off the ground. It was a disorientating yet oddly familiar sensation.

"Wonderful! You're doing this perfectly. Do you feel ok to relax now?"

"Yes" It was not so easy to speak, because there was a time lag happening in her head, thoughts coming to rest, breathing already getting slower.

Tilarnia passed Daisy a belt with two loops, and instructed her to put her foot through one loop, which she managed to do quite easily. Then a second belt put on her other ankle. Her wrists were to go through the other ends of the loops, which meant she was free to relax and just hang there, bat-like, upside down.

"Now you can let go completely, and I will gently bring you back when it is time."

Daisy nodded, her eyes closed softly, and her head felt amazing, hanging weightlessly like that. All the tension normally held in her neck just dropped away, almost like warm candle wax dripping from the crown of her head. She was aware of the warmth of the Tilarnia's belly, which was so close, yet not touching. There was a feeling of being back in the womb, the weighless suspension and slight sway. An enormously deep exhalation came out of her, and the normal need to inhale again did not occur.

A sense of floating came upon her, and she became a dolphin, free and boundlessly happy in the ocean. What seemed like minutes later another ultra-deep inhalation was taken involuntarily by her lungs. Somewhere, gentle hands were stroking down her back, and she was a baby again, relishing the contact. Then fingers were kneading the base of her neck and easing out the habitual tightness in the shoulder muscles. More ultra-slow breathing, and the sensation of floating deeper and deeper into the ocean which could have been space, not water. It did not matter.

Nothing mattered. Soon, even the part of her which had been chronicling these events released, and she was a free, tranquil, vast consciousness. Bliss. No incoming sensations, no arising thoughts. Just bliss.

All too soon, Tilarnia softly spoke, and rhythmically tapped on her shoulders, to bring her back into her body. Back into awareness of where she was, dangling upside down from a pair of feet. In an open tent, with a sweet breeze blowing. Wind chimes, bells, and the noises of surrounding festival activities filtered back. How weird that her head had not throbbed, nor her face felt flushed at all. Tilarnia asked her to slip first one, and then the other loop off her wrists and ankles. Then gradually, but before she could get in a panic about how she was supposed to dismount from this odd perch, the Base placed her hands under Daisy's shoulders supportingly, and asked her to take her feet apart and straighten her legs, all super slowly. The next thing, the Base had bent her own legs, allowing Daisy's feet to touch the mat. Daisy opened her eyes, saw that she was back to earth, and was effervescent with gratitude.

"Thank you so much. That was the best experience ever, just awesome!" Speaking felt a little strange, as the words came from her mouth.

"You are very welcome, now take it easy for the rest of the day, you're still in an altered state."

Altered state wasn't in it. Daisy felt brilliant! She had been taken out of her body, and yet paradoxically also more fully into it, at the same time.

"I have to do that again. You've got to try it" she said as she and Brian were walking away from the Tilarnia's tent.

"I could do that for you, I was watching, and I've got good strong legs to hold you up" Brian offered. He resolutely declined to have the inversion experience himself, though, no matter how gushingly she praised it.

"Very much a ground-dwelling creature is the Breen" she reflected out loud. "And yet has been seen to climb trees like his arboreal ancestors." Daisy spoke with her narrative voice, the one used by the great naturalists of television nature documentary fame. "And here we witness him for the first time stepping out into the unexplored territory of inner landscapes. Exactly what the Breen feel when they hang upside down may remain their secret......."

"The Breen declines to follow the Bedazzled One of a freaking cliff actually, and lives to climb another day!" was his final comment.

Daisy knew her friend well enough to realise that he never gave in. There was an admirable, if frustrating, stubbornness to his character she was long familiar with. Her nature was, by contrast, one of fiery enthusiasm which quickly faded, when the next interesting idea presented itself. Brian had learned to humour her in the first flush of her latest obsession, knowing that it would last only until the next exciting thing appeared. She had a childlike capacity to become completely engrossed in things which was very endearing, and which he envied.

His keen eye for detail and uncanny ability to work out how to do things soon had him master of any practical problem. Indeed he thrived on such problem solving conundrums, whilst Daisy rapidly gave up the struggle. "It gives me brain ache" she would say. Meaning that the harder she tried to think about it the more confused she became. Until she would induce a brain-fog stress reaction, which could deteriorate into a migraine episode if she pushed it further. Her mind simply didn't seem to work in that logical sequential way, and she often failed to think things through. So, when she needed help but couldn't bring herself to ask for it, she had developed a tactic of putting on her pathetic little girl's voice, and wheedling, "Oh Breeeeeen!" with an ascending scale of notes. Should he be already busy on some other task, she had a repertoire of silly noises, sighs, audible breaths and exhalations.

These sprang up from some deeper part of her, and were not entirely within her voluntary control. They were accompanied by facial megrims, pouting, eyelid fluttering, and fingertip wriggling, which could progress to hand flapping. The next stage might include a series of skips, pirouettes and dancing in order to dissipate the mounting tension she was feeling. If even these failed to elicit the desired response, she had been known to make loud explosive noises like an elephant trumpeting, a horse neighing, or an eagle's shrill cry. She really was very childlike and unselfconscious at these times, and had clearly never grown out of certain stereotypical behaviours. Either that, or she was acting out behaviours which had been forcibly repressed, ridiculed or punished in early life. What a tantalisingly delightful creature she was.

Brian had indeed learned how to fly Daisy from his feet, in Inversion, just as Tilarnia had done at the Natural Festival. Momentarily wishing that he was there on the riverbank with her, Daisy recalled why she had chosen to make this expedition alone. She had taken herself away from civilisation, society, and routine, specifically in order to get more in touch with her authentic self. And here she was, sitting beside the lazy river as it rolled its way between two grassy banks. In a verdant water meadow in the sunshine, naked as a jay bird. Commencing on a long overdue, much needed, water fasting retreat.

Her thoughts had dampened down, slowed, and receded naturally. Her breath, the air, the atmosphere were all one, continuous and unbounded. She was neither looking out from a set of eyes nor observing her surroundings from any particular spot. Everything was merging quite delightfully into a kaleidoscope of undifferentiated beingness.

So too with the listening mechanisms, normally tuned to the small band of accustomed, required, alert sounds; these became more relaxed. Gradually the unfiltered world of sounds being perceived was expanding, becoming keener and sharper. And even that part of her brain which had been taught to differentiate everything, name it and classify it, comparing it against every other catalogued sound it had memorised.........this too took a welcome break.

Feeling utterly safe in her piece of skin on her patch of good earth there was no need for fear-based watchfulness. She trusted nature, she trusted her intuitive self, and she trusted the higher guidance which had orchestrated this event. Forgetting her nakedness, forgetting her hunger, forgetting her ego identity, suddenly the desire to sleep descended like a blanket of further forgetfulness. Like a mouse slipping into its nest, she crawled into her little silver dome tent, sighing contentedly to find it so very warm and drowsy and soft................

What? Ripping through her reverie and slapping her awake, Daisy shot upright and saw an ugly male face grinning in through the tent flap she had left open. It had thick lascivious lips and coarse, wiry looking, dirty blonde hair. Aware of her nakedness, and feeling exposed, she reacted with defensive anger......."Get away! What are you doing here?!" she demanded.
"I'm the water bailiff of this river, here to catch fishermen without licenses" was his reply. At least he had taken his big ugly head away from her pudenda! Daisy got a most unpleasant flashback to the time, aged 5 and in hospital, when 5 white coated doctors had suddenly appeared around her bed, pushed her down and started poking about down there.......on the pretense that she had bladder problems, but they had not even had the courtesy to introduce themselves. Whose body was it?

Water bailiff indeed! He should think himself lucky she wasn't a fishing anorak, with a sharp knife at her side to protect herself. Lucky water bailiff that she was a pacifist. Calming down somewhat, she heard him walking away in his welly boots. 'He won't be coming back, its ok', she said to herself. But her meditatory bubble had been punctured, she felt mildly violated – after all, his face had been mere inches from her unsuspecting vagina! Shuddering as thoughts of what might have happened, dire prognostications about what befell lone women travellers, and that vile way men were predisposed to leer at women. Aaah! She was so not a happy bunny right now.

As if comforting a child, Daisy soothed her ruffled mind, and found it in herself to laugh at the situation. Nothing awful had happened, she was fine, hey she had probably made that water boatman's day. From that point on she would refer to him as the water boatman; one of those predatory skimming insects which rowed their spiny bodies across the surface of still waters, in search of unsuspecting fish to sink their fangs into. She rationalised with herself that shocks and sharp wakeup calls were an essential part of nature. After all it might have been a starving bear or a mountain lion peeking in at her, if she happened to have pitched camp in some far away wild country. And not a mere mile from civilisation. So called. For the first time she wished she had brought a kettle to make a nice reassuring cup of tea; one of the aspects of civilisation she was very addicted to. Which was precisely why she had not allowed it to herself. Right then, she might as well use this experience and have a dialogue with her various aspects.

"Listen up, whole self." she began, "We are here to come together as never before, to join up and be strong as One Being. Whilst showing gratitude to our ego who has valiantly run the show for so long, the time has come to allow everyone an equal say in what we, as a whole being, do from now forward. This means that some of us are going to have to be very quiet and still, to make room for the parts which do not know how to speak, to be heard. And here and now I make a promise, that we all shall be recognised and allowed a voice, that we all shall respect and not criticise or judge one another. Nobody is going to be out of a job, I promise."

She could actually feel herself responding to this rallying cry. In her mind's eye she could see a camp fire glowing in the centre, and the various disparate parts of her personality and psyche assembling and sitting down in a circle around the flickering flames. "We are One Being, whole and indivisible, and we are powerful! We have a right to be here and we have common purpose. Nobody will be left out ever again." She sensed a general nodding and agreement moving through her inner people, and she felt an intense love for them. Each and every one was as precious and necessary to her as her physical body parts were in their own way.

"This 'I' who is vocalising is not in charge, there is no leader, for we are One."

The deep truth of this statement rang loud and clear as self-evident. "Who shall be listened to first?" A reticent but exquisitely beautiful, delicate and translucent small child arose. She knew her instantly as her inner child: magical, innocent, pure and incorruptible. That part of herself which had split off and gone into hiding when she had been exposed to a paedophile at the age of 4. Oh what a wise child this was, for it clearly carried within its multidimensional perspicacity the repository of an eternity of lifetimes. "And a little child shall lead them" Daisy remembered the prophecy.

This perfect child, unblemished by any experience no matter how horrific, to any child in any place, ever, spread out its arms and embraced the circle wordlessly and all inclusively. It was pure love, no doubt about that, and there was no part of it that was not pure love.

A timeless time later, the second aspect arose. Oh no, thought Daisy, it's my Jezebel, come to rattle her chains at me for locking her away! For Daisy had deliberately encased in a trunk, deep in a windowless dungeon, padlocked and bound, weighted and suppressed, her sexual self. She had found it necessary to do this because she could not maintain control over 'Jezzy', who had the ability to take over in the heat of passion and by the insatiable power of her desire. This had led Daisy into a destructive and depraved first relationship, which had taken all of her strength and much effort, to extricate herself from. She had felt that she could not control the way Jezzy expressed herself, or the less than salubrious energetics which she attracted from men. Consequently Jezzy had been shut away.

"We are so sorry we did that to you", the rest of the circle were conveying. "We ask you to return to the whole as a much loved and vital part of us. It has been cold and colourless without your fire and joy. Welcome back!"

More group hugging across all levels of being then ensued. And so the meeting progressed, gaining coherence and massive healing as the external day became night. Nothing disturbed the solemn joy, the sacred gaiety of this intent.

In the morning there was a prevailing calm cohesion, as if all the scattered parts of her had been recalled, re-membered and reconnected. Many unknowns were present also, representing those vast parts of her Oneself she had felt it necessary to forget about in order to become this single person here appearing as a human female, limited in time and bound by the natural laws of 3rd dimensional space. It was obvious that 'she' was way more than this point of fixity. It was clear that there was a way bigger plan of events than could be envisioned from the game board of separation currently playing out on earth.

She had not gone mad, nor lost the plot, despite coming to a point of taking things less seriously than before. In the grand scheme of things, with the perspective of vastness, how could she have bought into the illusions and colluded with the delusions spun out on earth?

Very peripherally, Daisy had been ever so slightly aware that a Guiding Light had been also present, and assumed this must be her higher self. Then as she drifted as softly and gently as a leaf floating on a still pond, in between sleeping and waking, she imagined she glimpsed a loving presence. Perhaps the beautiful Lady who sometimes showed Herself, had presided over all the proceedings, ever watchful and protective, yet never interfering as Her children slowly awoke from their shadow play. Out of their dreams of separation and their delusions of rejection, their nightmares of conflict and the horrors of justification. Oh my goodness there was darkness about, prowling in bottomless insatiable hunger, that much was certain. But where the darkness seemed deepest, there the Light abounded and penetrated all the more: this, too, was obvious.

For all the times people had denied there could be a Power beyond themselves, or that there could be a beneficent, loving Creator/Sustainer/Source or Force, somehow permitting the evil which was seemingly allowed to run amok.

For all the confusion about time and circumstance, over and above the scurrying, compressed mentality of the human animal, Daisy had been graced with a rainbow echoing the covenantal ongoing Love which alone was everlasting while all else would pass.

And perhaps it had to be sufficient, for now, that she remained bewildered and felt isolated amongst people whilst feeling truly at home amongst the animals and plants. She resolved to redouble her efforts to love everyone, including Clara, whom she felt pity for, and no animosity, right now. Naturally her limited self-concept would continue to hold more questions than answers, but still, within what stillness she could occasionally attain, there at the epicentre of all spinning worlds, was a serene knowingness and certainty. There was 'a purpose to everything under heaven', and everything was unfolding exactly as it needed to. A sweet benign contentment, a poised equanimity, and an angel's feather of forgiveness rocked her to sleep.

It had been raining hard, and Daisy was chilled to the marrow. Huddled miserably in her drooping silver tent, all zipped in and cramped, the euphoria had definitely deserted her. All that day, and through the following night she tossed and moaned fitfully. 'Remind me again what I'm doing here?' She asked the blank walls of her self-imposed cabin. 'How much longer did I say I'd stay here?'
She had envisioned bright hot sunny days, idyllically dancing amongst the draping willows. Interspersed with refreshing dips into the shockingly cold river water. She had hoped to see the bright blue flash of a kingfisher, the silent slipping of an otter from air to water world. She had planned to swing from tree branches, and stretch in fragrant flower banks to the drowsy mumble of bees. But it was still raining.
Perhaps I have done what I came here for, she reasoned. Perhaps I can pack up and go home now. But the thought of crawling out of her tent and getting wet was not inviting at all. She was already wearing all of the clothes she had brought, and her bedding was damp. Right, come on! She decided that someone had to assert command here, to call an end to the fast and the inner journeying, at least for the time being. 'It's all going to be here another day', she comforted herself, and so propelled her unwilling body outside. In fact her body was only too glad to be allowed to move and warm itself up through activity. 'Hey I can leave all this stuff here and collect it later, can't I?' That was a much nicer proposition.

And so it was that she had not gone through more than the first two fences on her way through the clinging long wet grass, than she heard/felt another human approaching. It was Brian! Oh wow, she could not remember ever feeling more overjoyed to see him. Like a puppy dog with two tails she jumped about and threw herself on him, and hugged and embraced, and chattered for all she was worth.

Well pleased with his choice to follow his instinct to come and check on her, despite having been strictly forbidden to do so, Brian had in fact intended merely to creep up and observe Daisy's little campsite from a safe distance. She neither cared about this, not questioned his appearance.

"Might the Honourable Gentleman have the makings of tea about his person by any happenstance? One could murder a mug of cha!"

"I might have." he responded.

"Oh you star in my firmament! I'm chilled t'ut marrow."

Linking arms with him and skipping along in haste, she added, "I'm starving. Don't suppose you've got any fruit?"

As luck or design would have it he was able to produce a bag of pears and two bananas with a flourish. "Oh you absolute lifesaving angel you!" that gained him another massive hug. And so the two, momentarily oblivious to the drenching rain, shared a rare and precious kiss, there beneath the dripping trees. Then they hurried along to reach the road, where Daisy had been steeling herself for the long bike ride home.

"Your carriage awaits, Ma'am" said Brian with a flourish, a doffing of his invisible hat, and a deep bow.

"Oh tremendous! How does it get any better than this." Brian had borrowed his brother's car, an old, lovingly restored Rover P6, in beige and cream. Her Father had had one of these when she was a child. Refusing to sit in the front seat she vaulted herself into the back, where a thick travel rug lay waiting.

"It even smells exactly like Dad's car used to." She felt so very happy, safe, cossetted and cocooned, and fell asleep immediately.

## Chapter 15

Shit shit shit! Why hadn't she seen this coming? Why hadn't she been able to stop it? Excuse herself all she liked, and beat herself up all she might, nothing could alter the fact that she had ended up in bed with Brian. Damn you Jezebel! Now you know why you were kept locked away.

But Daisy knew she could not blame Jezzy. It was only natural, and one's hormone driven sexuality did not come equipped with emotional overrides – that was someone else's job. So whose fault was it, then? Who in their weakness had allowed this to happen?

Did it matter? The important thing was how was she going to get out of this? Even as Jezzy had lain there indulging herself, and the rest of her had enjoyed being pleasured, there remained, aloof and on the ceiling, averted in judgemental disdain, that part of Daisy which she had never been able to either incorporate or gratify. It was some high faluting, transcendentally removed, detached part of her. It's only remit was freedom.

Yes, well what about her freedom to have a bit of mutual consensual lovemaking? But she knew this wouldn't cut, for she already felt the barn doors swinging shut to trap her in some cosy relationship status which would stifle and suffocate her, she knew it. Already her legs were thrashing away underwater kicking for the surface, to breathe at last after the smothering, cloying, disgusting act was finally over, and she could run to the shower.

"That shouldn't have happened, I'm sorry Brian" she began her preamble.

"Well I'm not, it was about time" Yikes! He still had his clothes off, and was enveloping her again with his pheromone thingummies....

"It can't happen again" she said firmly, "And nobody's to know about it, alright?"

"I promise I won't tell a soul" Brian murmured into her hair as he grabbed her from behind.

What was this overriding impulse – dammit, SHE was a celibate girl, she didn't go around..........

"Blast it, no! I said............."

But it was too late, the stronger devil of her nature had seized the moment and ran with it. Too fast to be caught, giggling and peeking, posing and revealing itself in the most shocking and delightful ways. May as well give in and accept defeat, deal with the consequences later.

And so it was that the next morning Daisy went off to the doctor's for a precautionary morning after pill. And back at the flat she threw some clothes into a bag and excused herself, off to visit her Mum. She felt really mean treating her best friend like that, but there was no way – why, already last night he had been all over her like a rash, making plans for their future together...oh my goodness no! Thankfully there were still several weeks of holiday left, and she had some work lined up at her friend Jennifer's stables; mucking out, grooming, and exercising the horses. She could stay away a good while and forget it ever happened. Back to denial? No: backing away from delusive compulsion.

The more distance she could put between the night's proclivities and her normal, prudish, self the better. She had to get that Jezzy back in chains, and quickly. It was too chaotic and uncontrollable to ever go down that slippery slope back into sexual activity. Like any other addiction, she had discovered by painful past experience that it would grow more demanding and outrageous every day. Her Buddhist study confirmed this, and said that sexuality and spirituality were incompatible.

Brian was of the opinion that she was repressed by Catholic guilt, and shame about her body. Yes, well there was that too. Catholics weren't anti-sex actually: why did he think there were so many of them? They taught that the act of love was a holy event, designed by a loving God for the gift and blessing of bringing new children into the world. It was sacred, and of course only to be unwrapped after marriage. A marriage which was indissoluble. This scared Daisy more than anything, for she had unfortunately grown up listening to her Mother screaming at her Father, saying he had imprisoned her and stolen her life away. She had yelled out: "These kids are the product of Papal rape!" before

Daisy had any idea what that meant. Clearly, then, Daisy had taken on much of her Mother's anguish, her mother's terror of having a third child when she could not cope with the two she already had. "The Lord has not provided for the ones we've already got!" ran another of her Mother's rants.

Her Mother had had a nervous breakdown in the end, and turned increasingly to drink, leaving Daisy as the only girl in the family to take on many of the household duties.

Jean rang, and they met in a local tea shop for a catch-up. It was in a converted ancient cow byre, with low oak beams and lovely antique crockery, all mismatched and quirky. Best of all it made all of its own cakes; and there was always at least one, and often two of them, which were not only vegan but gluten free. The very first thing Jean said was, "You're looking chipper and bouncy – been having some fun?" And then she had collapsed into fits of laughter as Daisy had tried to describe her predicament. "Thought you'd got lucky, your base chakra is wide open and winking!"

Daisy shrieked loudly, blushed scarlet, and attempted to cover up her lower half with her violet pashmina.

"We're in the 21$^{st}$ century, woman, the days of puritanical guilt are over. Give yourself a break!"

Then seeing how genuinely upset her friend was, Jean reached over and touched her arm, "Forgive my insensitivity; come on, let me take your mind off yourself for a while and tell you what I've been up to – and with whom. Unless it's going to offend you, that is?"

Now it was Jean's turn to blush, as well she might, considering the extremity of her promiscuity. She shared that she had been away on a very wild, uninhibited holiday with some paraplegics and their carers. "These guys were blown away to discover what orgasms they could achieve from the neck up with a bit of encouragement" she said, "Are you shocked?"

"No, no I'm actually really in awe of you, for being so generous and loving – those poor guys, I guess nobody wants to think about what they do for gratification. They have needs like anyone else does." Daisy genuinely did not have a problem about this, and would never presume to judge anyone as harshly as she did herself.

"Yes, more than, in some ways Daisy - not being able to relieve themselves in the normal way."

And just before Daisy hoped that Jean wouldn't give her more graphic information, their tea arrived, and the subject was changed. Jean asked about Daisy's painting, and Daisy asked after Jean's sister who had her hands more than full with a new baby plus a set of twins just starting to crawl everywhere. "Phew, that won't leave much time for anything else, I bet." she shook her head at the enormity of the responsibility. Then Jean looked searchingly into her eyes and said: "Are you sure you don't think it's wrong for disabled people to have sex?"

"No of course not, it's just that it's nobody's business but theirs what they do or how, is it? I think the imagination is vastly underused, and it might stop some of the pornography exploitation if people could be less visual and graphic about things......." that sounded wrong, not the way she meant it to...... she was trying to defend women from being used as sex objects.

Jean continued, "Not everyone is visually oriented, or kinaesthetically predominant either, are they? And then there's the wonderful way that nature provides compensation for apparent incapacity, by enhancing other senses or skills".

"Really? Oh that is such a relief to hear; you know I knew that from being around you, because you have such a sparkle and strength not available to us mere mortals."

"Thank you for noticing! Well I've been thinking that with your phobia about men's willies and everything, you might feel safer exploring your sexuality with a man who's willy doesn't work at all." She paused, waiting to see how Daisy reacted, which was with unreadable silence. So she continued, "I could introduce you to some really good looking guys, if you like? Now that you've reactivated your libido...."

Daisy took a deep breath, "My problem is that I'd like to forget all about sex and entanglement. You know I used to think I was afraid of entrapment, but to be offered a no-strings fling wouldn't be right either. And commitment has never been a realistic idea for me – I think it's great for other people, but I guess I'm just a loner with other priorities."

"Fear of intimacy, that's what it is, my darling. And I don't know how you can get around that, it's as if you've double bound yourself to make sure you don't give it a chance."

"You know that's exactly what it is. Fear of intimacy, that's it! Sounds so simple, but I never worked it out before. And the fear is so overwhelming I just have to cut and run."

"Never mind, you're still young, with everything going for you. Maybe your path really is a solitary one."

"Well for sure I never thought about babies and having kids like most other girls, if that's anything to go by. What about you?"

"I could see me with a baby, yes actually, and I love cuddling my sister's children, but it wouldn't be fair as we Para's usually don't live very long......"

"Oh." Daisy had never even considered what Jean's physical situation was, had never wanted to ask in case she didn't want to talk about it.

"No I don't want to talk about it, just live day by day, you know. But I get a lot of infections, kidneys and things, due to the waterworks not functioning; catheters and stuff......."

Daisy was trying unsuccessfully to hold back the tears which came at the thought of Jean's unseen struggles and prospect-shortened life.

"Its OK really; you know it makes us appreciate what we *do* have more than other people can, and to live twice as fast" Jean tried to soften the truth.

"Ah, yes: 'live fast, die young'; there's a strong attraction in that. I hate the thought of getting old and decrepit anyway." Daisy had chilling memories of seeing elderly people reduced to shuffling, mumbling, drooling incoherence.

"Well honestly, I don't relish endless decades of watching people consuming the planet to a stinking cinder myself. Get mighty depressed by it sometimes." Daisy went on to admit.

There was a pause, where each reflected in glum silence.

"Anyway, we're young and bright and beautiful, and we may just get to turn this ship around yet!" Jean retrieved them from descent into the doldrums.

And the two friends shared a long, heartfelt hug, finishing by spontaneously putting their foreheads together, third eyes touching gently.

"I realise you have to take antibiotics a lot for the infections, but do you know about taking probiotics to repopulate your friendly flora?" Daisy asked.

"I eat yogurt if that's what you mean" replied Jean.

"No, there's way more than that you can do, I grow stuff called kefir which is a cultured milk product that has been used for centuries in Baltic countries like Russia. It kept them alive through the long hard winters when they ran short of fruit and vegetables. I've managed to get it to adapt to living on soya milk, so its vegan. I'll bring you some; once you have it you just feed it on fresh milk every day and it keeps on growing. It's not difficult, and costs way less than buying those probiotics from the health food shop."

"Oh that sounds great. What does it taste like?"

"It's really mild, so it goes with anything. Oh and I make other fermented foods, sort of like pickles, only they're got actively living enzymes in them –they're super easy to make, you just need a tall jar or big crock, or the old fashioned kilner jars. You chop or grate your veggies and squash them in the jar, and keep them covered by salty water, and they last for months."

"Wow! Why haven't you told me about all this before? You know if you talked about these things and less about why meat is murder you'd get lots more people interested – uh, sorry didn't mean to criticise or demean....."

"No its fine, you're exactly right. I've actually been planning to start up a vegan foods class at University next year.... show them what they're missing, get them by the back door method."

"Sign me up, I'm definitely into it. I love your sunflower pate, and that banana ice cream you gave me is so tasty, no one will believe its fat free, or made of banana."

Wonderful, Daisy had a new project to immerse herself in. She went back to the flat brimming over with ideas to share with Brian, and deflect any residual embarrassment from that which must not be mentioned. She realised that she could pour herself into her prime directive which was the spreading of peace and kindness, towards people and animals. The desire to huddle up with one special someone and blot out the raging world just would not work for her. There was a reason why she could not lose herself in that way. Another, higher, grander cause was forcing its way through her; it was bigger than that distracted disillusionment.

Jasper had encouraged her to write, and asked for the privilege of being permitted to read what she had to impart. Thus encouraged, and picking up her pen, Daisy began to write. It began as a psychological excavation, which grew into a cause. She watched as it ran across the page like a sparkling river of light. She was discovering her gift, a way of transcending black print on white paper which would touch and ignite everyone who read it, inspiring them to pursue compassion as it had been pursuing her. She had been hunted down and caught by the desire to see a new world of genuine care and love in action. The promotion of peace from principle to practise. Stunned by the power of words which surely came not from her but through her, Daisy borrowed her flatmate Lilian's typewriter, and typed out her first page. Before she could mess with it or modify it. Then she took it to the college office and had copies made.

Already she was getting feelings of exposure and self-disclosure which tempted her to run home and avoid putting herself out there, for so it felt. Quickly she distributed the sheets of paper, before she could back out. Maybe nobody will bother to read them, she reasoned. Maybe nobody will get my message, even if they do, she comforted herself. Only then did she allow herself to sit down and read what she had written that afternoon. Trying to read for the first time, as if she knew nothing about anything, to gauge the possible impact.

## STRUNG UP ON ENTRAPPED MOMENTS?

*Observation tells me that most people's field of possibilities and self-allowance not merely contracts – it collapses, in around them with age. Should it not rather be a process of continual expansion following the relative strictures imposed upon youth, and the relinquishment of the responsibilities of middle life? An outspanning into potentially more, not less, freedom? Instead, people buy into the myth of linearity, believing themselves on an ever shortening slide into death.*

*But if we deliberately recapitulate past and future, freed from the tyrannical prognostications of memory, and if we remorselessly scrutinise and challenge routines and patterns, the opposite happens. Unfettered by the routine of entrapped moments, into the totality of the expansive now. Aligned with consciously chosen intent in its fluidic unfoldment, one's centre is free to dance along the path of potential. Unfettered by the shackles of habit and expectation, the gift of the present unwraps itself. By not preparing for outcomes, and disbanding conclusions from what has gone, and ruthlessly deselecting time pressure, bright fresh potential is birthed into being.*

*Caution and timidity paralyse the fresh seed germinating inside one's fruit, whereas boldness and courage fuel the ongoing journey. I have lived on the edge, fearlessly throwing out the sense and safety which stole the lives of my parents. They put me in a cage in a dark place alone to face dreadful demons and certain death – for babies there are only two states of being : warm content and happy, or dying. That's it. So daily I learned how to survive. Thank you so much parents; only someone who loved me very much could have facilitated such a desperate introduction to the school of hard knocks.*

As my body developed I learned how to grab onto the bars and haul myself onto my feet, and exert with delight a bit of control over my environment, by violently rocking to and fro. My cot ship slid across the linoleum floor of the second layer of my prison, an upstairs bedroom where my screams of abandonment would not disturb my parents. Eventually I was able to explore the margins of this prison by directing my momentum in different directions, picking up speed across the lino and slamming most satisfyingly into one wall or another. But my joy was to be short-lived: the noise of this activity, and the real or potential damage to the paintwork and wallpaper induced my father to remove the wheels from my cot.

I have never really got over this most despicable parental crime. All that was left to me was to rock in place, making comforting noises to myself like the demented animal I was. I still catch myself lapsing into this regressive but reassuring habit to this day.

Is it any wonder then, that in adolescence I developed a burning compassion for any creature imprisoned in a cage? I turned vegan and spoke for animal rights, to any and every one I met, never missing an opportunity to bring this awareness into the conversation. Lightly, gently sowing seeds. The lack of tangible fruit from those seeds is explained to me by a guiding Lady as not conducive to my higher welfare, as it would merely feed the ego in me. And egos don't help causes, they only think they do.

Why is it that abused children may grow up and become abusers? A form of throwing out from themselves the trauma, and providing temporary respite from the locked down suffering which continuously re-enacts itself otherwise? For there is a part of Daisy still imprisoned in that cot in the darkness, in a totally real sense, because the psyche does not recognise time as linear, and my compensation is to be a voice for the voiceless innocents daily tortured and killed, in factory farms throughout the world: 58 billion land animals alone each year, and rising, as the human demand for meat and liquid flesh (dairy and eggs) increases with the accelerating human population. It seems ironic to me that I should appear to be a human being, the most deadly predator ever, when inside I feel to be a fabulous, fleet of foot, wild, four legged, herbivorous creature. Born to run free with the sun on my back and the wind in my hair. Yet here I sit saddled with a mind which incessantly goads me to reach out and speak the creatures' plight. And the human's plight also, for in truth they are the same. We are a parody of our birth right condition. Life is lived backwards, and upside down. Duped into swallowing torment and lies by the vile learned habit of drinking the secretions of a grieving mother whose calf has been stolen and murdered. That's where it starts: the disconnection from the cruelty of incarcerating, commodifying and killing whole races of beautiful, sentient beings, needlessly. How can anyone gaze into the liquid, amber, trusting, harmless eyes of a bovine, and not feel its pain? How can anyone stare at the squealing tortured piglet with utter dispassion whilst cutting off its testicles, tail and teeth with no anaesthetic? This is standard practise in factory farms, should you be ignorant of the price of cheap bacon. The very same shut-down compassion is operating here as was at work in the Nazi death camps. How chilling a realisation is that? So please open your loving caring heart, and say "Not in my name! No more!" Please go vegan, and encourage others to choose the kind option at their daily opportunities to demonstrate who they are: for every meal says something about what you stand for, what you tolerate, what your money supports. It ought to be clear by now that world peace will only descend to earth when the killing stops. Full stop. It is the only way. So, use the power of fork over knife!

Begin now, to atone for the suffering you have been funding, and unwrap the joys of the gentle cuisines from around the world! It is exciting, it is liberating, it is life giving, and I am filled with optimistic joy at this turning point in humanity's purpose. We are awakening to our individual and collective force for good. The era of slaughtering other species and ravaging the environment is passing away. A weighty miasmic cloud is lifting from our beautiful planet: departing, never to return. What an immense privilege it is to be alive, here and now, and be a part of this evolution!

*I use this piece of communication to challenge assumptions and conditioned habits. I fly the flag of liberty, equality and fraternity in its widest sense, as a Guardian of all life on earth. When all the boundaries, cages and walls which have incarcerated the jailers every bit as much as the inmates are demolished. When swords become ploughs, and cots become cradling arms. When fake boundaries between us are rubbed out, nobody need feel marginalised, separate, terrified, or alone, ever again.*

*The Peaceable Kingdom where lion lies down with lamb, and there is no more killing on any holy mountain, valley or plain, and all the land is sacred.*

*Peace shall descend like a dove.*

*Let peace reign in your heart, and let your heart lead your head, and your actions each be harmless and loving.*

*Begin now, in the serenity of your inner sanctum. Be joined-up inside yourself, discard everything which does not promote peace, and refuse to relinquish love as your prime directive. Nothing else matters. Only love is real, and shall endure. The nightmares will vanish in this brave new dawn.*

*I am Vegan, and our tribe is growing, our power arising, unstoppably.*

*We are everywhere, Warriors of kindness, moving our conjoined world into Unity.*

*The time has come, and nothing can silence us now! PLEASE JOIN US!*

*Go cruelty free today ~ ask me how, I don't bite :)*


Brian was the first to give her feedback, and it was not encouraging. "You use too many words, it's too flowery, and you dilute your message by trying to be clever" he said.

"Oh." Daisy felt very deflated. She loved words, and using them creatively, descriptively, and with verve. But if it failed to reach her best friend, the one person in the world who really knew who she was and what she meant, what chance did she stand of reaching anyone else? Perhaps she ought not to show it to Jasper after all, because he was a proper writer, and criticism from him would be even worse.

"OK then, I'll put my energy into the cooking demos" she said, but was secretly crestfallen. She knew she did have a way with words, a flair for using language, it just needed shaping. Maybe poetry was more her style? At the very least, it would be an outlet for her personal angst, and with luck it might serve to alleviate the inner anguish of others less capable of describing their pain.

For sure she did not want to hand Clara ammunition with which to tease her, so why had she shared that she rocked herself to sleep? 'Because your strength lies within your vulnerability' the thought had been placed in her mind.

Even though she had no comprehension of what that could possibly mean, she trusted the source of the message, which she sensed was the Lady who had come to her in her time of desperate need in hospital as a five year old child. The Lady who came to her sometimes and aided her. In some ineffable way, Daisy felt she was being gently guided through the confused processes of life. Discernment was what she truly needed; the ability to know which choice was the best one, in every moment.


Jean came hurtling up to her at full speed in the refectory the next morning, her wheels screeching to a halt most impressively. Daisy looked down to check for skid marks on the shiny yellow floor.

"Wow, I didn't know you could do wheelies in your chariot, Jean!" she said admiringly.

"Not bad eh? One of my para mates shared how to get the engine souped up —quite illegal of course! Drains the battery fast, but its great fun. Listen, I've found out that your dark Adonis is in the Arts Department, and I'm friends with one of his friends, who happens to like you........SO" she continued before Daisy could flap or fluster, "I told him you liked painting, and he's invited us to use the facilities there. How good is that?"

"But I'm crap at art! We didn't even do any at my convent school. If you were in the 'A' stream there was no time for domestic science, crafts, or art – we had to do Latin, theology and physics instead. I can't draw a circle or a straight line."

"We're meeting him, his name's Derik, over there at 2 tomorrow. Don't be late. And wear something revealing." Jean dismissed all objections with an imperious flick of her one moveable finger, and off she sped, leaving Daisy with an uncomfortable feeling of mixed hope and dread.

On the way home Daisy went into the local library in a desperate search for arty information. Grabbing the largest tome she could find, she started looking through it, thinking she could cram the history of art and its various styles and genres into her head so as to not feel like a complete fraud.

Her ignorance was lamentable. The quintessential Constable print found in so many houses, usually opposite the mantelpiece with its trio of flying ducks. The modern stuff which looked as if a child had drawn them. The Picasso weirdness that looked as if he had tried too hard to be deliberately different.

Like everyone else, she knew what appealed to her, and what did not. She could gaze at Monet and Degas with their restful colours and softened lines, all day. OK these were called Impressionists; righty ho, she could trot that name out. What else did she like that she could recognise? Did pop art count? She found some album covers to be wonderful, clever and intriguing. She loved sitting on the bean bag at Jean's flat, going through her old record collection and gazing at the imagery. Especially how they told a story which progressed through the inside flaps of the album cover. Funnily enough the best ones seemed to coincide with her favourite music, too. Like Yes and Pink Floyd, Led Zeppelin and King Crimson. Feeling a little better prepared, she went home and chose a denim jumpsuit to wear, and smartened it up with a wide orange belt, a yellow and orange scarf, and the plimsolls she had decorated herself with shiny sequins.

Jean was already waiting for her outside the Art Department, and complemented her on her bold, if safe, clothing.

"What do you mean, 'safe'?" Daisy said defensively.

"Well you're all zipped into that suit as if you're going sky diving." Jean teased her, and she couldn't help laughing. "I've seen your legs and they're not bad at all – I tell you if I had legs like that they'd be well on show!"

Derik was not there to meet them, and by herself Daisy would have slunk away quickly and pretended she hadn't bothered to turn up, either. Not Jean though, who was clearly enjoying the excuse to go exploring a new part of the campus. The first thing that struck them both was the smell –obviously all the paint and solvents they used. Following some invisible lead or other, with Daisy trailing behind reluctantly, Jean nipped along corridors and pushed open doors to peer inside. "Ooh, this looks exciting!" she said and went straight into a large airy room, with all manner of strange sculptures in various stages of construction. There was only one student working there, and Jean sang out "Hi there, we're looking for Derik, have you seen him?"

"Yeah, he's through there" replied the stocky unkempt person who was up to his elbows in papier mache'. He was working on a large otherworldly creature, busy building flesh onto its wire bones.

Daisy hadn't even thought about other forms of art than painting and drawing. This looked great, wow! She couldn't imagine having the time, space, and materials – and the permission, to play like this. She had never been allowed to make much mess as a child, and the highly polished mahogany dining table was no place for glue and scissors. She could use the kitchen table, between meals and when not being used for the many activities which went on there, to quietly do things though, as long as it was all tidied away in time. One thing she liked doing was cutting out pictures from magazines, then making them into colourful pictures – collage, she thought that was called. The other thing she liked was tracing on greaseproof paper taken from the kitchen drawer. She had saved boxes of her tracings, intending to use them someday, but when she left home to come to University everything had been thrown out. Her Mother needed her room to rent out to lodgers, to help pay the bills. Remembering this, Daisy suddenly felt all flat and glum, and the colour leached out of her day.

But there, in the next room, stood Derik, bent over some piece of work. He looked up with a start, and said, "Oh is it that time already? I'm sorry Jean. Well done for finding me."

He was tall, about 6' 2", very lean, and black. Having finished hugging Jean, he straightened up, and looked directly and appraisingly at Daisy, making her self-conscious. Darn it, she could feel herself blushing. I wish I was black, then nobody would know if I was blushing or not, she thought.

He leaned over with his arm extended and shook Daisy's hand. He had a lovely smile, which she returned, and dropped her gaze immediately. One thing she could never do was hold eye contact, especially not with men.

"Have you ever been in a darkroom?" he asked. Was Daisy ever glad to have Jean with her. Wasn't that a bit forward, she wondered. But Jean was all for it, "No I haven't, but I'd love to see how you develop films. What about you Daisy?"

"No, never" responded Daisy who could care less about it, and was still feeling uncomfortable.

Without another word, Derik led the way through another door and into a room which smelt really badly of chemicals. Eugh! Daisy hated it and wanted to be outside in the fresh air, surrounded by nature, and in her own company, quiet and relaxed.

Derik was showing Jean some photos hung up to dry like washing on a line, and explained that although it had to be completely dark to be safe from spoiling the film, they could use an infra-red lamp to see what they were doing. Daisy was starting to feel nauseous and claustrophobic, and was about to excuse herself and get out of there, when Derik took his camera washing off the line, and turned and led the way out. Great! Back in the large bright room, he showed them that he was making a decorated box to contain washing powder, for his current project.

"Ah, I never really thought about it being someone's job to make things like that" she thought out loud, rather less than impressed.

Derik at last noticed her complete lack of enthusiasm, and suggested they go for some coffee. She really could not envisage herself trailing up here pretending to be an artist. What had Jean been thinking about? On their way out, several people acknowledged Jean with a smile, and often a gesture. She was a very tactile person, considering her immobility.

In the refectory, Jean announced that she was modelling the next morning for a life drawing class back at the Art Department. "They need models, Daisy, how about you? It's good pay."
Daisy did not realise at the time that this meant being naked or she would have blushed again. As it was, much as she could use some extra money, she wouldn't have been able to cope with being critically stared at and drawn. What if they made her look really fat or ugly? Sitting still wouldn't come easily to her either. She worked on a market stall on Saturday's and holidays, in exchange for some cash and two enormous bags full of leftover fruit and vegetables. It was very tiring, being on her feet all day, lifting boxes of apples and sacks of onions. And doing all that adding up in her head, plus being polite and patient to customers whilst swift about her job. But modelling, no way! Later on when Jean explained that life drawing entailed taking her clothes off, Daisy wondered, not for the first time, if Jean was constantly trying to push her out of her comfort zone in order to force her to 'get over herself'. Either that, or Jean truly did not realise how uncomfortable she felt around strange men.

She could not believe it when Derik turned to her and invited her to visit some friends of his from Trinidad that evening. She felt sure he was never going to speak to her again because she had been so miserable and hardly said a word. Derik was saying that these friends did not know any white people, and how he wanted them to meet her. 'Why me?' she thought but of course she did not say that. She said, "Yes, that would be lovely, shall I bring some food to share?" Jean had told him she was vegan, hadn't she? It would be so embarrassing if she had not.

"They are fascinated by your eating no animal products at all, and your activism, and want to learn all about it".

Oh, how could it get any better than this! What a lovely couple Derik's friends were! Boule and Hanta had only been in the UK for a few weeks, and had seemingly not travelled about much yet. Daisy felt accepted by them exactly as she was, in a way which was very rare amongst her fellow Brits. Normally she had to wait patiently for the conversation to touch upon a subject where she could slip in an animal rights comment. But here she was being actively requested to tell them all about her beliefs. Before she could restrain herself, she was off on one of her fact-delivering "Why not milk" monologues.

"To be frank, I wonder why vegetarians fail to see milk as the liquid flesh it is. Milk is not white water: it's billions of body cells and tissues from a grieving mother cow whose baby had been stolen away and murdered. And the milk from modern intensive dairy farms is the worst of all, because the cows are forced to produce up to 7 times the amount of milk that their one calf would drink. These cows are fed a high protein, unnatural diet, including fish and animal by-products, and even the blood of other murdered cows, to increase their milk output. They frequently suffer from mastitis, meaning there is pus and blood in the milk. Dairy Industry standards have had to be relaxed to permit so many parts per million of these as it is an unavoidable consequence of mechanical milking and maximised lactation. And of course, no cow can keep up with the high milk yield demanded of them, so they inevitably face their own slaughter after 3 or 4 years. But not before becoming crippled with brittle bones due to the calcium which has been leached out of them to make so much milk."

Boule was clearly horrified to learn about this hidden cruelty, the product of greed and the illusion of cheap nutrition. She said that the cows in her village back home looked very different, roamed about freely and were allowed to keep their calves for the first few weeks following birth. She had noticed the massive, stretched-to-bursting udders of the cows here, and the difficulty they had just walking. "I don't like the way milk here tastes either, but what can we use instead?"

"I make delicious plant milk from almonds; it is so easy, you just soak the nuts overnight, which make them more digestible, then put them with fresh water in a blender, and strain through a muslin bag. You can add vanilla or sweetener in you like. Other nuts or sunflower seeds make tasty milk too."

"Oh what a great idea! I'm so glad Derik brought you round to meet us. Please tell me more about what you eat. Honestly the meat here doesn't taste right either, and now I understand why."

The two women talked for hours, about women's things, and living closer to nature, the future for children, and the difference between sacredness and religion. Boule's family had been influenced by Christianity, but still continued many of their traditional ways, which she guessed could be called 'pagan'. Daisy was overjoyed to be spending time with someone who had grown up so close to nature and admitted that she had not had the opportunity to form friendships with non-white people before. Was it because they preferred to keep themselves separate, or they did not think white people were friendly, or for some other reason, she asked.

"Henta noticed the distance between races here, and we decided to make friends with local people. It feels good to be part of a mixed community, and we think we are going to be happy, even though we are missing our families very much."

Daisy suggested that they get together and make a meal for a group of friends, sharing their ideas. She was excited to be discovering new recipes, and promised to ask the market trader she worked for if he could find some cassava, breadfruit and darsheen leaves. She was intrigued to learn about young coconuts, containing soft gel flesh and excellent milk, very different to the mature coconuts she was familiar with.

On the way home, Derik said he was very happy to meet 'the real Daisy', and asked her if she thought they might become more than friends. She was glad he had asked her rather than assuming anything, and felt respected and honoured. She tried to explain her fears about relationships, without going into detail, and he told her he would give her as much time as she needed. It would have been awful to admit to him that she had only wanted to meet him in the hope of getting paired off with "Adonis", who she had actually not thought about so much recently. She had to admit to herself that it was probably more lust than genuine attraction, and how superficial and unspiritual was that showing her to be.   Meanwhile she liked Derik, but did not find him remotely sexually attractive. That was because he was way too nice, she thought with a shudder of realisation.

Telling herself firmly to stop worrying and criticising herself, she ran a deep hot bath laced with essential oils of geranium and frankincense. She lit some night lights and placed them around the bathtub, and luxuriated, because the whole house was asleep. It was very rare for her to be last to bed, and it was with a very light heart that she finally turned in at 3am. She fell asleep with a smile of contentment on her face, and greatly renewed optimism in her head.

# Chapter 16

Daisy re-read for the twentieth time the letter from J.B. Ballard, Mr. 'Wholly Cow' himself. She was still unsure if it might be a trap to get her back for her years of relentless activism. "Much as I am loathe to admit it, the years I spent following my family dairy business have never made me happy – wealthy maybe, but not satisfied. Then my daughter Clara gave me your booklet "Why not milk?" and the whole way of life I had never challenged before suddenly came into clear focus. I regret intensely my exploitation of so many cows for so very long, and I would welcome your opinion and assistance in turning Bothies Grange into a sanctuary where the remaining herd could live out their retirement."
"Wholly Cow" to "Holy Cow", what a wonderful concept!

Daisy cycled through the ornate gold and black painted gates into the Grange, and followed the sweeping drive as it made its manicured meander through 200 acres of prime Derbyshire farm land. Even though she had already firmly decided not to take up Ballard's request for her to devote herself to the handful of cows he wanted to assuage his conscience with. To say she was not tempted would be a lie, yet she equally well felt that her path lay elsewhere. Nice to be asked though, as her Mum used to say. Still had someone answering the door for him then, she observed wryly as she was ushered into a bright capacious hall. Meaning that he still needed waiting upon. She felt a sneer of contempt for everything his class stood for, and determined not to be nice to him.
The entrance hall was predictably sombre and smelled of its 300 years of privilege on the backs of others. There were no gloomy family portraits or beheaded stuffed creatures here though – how very refreshing. Not what she had been expecting at all.
Ballard was as tall and gaunt as Daisy was small and round. There was a severity to his chiselled expression which put Daisy in mind of an army General: someone fully prepared to do what had to be

done, unflinchingly. A man of very strong principles, clearly, however she might disagree with them. Daisy was not a subscriber to the notion that ends could justify means, nor that the greatest good of the greatest number ought to decide things. For her, each individual was unique and valuable in their own right, regardless of species, race, age, sex or means. Indeed she had more interest in redistributing the remaining resources of the planet evenly around the world to be conserved for the common good. She had a deep loathing for empires and corporate power structures.

"Call me Julian" said Ballard, thanking her warmly for her visit....... she was a very busy person, he realised.
"Yea yea, so let's get to the point shall we?" Daisy heard her voice cut in. Oh no, why was she so deficient in social skills! The fact was, she was rather more impressed by this man, whom she had harboured such strong aversion to, than she wanted to be. She felt as if she needed to put on a suit of armour in order to block his energy which was disconcertingly pervasive. Julian seemed to deflate a little, as if he well knew the effect he could have on others. He diminished himself somewhat then, into a low easy chair, opposite the high backed one she took, when they entered an adjoining room where he had indicated with a broad sweep of his arm she was free to choose her own place to sit. Not safe behind his desk, then, formal and in control, for this spacious room was clearly his office, the hub of his business life.

Not for the first time she asked herself what could have happened to turn him around? Much as she prized her way with words she knew that without prior preparation a man like Ballard would not be swayed by mere concepts in a fringe publication. "Leopards don't change their spots" her mother would have said. Ironically her mother would have been all over Ballard like a rash – having been raised on a large country estate herself she had come to regret her impulsive decision to "marry beneath her" to oppose her own overbearing stepmother. Mother would have weighed up what the antiques in the hall were worth at first glance, Daisy thought wryly, whereas she herself was less than indifferent to what she described as useless clutter that people prized so highly. Contempt would be nearer the mark.

She must never permit herself to lose touch with the level of cruelty which Ballard had promoted at Bothies Grange. He had been so very proud and boastful about making it the most mechanised dairy in the country when it had opened five years previously. The poor cows never got to graze in open fields on fresh green grass, but instead were fed precisely rationed unnatural food scientifically designed to maximise milk output.

"My Clara is dying." Julian's words sliced through Daisy's train of thought, sliced through her veneer of aloofness, and indeed sliced right to the quick of her heart, which skipped a beat and lurched in her chest. Oh so that was it, the reason for the suffering etched so obviously upon his face. The reason for his letter, too. Instinctively Daisy leaned forward in sympathy but he waved her back. "No, it's not what you think, she accepts it, is ready to go - it's what she wants."

Briefly, and with alarmingly frankness, Julian described the gruesome process of his daughter's battle with cancer. The poor woman had gone through so much suffering during the diagnosis and attempted treatment of her disease, and naturally no expense had been spared, but eventually she had accepted the inevitable. She wanted to make her peace with life. Like Daisy she had never married, though for very different reasons. Daisy had been so committed to her calling to speak out for human and animal rights that she had never managed to devote herself to any one relationship. Clara, she was now being told, was a secret lesbian who so rejected this aspect of herself that she had lived in denial of it, giving her time instead to breeding horses and dogs.

Oh. Suddenly the dynamism between the two of them which had grated since the outset began to make sense. If Clara had secretly fancied her then she would have deliberately taken every opportunity to drive her away, but as they were forced to coexist in the same place at University for 3 years she had resorted to those verbal attacks on her. This realisation put a tight tourniquet on Daisy's heart, and she was having difficulty breathing. What safer place could there be to hide unrequited forbidden love than under the dark mantle of hatred? Suddenly, so much became crystal clear. Daisy had assumed that Clara had behaved so contrarily opposite to everything she was and she stood for out of loathing; hence her cropped bleached hair and her superficial material principles, which contrasted so strikingly with Daisy's own long dark hair and deep spirituality.

To say that Daisy was disarmed by this revelation would be a complete understatement. She felt more effectively pummelled, dismembered and shrivelled than any number of direct physical blows could have reduced her to. What a stupid waste. What a ridiculous parody of the way life could have turned out. They might have been friends and joined forces together to change the world! The reality that so much of her life had been built on denial and deceit left her numb with poignant sorrow.

The parallel between this intensely personal state, and the way the world at large continued acting out its feuds and reprisals, had not merely stopped Daisy in her tracks, but she felt quite derailed by it. She could no more have got up from that chair and carried on with life as normal, as fly to the moon.

Ballard was explaining that because of their strict religious beliefs, Clara had always rejected any possibility of accepting her gay nature. Indeed she had gone the other way and proclaimed her disgust at such practises being tolerated by modern western society.

"Can I see her, speak to her?" At last Daisy found some words to say.

"She could not bear that, she is in Switzerland and has chosen to close her life by her own hand as her last self-willed action."

"But that's insane! I can help her, I will help her.......I know a lot about rawfoods and how they have healed many people of otherwise terminal conditions including cancer. Bring her home and I promise I'll do everything in my power to get her well." Daisy was feeling overcome with guilt at the way she had so harshly judged and disliked Clara whilst they were at Uni, and determined to make up for it.

"Clara said you'd think up some excuse to stop her, but her mind is completely made up, and she has made her peace with everybody. Everybody, except you." Julian's searching look told Daisy that he knew his daughter had been forced to live with hopelessly unrequited love on account of her. "She timed it precisely so that you were here with me when she died....... by the time your green tea arrives it will be over".

Automatically, Daisy's eyes darted to the door, "Then it's not too late! Ring her! She's just depressed; we can help her........please!" Daisy had leaped up and was shaking him by his shoulders. The door swung open and a maid entered, carrying a silver tray........"NO! This is sick madness, how can you, she's your only child for God's sake........"

But Julian had pierced her eyes with his, locking her down with the dreadful force of his acquiescence to his daughter's last wish. "Yes, life is precious and sacred, but what Clara went through because I forced her to cling to life long after she naturally would have died, that had to stop – don't you see? She suffered things that you of all people would never allow an animal to go through – it's been hell for her – torture......."

Daisy wanted to be far away from this place and these feelings. It was so completely messed up. In its way it felt worse than the things she had steeled herself to witness happening to innocent people in poverty stricken places, war zones, and disaster situations. This, here, screamed out as just plain wrong. There was something so perversely not right about calm, deliberate self-killing, regardless of the weight of reasoning that made the decision.

Yet who was she to judge? Had there not been times in her own life when despair at the sheer insurmountability of the world's cruelties had brought her to the very brink of suicide herself, and she in perfect, vibrant health? Her mind slipped back to the dreadful time when her mother had tried to kill herself, and the numb disbelief and denial which followed.

A cup of green tea had already been poured for her, and a whisper of steam silently escaped from it, rising until it vanished from her sight precisely six inches above the rim. She realised she was staring fixedly at it, and that part of her mind was engaged in computing these pointless facts, pondering upon where the essence of the tea went, where Clara's very soul might even now be hovering. On the brink between life and death.

In her own way, Daisy and, she dimly sensed, Clara's father, were having their own near death experience right here and now, and separately yet oddly united. So very different yet joined together by the twisted knot of inexpressible connection which hung in the room all around them. In that instant Daisy realised that nowhere would be far enough away to escape this experience, and that simultaneously it unlocked a deep secret from within the vaults of her own heart.

An uprising of compressed emotion hit her like a tsunami, and against her will Daisy found her eyes turning to meet his. Such a picture of grief and regret, rage and dis-empowerment flashed before her in his face. It was as if she was granted access to his passing lifetime of stored memories suddenly downloaded into her awareness. Unstoppable, ungraspable, a flowing molten lava of love. Inexpressibly shared, impossibly silenced, terminally crushed. It was racing through her like a steam train. Complete with eerie, howling whistle.

For, like an owl's hoot piercing the dense air between them, a cry escaped from the one throat in this tragic triad at last no longer closed down, muted and muzzled. Clara's last gasp resounded as if she were right there with them in that room, for in a true sense she was. As, freed from the prison of her wracked body, Clara's spirit had indeed instantaneously appeared.

She had come to acknowledge their respecting of her final wish.

She had come to say farewell.

She had come, with an indelible smile of serenity which Daisy would ever retain upon the inner gallery of her mental landscape.

Already Daisy's hand was involuntarily making the delicate strokes of pastel on grained paper required to depict this vision which she knew would hang in this very room. Into this picture she would pour the thousand words and more which had gone unspoken in this moment. The first of many tributes she was to make to Clara, many of them against her better judgement.

Some moments, some searing glances, are so very loaded and suffused with meaning and feeling as to be eternal. In some ways Daisy and Julian were being trapped in amber, even as they felt the passing of a soul moving freely up and away, ascending in liberty at last, expanding and escaping the cramped confines of earthly life. Clara had seized her own freedom, conferring in the process upon her father and her old adversary the weight of her life.

The twist in the tourniquet upon Daisy's heart unravelled, and she began to weep. Decades of unshed tears now took this chance to pour forth, unstopped and inappropriate, excessive and overwhelming. She howled and dissolved herself into a liquid realm of uncensored sensation. She cried for the whole world in its wobbling weirdness. Her tears joined the tears of women weeping inconsolably for their lost children, their sundered love, the impossibility of happiness in this benighted life. Her tears and the wailing of women the world over throughout eternity were the same sobbing. She abandoned herself, she had been abandoned. She murdered herself, had been murdered, over and over, a hundred times in a hundred lifetimes. Clara her worst enemy, Clara her nemesis, had been in love with her all along.
And yet here she still remained, crumpled and sundered, left behind after the storm had passed through her. Like women the world over, who somehow have to find the strength to get up and do what must be done. Help the mothers, feed the children, comfort the afflicted, console, rebuild, teach, stand up and keep going. It mattered not whom she had shed tears for, whether for a person she had found it impossible to like or respect, or for that person's father who sat before her now, incapable of releasing his own tears.

Daisy spontaneously got up, crossed the little space that strangely united them, and wrapped her arms around Julian. Right now they were not apart, right here they was no Julian or Daisy, stitched tightly within their separate skins. United with the intimacy which links gladiators in the ring facing the inevitability of death and the finality of its falling upon them. In the next instant she hoped he would not reciprocate her touch, she shrank from the thought of it, and pulled herself away, retreating back into her familiar fear and distrust of father figures, and men, and her issues with authority..........slipping away from the terrible risks of intimacy. But Julian's hand was closing tightly upon her retreating arm as he unspokenly commanded her to look at him. The very nakedness of conjoined grief welded their eyes and she felt herself falling from a great height, found herself tumbling off a cliff of false isolation, plummeting down a precipice in the grip of an avalanche from which she could never escape.

Caught between the horns of the dilemma of all ages – to run away and retreat, and to cave in and stay were the same thing, or rather they reflected the same split within herself. All persons had their own version of this dichotomy: the impossibility of surrender versus the impossibility of denial. So much that was not okay had already happened here. So much that was beyond surreal, so much that shook everything she thought was secure and sacrosanct. Julian had his arms around her waist and his head buried in her chest, and he was gripping onto her like a drowning man. Daisy felt that she could neither move, nor say anything. She both feared and hoped that he would give way to tears himself, but she knew that men were not like women in these things, and that he was holding back his grief.

He had known about this before she even came here today. It was all pre-arranged. She simply couldn't get her head around it, and as for the rest of her, she wondered if she would ever feel normal again.

After what felt like an eternity of holding her breath, and feeling at one and the same time turned to stone like a statue, yet dissolved and boundary-less as an ocean, at last Julian let go. Numbly, Daisy returned to her seat, and watched her hand reach mechanically for her cup of cold tea and bring it to her lips. She would never forget how intensely alive she felt, or how intensely dead she knew Clara now was. The image of Clara's face, that final un-fazed and unfading smile, had left the room, but become emblazoned upon the back of Daisy's retina. She would have to paint it, in the hope of erasing it. She wondered if Julian had seen or felt his daughter's presence. Was Clara still here in this room?

At last Julian broke the silence and said in a cracked, soft voice, "Thank you so much for staying with me, you've no idea how grateful I am."

Daisy managed to rise to her feet, seizing the moment, and reached for her bag. "Shall I come back tomorrow, see how you are?"

"Would you?"

She managed to look at him, and forced the smallest smile of reassurance and a nod, "Of course I'll come back".

Somehow she got herself out of that dense atmosphere and found her way through the hall and let herself out. Thank goodness there was nobody about. Grateful that her legs knew how to walk all by themselves, but feeling incapable of cycling, Daisy pushed her bike across the scrunching gravel and away down the drive. It was impossible to describe how she felt – that same mixture of numb yet hyper awake, exhausted and wired at the same time.

# Chapter 17

Brian could tell from her face, and the stoop of her shoulders, that something extraordinary had happened to her. He knew better than to immediately fire questions. He simply and very gently put his arms reassuringly about her, steered her to the couch and brought her some tea. His old white cat, Krysta, had known just what to do, and was purring loudly on her lap with a vibrancy and noisy insistence which both grounded and soothed her.

"What a beautiful wise old pushcateeny you are Krysta." were Daisy's first words. "Is it OK if I don't talk about it right now?" she asked. Seeing how fragile she was, Brian immediately bustled about, grabbed a DVD and said, "Of course, I've been wanting to share this film with you for ages – you up for a distraction?" Oh what an angel he was. He always knew exactly what to say.

Amazingly Daisy managed to sleep that night, after praying for Clara and her father Julian, and awoke without remembering any dreams. She was deeply contemplative, thinking about past relationships, remembering how she had both cared with a fiery fierceness for her first lover, yet simultaneously had been brought to a place where she felt prepared to kill him if he did not leave her alone. One of those 'can't live with them / can't live without them' knife-edge, passionate, impossible relationships. She who preached to others about transcending polarities, she who had watched her own Mother's lifelong struggle with rejection and abandonment. She who's every effort to heal her Mother had failed, because her Mother had been thrown away as a two year old by her birth Mother. Daisy had been condemned to a life of futile and hopeless rescue efforts because she could not fix so primal a wound.

Eventually her Mother had been pain and rage held together by alcohol and cigarettes, and the closer Daisy tried to get to her, the more viciously she had been spurned and spat upon. Knowing that, Daisy eventually withdrew her offers of love and her efforts of care, and bowed to her Mother's desperation for fulfilment of her own belief of unlovability. Where her Mother had chosen slow poison and desiccation, Daisy chose an impossible cause. Being a voice to the voiceless mute members of the animal kingdom whose chance of life was ruthlessly denied. Not for factory farm animals could there be any hope of a natural existence under the sun, following their instincts, roaming, nesting, socialising or interacting with their environment.

Countless billions of creatures were callously artificially inseminated, coldly raised purely for human use, with never a shred of consideration for their inherent natural life. Billions of chickens the world over were deliberately deprived of freedom, incarcerated and kept apart : mothers from chicks, and male chicks ground up alive because they could not lay eggs and would not grow fast enough to make the breast meat humans craved.

With a sudden stab of realisation, Daisy saw the separation of human families similarly torn apart by inherited dysfunction. Children raised intensively in conditioning chambers called schools, and the males packed off to be ground up by war machines. The whole, sick cycle seemingly self-perpetuating and accelerating as it grew. So the intensive factory farms, where individual creatures were not recognised as sentient beings but mere commodities, were run by compassion-less automated men, taught to kill and dismember without a thought. So, too, with the soldiers, who if they ever did stop and question why, found it too late to avoid the inevitable mass slaughter which had been prescribed for them to perform.

Daisy, in the fervour of her pacifism, could not understand why all the soldiers did not simply refuse to fight. For her, it took more courage and honesty to say "No" than to follow the herd trustingly, as a lamb bleats its ineffectual plea, even as the knife strikes at its defenceless throat. Daisy had been mourning for these unknown victims of unnecessary destruction and violence her whole life. In her lowest moment of suicidal despair, the only thing which had stopped her was the thought that her death would have no meaning, just as the lives of all of these victims had not been permitted to have any meaning. She got angry when people tried to justify all the killing by saying that 'none of the animal would go to waste'. As if it lessened the terror and pain inflicted upon them in any way to then have their bodies hacked to pieces, shrink wrapped and distributed. They were waste products from the start, the whole bloody business was a violent waste of potential.

The other reason she had stayed alive was the realisation that she had been granted a voice, and the ability to use it on behalf of the innocent mute.  Such had become her motivation as she poured out her impassioned plea in her writing and her outreach. She never knowingly missed an opportunity, either, to awaken the spark of compassion in anyone she met. She truly believed that human beings were not by nature cruel, callous and destructive, despite all the evidence for it. She considered herself to be a great optimist, and had beautiful visions of the way life could be, in the Peaceable Kingdom of Vegantopia, as she called it. Her Mother had been the first of many to tell her she was "away with the fairies", to which her usual response was, "If only! Don't I wish."

Daisy totally believed that the violence in society was a direct result of the unnatural predation upon fellow, non-human earthlings. To her it was obvious that because people shut down their feelings, and disconnected from their innate kindness in order to kill and eat animals, they by extension became closed hearted towards one another. She also felt that there was an inexorable process of continuing evolution going on, which was carrying humanity towards deeper connectivity to each other. A fateful movement towards an awareness of their link with all other life on the planet. Many seemed to see the world becoming more savage, selfish, and dangerous. Daisy, however, persisted in her blithe, trusting faith in humanity's higher nature. She felt she was on a sacred mission to help awaken the unenlightened, and be a force for peace. Encouraging the power of gentleness to supplant fear and control. Ultimately, this was the only thing that made any sense to her.

Daisy wondered if Julian Ballard had actually read any of her pamphlets at all. She worried about how awkward this visit was going to be, as she dressed in preparation. She was aware that she was taking special care with her choice of clothes – wanting to appear respectful and sombre, yet reluctant to wear dark colours. In the end she wore a deep green velvet jacket, over a fawn and cream floral, loose fitting, button through dress. The dress reached to her calves, and as the day was mild with the approach of spring she left off her customary boots, and instead wore sandals over her emerald green tights.

Spontaneously, as she left the house she took her favourite orchid plant in its special ceramic pot, as a gift. The pot fitted well into the basket of her bike, and she immediately felt much happier as the fresh cool air passed across her face. Cycling nearly always soothed her, something about the rhythmic ease of it, the balance and the speed was just right. Especially along leafy country lanes and easy trails such as the eight miles of cross country which she easily covered in half an hour.

Passing through the ornate, open, gold and black gates to the Grange she had a sensation of great familiarity, and got the distinct impression that she would indeed be making this journey routinely, though how that would happen she could not say. It was almost as if the Grange was adopting her, drawing her into itself. She was not sure she liked the sensation. After all, freedom was her middle name, and entrapment her nemesis. She had been so certain she would refuse Ballard's request for her to create a farm sanctuary here, but maybe fate had its own ideas about that. She was still very unsettled from the previous day's events, and decided that it was her duty to place Julian at his ease, and determined to be some comfort to him if she possibly could.

Suddenly she had been swallowed up by the drive and was leaning her bike against the wisteria-covered wall next to the heavy oak front door. It swung open before she could reach the bell, and Ballard himself was standing there, looking pale and gaunt in beige linen slacks and a green checked shirt, topped with an open waistcoat of pale green corduroy. He smiled warmly and accepted the orchid graciously. "You must see the orangery" he said, "if you're fond of plants." Walking ahead to lead the way, he crossed the large tiled hall and took the passage on the right, towards the back of the house. A grandfather clock pendulously marked time as she passed, and she noticed a delightful library on the left, rich with the promise of endless reading pleasures, a rare luxury for her these days.

There was so much lovely natural wood everywhere, none of it dark and oppressive as in the hallway, but light and warm, as if glowing from within, almost as if it might still be living, breathing trees. 'Daisy Fethergill what are you like', she said to herself, catching her own reverie.

The next moment she felt that she was walking into Kew gardens, for they had entered the orangery: a lofty and breathtakingly beautiful Victorian splendour. Tree ferns reached up to the sky beyond the glass roof, and she recognised a banana tree and several other exotics as they arrived at the central open space. Now you're talking, she thought, as she saw the provision for tea making discreetly organised behind a walnut wood bar, and a lovely table simply set for lunch.

"How are you feeling today?" Daisy enquired.

"Actually a lot better than I thought I was going to" he replied. "Having you here yesterday was such a blessing, I can't tell you..... I'm flying over to Switzerland to collect, to bring Clara....." his words faltered and he fell silent. "She was very organised, like her mother before her, and would have hated any fuss. It makes it easier, somehow."

Daisy had no idea of course, what he must be feeling. She guessed that the wolf hound lying at his feet had been one of Clara's, and marvelled that the dog had not come over to check her out as most dogs would have done. It had not so much as acknowledged her presence. It was a magnificent creature and fit perfectly into the room. Perhaps he too was processing his own grief?

"I just got some cold things from the deli, hope that's alright for you?" Julian said, "I made sure there were no animals in any of it." The food was really tasty: dolmades and olives, hummus and an assortment of breads, baby salad leaves and vine tomatoes – simple and delicious.

"It's perfect, thank you, some of my favourite foods" she smiled warmly. The conversation then began to flow around the subject of food, its importance and significance. Daisy admitted that she regretted not being able to share a proper meal with her Mother from the fraught time when she had announced her decision to turn vegan as a teenager.

"She never accepted my veganism, saw it as a personal attack on herself and her values I suppose, and she would never try anything I made. She's a plain 'meat and potatoes' lady, white bread and butter, you know." Daisy sighed.

Julian surprised her by saying that he had disappointed his own mother by refusing to go in the army which was her family's tradition. He couldn't meet Daisy on her pacifism, however, and admitted to having shotguns on the premises.

"My uncle Sam had a shotgun, he kept a smallholding." and she found herself telling Julian the story of how when she was just 3 years old and they had been staying at his home, she had disappeared, causing a panic for over an hour, only to be discovered asleep on the belly of a large white sow amongst her litter of piglets. Her uncle had been the old fashioned type, so yes the pigs were raised as meat, but he always prided himself on keeping them clean in fresh, deep straw. Julian laughed when she told him how her uncle used to stand her in his wellington boot, and it came up to her waist. Visits to Uncle Sam were her happiest childhood memories.

Now, here before her, was arguably her greatest chance to be an agent of change. By dint of personal loss, one of the leading agents of animal exploitation and her former nemesis had experienced a change of heart, an awakening of compassion.

Julian Ballard's daughter had been taken from him, and had laid her last wish upon him – that he fulfil Daisy's mission to halt the holocaust of dairy farming which he had made it his own life's work to promote up until this point. Daisy had written passionately in her booklet "Why not milk?" about the cruelty of severing the sacred mother/child bond which the dairy industry was based upon. How else could they steal a mother's milk away for themselves?

Not merely that, but these factory farmed mothers never knew a herd life, never met the bull which sired their calf, would never feel the earth beneath their cloven feet, nor taste the sweet richness of living grass between their teeth. As if these crimes against nature were not enough, modern cows were forced to secrete up to 7 times the volume of milk in a day that their one calf could ever drink. Mastitis from this, plus crippled feet and joints from the unnatural slatted metal flooring, plus grief for her murdered calf, took their inevitable toll. The interminable cycle of annual insemination, the simultaneous burden of pregnancy and lactation, wore them out way before their natural lifespan of 25 years would ever be reached, and most only lasted 5 or 6 years of this punishment.

Added to that, the antibiotics, growth hormones and fishmeal in their high protein food gave them indigestion and hugely increased the methane their bodies belched out into the atmosphere. Acres of toxic ammonial effluent from their waste damaged the soil and waterways from the 40 billion cows raised and slaughtered yearly on the planet. The wider picture showed the human and ecological cost of the soya beans and grains fed to the cows, where old forests had been cut down to grow them, plus energy to transport them to the farming units. Meanwhile as a direct result, indigenous people were starving as their lands turned to desert. The energy required to process, refrigerate, package and transport all the resulting dairy products around the globe far exceeded that used for any other purpose.

"Have you even read my pamphlets?" Daisy had to ask. Julian had to admit that, no, he had not read them cover to cover, but that he knew the bottom line was the call of vegans to animal exploiters to end their practices. And he wanted to do that as soon as possible as his tribute to his daughter, and in fulfilment of her last wish. He told Daisy that he needed her advice about how to go about dismantling his farm in the least harmful way possible. He understood that the animals on his farm were his responsibility, and that moving them on, and shutting down the machines would not be the best or easiest outcome for anyone involved, including his workers. He liked the idea of turning the farm into a sanctuary and keeping what remained of the herd in retirement, in as natural conditions as possible for the rest of their lives.

He asked Daisy to run it for him. She said no, that she had her own life path and could not just turn aside from that and take over his responsibilities for him. She told him that it would not be as simple as throwing some of the money he had got from exploiting animals back into the welfare of a token few and then assuming his conscience would be quiet. She said that if he was sincere then he had to walk his talk by going vegan and by encouraging as many people as possible to follow him. She cited the example of the American cowboy who had turned his back on his past and was an inspiration to many, as well as making up for the harm his earlier life had caused. She asked him how far he felt capable and willing to take this.

There was a very long pause. "I think I would feel great about it if you were on board, but without you it's not going to happen." Seeing her expression accusing him of emotional blackmail, he went on, "Well you asked me a direct question and I'm trying to be as honest as possible. This is all so new to me, remember, whereas you have had years to get used to it. I really don't want to be an activist, and can't see myself doing what you do."

Seeing Julian passing his hand across his furrowed brow, Daisy simply had to soften, "OK Julian, I'm sorry I've been really hard on you and expecting too much, and it's not fair or kind. You are right that this has always been my path, not yours. Please let's stop right here and do something completely different, go for a walk or something, and relax."

Julian had never felt so relieved. So the antsy activist did take time off once in a while. He gave her a quick guided tour of the house, stables and gardens, and told her that she must feel free to come and use the indoor swimming pool any time she liked. It was going to take a lot of organising to complete the ambitious changes they needed to make.

As time went by, with Daisy visiting Bothies Grange almost daily, they learned to relax and accept each other as they were, which was quite profoundly different people. The only important thing was the vision they were working on between them.

One particularly cold and rainy day, enjoying the warmth of the pool, Julian suddenly had a boyish expression and deliberately splashed at her as he swam past. Daisy retaliated instantly by thrashed the water with her legs in a vain effort to splash him back, but he was much too quick in the water to be caught. The playful exchange broke the ice between them, and they both felt that the dynamic had changed. It was always going to be a very unusual relationship, but it had imperceptibly entered a more mutually trusting phase. She still felt as if she was in an enemy encampment, guiltily realising how it might look to her vegan friends. Julian was not going to give up his shooting and fishing and hunting just like that, if at all. But it was much too late to regret having ever gone to the Grange. Fate had presented her with this opportunity and she was not going to walk away. The only way out had to be through, even though it was inevitably going to take her away from her usual form of activism. If she played it right she could bring her friends into the enterprise too. As Julian had stated that he required his existing workers to be given jobs in any scheme that Daisy came up with, she would need to use care and sensitivity.

"I have a great idea for transforming the dairy into a cruelty free place" Daisy began, over a very tasty supper of Thai vegetables and cashews with rice noodles.

"I've experimented with making cheesy things using plants, and the principles are the same as dairy products. You need milk, a fermentation agent, a warm place to let the flavours develop, and some way of pressing out the water to make it solid."

"What do you use instead of milk, then?" Julian wanted to know. So he hadn't read her pamphlets then, just as she suspected.

"Nuts can be soaked overnight, mixed with water and liquidised. Then you strain them through muslin and you have milk. The solid residue is very nutritious and high in fibre and protein and makes lovely burgers and sausages".

"Ah, so you're thinking the cheese making equipment we already have can be used to make non-dairy products instead? That's an excellent idea."

"Yes, and yogurt can be made using the same liquid, mixed with cultures. Soya beans are hugely versatile too, and make great cheese."

"The market for these things is growing fast, what with health consciousness and the increasing number of lactose intolerant people. We were approached by someone with interests in producing lactose free milk quite recently."

"I would like to be assured that if I get involved with the new dairy there won't be any cow products used whatsoever. Both to avoid cross contamination and from an ethical perspective." Daisy was concerned about the purity of what she put her energy into.

"These decisions would not be just mine or yours I'm afraid, because it's no longer classed as a small family business." Julian was hedging.

"What if I just give you a few ideas and recipes and leave you to get on with it then, as I'm definitely not a business person." Daisy was acting as if she was prepared to bail out.

"No, absolutely not, I need you to lead this thing Daisy. Please, I want you to move in here and let's make it happen."

"Move in?" Daisy was incredulous.

"Why not? It would make it so much easier, and more convenient all round, and there's plenty of space here. You can borrow one of the cars any time you like so you won't feel trapped. And I'll give you a company debit card to use, and a generous personal allowance. Do say yes."

It was simply too enticing an offer to turn down, and Daisy had always been a spontaneous decision maker.

"Yes, I think it makes sense too, but I don't want any money from you. That wouldn't feel right. If I have my basic needs covered I'm happy to be here and do this. I can really focus on things and not get distracted. I hate dealing with money, so being able to forget about it would be fantastic."

"You remind me of Clara when you talk like that. She went off doing voluntary work in Thailand and didn't let me know she'd got into a bit of trouble. Very independent and resourceful the both of you. Whatever makes you feel comfortable is fine with me. You'll obviously need clothes and toiletries and things so you must use the card to cover whatever you want. And I've already set up a fund for you to use at your discretion for anything related to the sanctuary."

"Really? Oh my goodness, that's such a generous offer. I promise I won't ever buy anything unnecessary or extravagant. I hate shopping anyway, and get more joy out of making do and recycling things."

Brian was flabbergasted. "Move in? Wow! But you should be getting a salary, Daisy, think about your future."

"Oh the future doesn't exist, and I know that I'm being taken care of. Divine Providence is smiling on me because I'm doing something really good. That's the way it feels anyway."

"Be careful you're not being used, even if it is as a daughter substitute."

"I'm only too aware of that element, but at least he's not trying to get me into bed, now that I couldn't cope with."

"So what car are you going to be allowed to drive, something economical and safe like a hybrid Prius?"

"I'll choose something flashy and fast given half a chance. Only for vitally important business use, naturally" Daisy grinned.

## Chapter 18

"Come on, time for another green smoothie!" Daisy said, as she sprang from the water towards the counter which she had helped to set up with juicers and blenders. She had taken it upon herself to improve Julian's eating habits, along with educating him about raw food principles.

"You know just how to tempt me, don't you" he mockingly said, curling up his nose in dislike.

"Can't you just feel it doing you good though!" was all the sympathy he got. Daisy wondered whether her increasingly frequent bossiness was tolerated only because she was becoming a daughter substitute. It did not matter though, because the effect was that the cheese making equipment at the dairy was all being adapted into making amazing vegan cheeses. Using cashew nuts, sunflower and sesame seeds, flavoured with nutritional yeast and coloured with turmeric and beetroot powder. She had done lots of research and experimentation to develop tasty viable products, and the "Holy Cow" dairy free brand was arising from the ashes of the former "Wholly Cow "product line. It was going to be a win / win result for Julian Ballard, and for the cow nation.

Daisy had made it absolutely clear that she did not want her name associated with the product, that this was to be seen as Julian's own personal transition, and his tribute to his daughter. Whilst she was very happy to be helping behind the scenes, she was adamant that her major and prime purpose was her own activism.

"Leopards don't change their spots, Daisy; that Ballard is a hard-nosed business man". Brian was neither impressed nor convinced by the events so rapidly unfolding in Daisy's life.

"I mustn't expect too much of him Brian, he's been through so much. And we must never forget that these ordinary people are not motivated by missionary zeal to make things right in the world like we activists are."

"What does that mean? You're making yourself sound like a religious fanatic."

"Don't you realise that's how most people see us, Brian?"

"Even though some activists have strong faith backgrounds, many are atheists. In fact I'd say that it's because I don't have the comfort of some god coming along and making everything humans have ruined all better again, that I'm motivated to get cracking myself. If not us, who? And maybe more than a few of us aren't getting enough sex so we pour our passions into other things!" Brian leaned over and made a leery lunge for Daisy with a mock slathery drool on his face.

As a shrieking Daisy dodged deftly out of reach, he added, "Yes, I know: 'I'm too busy to be bothered, stay on task, Brian!'" he completed her sentence before she could even mouth it.

From the kitchen she shouted, "We can't turn him into a Mother Theresa. Just because you would turn his billiard room into a food distribution depot and his lawns into salad! The Grange *is* his home you know. I've already taken over one of the greenhouses with my experiments for grafting fruit tree branches onto the deciduous trees. My idea is to perfect a technique that could cheaply and simply be used to convert all non-edible native trees into fruit bearers. What a wonderful contribution to the world's food needs that would be. Grafting means that existing trees could start producing fruit within as little as two years, instead of having to wait decades for an actual tree to grow from seed."

"But you could be working for someone and earning a good salary doing that, instead of pottering about in Ballard's sheds. He has other places to live, and heaps of money to stay in hotels, and paid staff on tap. Stop pandering to him Daisy. I'm beginning to think that you're enjoying the country seat lifestyle rather too much yourself, from the amount of time you've been spending up there."

"Listen Brian, part of the deal was to turn Julian's health around, and I can't do that without being there to make sure he's eating properly."

"So Ballard has his very own, tame, green smoothie maker. Everyone has their price I guess."

Driving away in Julian's cute little green Lotus Elan, Daisy wasn't sure if she was more angry than sad. Was Brian jealous? She found it impossible to turn the tables and imagine how she might be feeling in his shoes. She did not want to lose his friendship, and yet the bitterness coming from him whenever they met lately seemed to be leading to some sort of terminal argument. There was no way he would see her side of things, and no way would she give up the Grange now, even though as Brian said she had already lost much of her former free life. Maybe he was right; there was a price to pay for everything.

Daisy sighed deeply, but the weight in her heart only sank deeper. She felt as if she were expected to juggle an impossible number of balls. If Brian refused to accept her new life she might have to let him go. But that felt dreadful. Like a betrayal. She rationalised that everybody's life took so many different turns that sometimes people had to go separate ways. She mustn't dwell on it, there was so much tugging at her now. And anyway, it was him who had changed too, in response to how her life was turning out.

She could not even remember what her old life was like. Had she really caved in and begun to act like a lady of the manor as he insinuated? But if her prime motivation was still saving the animals why was she giving so much of her energy to Ballard? It did seem like whenever she intended to get down to focussing on the next stage of her rather fuzzy plan of action, some distraction would crop up.

It was so unfair! Brian knew her skills did not include continuity and seeing things through; she was the ideas person. She had always relied on him to carry out the practicalities, and now he was refusing to be part of it, and being thoroughly obstinate, as well as frankly quite obnoxious with her. Why couldn't he just flow with the way things went as she tried to do? Why couldn't he be happy for and with her? It was so maddening.

No sooner had she parked the car in the garage and entered the Grange, than Julian's bell sounded, putting a stop to her thoughts. She was beginning to regret her light-hearted suggestion that Julian strike the dinner gong to summon her attention! She had an aversion to carrying a mobile phone around and being instantly contactable.

"Where were you Daisy? I've been waiting hours for you to give me the menus for the summer party, had you forgotten? If it's not important enough to you I'll just get the old caterers to come in, but they don't have much clue about veggie stuff".

"I'm so sorry Julian, I haven't quite finished them yet, but I promise they'll be on your desk before your breakfast meeting tomorrow". Darn it, all that messing around and a wasted journey to Sheffield. Now she'd be up all night getting it done.

She was finding it hard to remember how she used to feel in her old life, just that it had been so much simpler. That was because she had been more her own person, whereas here she had to constantly refer to and go through Julian about everything. But the potential gains for her cause were so enticing. This summer party for example, it was her chance to present the animal rights message in an elegant relaxed way, so very different to standing on street corners trying to attract the attention of passers-by. Yes it entailed a lot of work, but she couldn't turn down such a golden opportunity.

Needless to say, Brian saw it differently. Why could he not appreciate that whether he liked it or not, the wealthy people Ballard mixed with had power and influence which might be turned to good use. In fact it was very rude of him to insinuate that she had any other motives for being there.

"Well what about your writing Daisy? You haven't written anything for months!" Brian had flung at her accusingly.

"Maybe, but I'm actually doing things now, rather than just writing about them!" she had bitten back at him, before spinning on her heel and resolutely walking out. But his words had stung her. She couldn't see clearly what her priorities ought to be. She couldn't face looking for a proper job and living a normal nine to five existence. She liked the lifestyle she was developing here, with lots of flexibility and opportunities, and not much responsibility.

Oh why did every meeting with Brian lately end up as a row? She was so tired of it. They had always been so easy and relaxed together. Why was he being so resistant to the necessary changes she was going through in her routine and life? He was so not going to like it when she went off to Switzerland with Julian next week. She hadn't dared to tell him about it. But hang on a minute. Was she her own person, or wasn't she? What did Brian's opinion have to do with it anyway?

Once again Daisy felt torn between conflicting pressures. Why should she feel this way? Surely it wasn't necessary? Why couldn't these opposing poles of her life come to meet and agree? They were not truly in opposition were they? It was so very confusing and brain-rattlingly annoying that she could not stand it. If Julian expected more of her attention than Brian had ever done, it was because he was accustomed to getting what he expected, whereas Brian was used to putting up with whatever might come his way. Two very different outlooks. It didn't make one right and the other wrong, it was just a matter of approach. And balance. It wasn't about being fair. I mean she couldn't slice herself cleanly in two and give exactly half of herself to each of them, now could she? That was ridiculous! And beneath it all, there was a growingly loud, internal voice saying: 'What about ME? When does Daisy get to say what *she* wants, instead of trying to figure out how to keep everyone else happy?'

For a moment she allowed herself to contemplate running away from not just Ballard and Brian but from the whole lot of them. Yeah, go off to India for a few months and let them all get on with it. Oh what a temptingly delicious prospect. But then this whole precarious pack of cards would probably come tumbling down, without her to constantly keep them delicately balanced. Wryly she realised that she did not have the means to buy a plane ticket, let alone money to live on, if she did go away. And of course she would not have been able to justify the ecological cost of a long plane journey purely on a whim, now would she. And then she had played right into Julian's hands by refusing a salary for her work. "Oh no." she had loftily said, "I don't evaluate myself in cash terms."

Daisy had bleated on about how she hated money and thought it was obsolete, and that as long as her basic needs were met she had no need of it. Fine and dandy, but in real terms she had dis-empowered herself and given control over her activities into his hands. Surely at first it had been a big relief to not have to think about where the money was going to come from to buy the next sack of seeds, or ethical toiletries. And yes, admittedly she did have access to a few more luxuries these days, but nothing she couldn't easily give up again. It wasn't her fault that the natural, cruelty free stuff cost so much more than the chemical, animal tested brands.

She comforted herself that as society's values changed, and people demanded ethical products as standard, and the government were forced by public pressure into ending their subsidies to the big exploitative companies, food and commodities would reflect their true cost and value. Fruit and vegetables would be the cheapest things, and meat would cost more like what its true exorbitant price actually was in terms of water and land usage, effluent, and the energy taken to prepare, transport and refrigerate it.

"Yeah and how much closer is that now than it was when we were at University? Wake up Daisy, it's not happening!" Brian's jibes kept replaying in her head. He wouldn't come to visit her at the Grange, and was mean to her when she made the effort to go and see him. She didn't know who he was any more, and he really was becoming quite insufferable.

Not for the first time in her life, a slow, sliding apathy was enveloping Daisy. Was she slipping between two tectonic plates here: if nothing she had ever done had changed anything, and if what she was doing now was in fact merely shoring up the status quo, then it was all pointless, wasn't it? Who the hell did she think she was anyway? Brian's parting words were ringing round in her head.

"Agent of change my arse! You've bought into the system completely and you're even been caught by one of the enemy – you're a corporate slave now and you don't even know it! You're prostituting yourself Daisy, every day, and you just can't admit it."

Brain was clearly jealous, and so she forgave his harshness towards her, from her ample largesse of abundance. He was entitled to his opinion after all, but in her heart of hearts she knew that she had been brought to the Grange to fulfil her destiny, her sacred life's mission. If most other people were simply not in touch with their life's purpose, that was their loss. Wasn't this the way it always must feel for everyone striving for massive changes in society? Unappreciated visionaries with unwelcome messages? She mustn't allow herself to give up now. Maybe real transformation lay right around the next bend, with the next enlightened Member of Parliament and the next vital piece of legislation. It wasn't really the government's fault anyway; they merely reflected the values which the majority of the society they worked for held. She had always thought that, and consequently devoted most of her energies towards awakening the public to what their daily food choices were costing. She had not lost her faith in the basic decency and kindness of people, even though this was so covered up by the constant petty trials of getting through to the next pay day, and covering their bills. Most people were too preoccupied in paying their rent or mortgage and providing for their children with half a glance to their own future situation to really evaluate the origin and spiritual cost of what lay upon their dinner plate. Of *who* lay on their dinner plate, in fact, lest it be forgotten that he or she was a sentient being, a person not an object.

Looked at from one perspective, life was actually getting worse for animals rather than better. It didn't matter that a handful of veggie alternative foods had become mainstream, people were still eating billions of animals, and the human population was growing all the time. America had taken steps to protect the powerful meat and dairy corporations' interests, by bringing into effect a law allowing them to incarcerate and detain, indefinitely without trial, anyone deemed to be a potential 'terrorist'. This included people attempting to obtain or show images gleaned from illegal covert filming or investigations. Daisy knew several good people who had already been snatched up by this merciless eagle's claw and its obsession with "homeland security", which was so clearly a thin veneer of big brotherly control. Having always side stepped any overt political agenda, and never participating in long conversations about politics, she had stayed resolutely focussed on the animal rights issues. She refused to get caught up in opinions about policy or parties. It was a waste of time anyway, because all the arguments only ever reinforced the polarities and never seemed to convince anyone.

No, for Daisy, life was very simple and direct, and boiled down to 3 simple questions: is it kind and equable; is it demonstrating compassion; is it sustainable and ecologically beneficial? She had always been an idealist, but a much grounded one. She thought of herself as a visionary, yes, because she had such clear images of the way life could be, and would be, if only she held onto, and held aloft, those cherished ideals. She sensed that if she slackened off even a tiny amount, then the progress already made might be lost. And she was acutely conscious that every day, millions more innocent animals suffered and died. So she simply could not let up the pressure she put upon herself, to speak out for them, to raise awareness of their plight, to encourage others to change their behaviour to more closely resemble the gentle society she longed to belong to. Being wholeheartedly committed to the cause had to be better than lukewarm, ineffectual lip service.

And now Brian had the cheek to accuse her of playing the lady of the manor and sucking up to the local elite. How dare he judge her so? Didn't he realise that she was making effort to convince these influential people that she was not fanatical, precisely to win them over? If all you ever did was blame and criticise you wouldn't be much of a change agent, would you?

Daisy had never subscribed to the belief that money was necessarily evil. It was purely an energy system still very much in use across the planet between humans, and could be turned as much to positive, benevolent action as to greedy and destructive ends. If Brian for a minute even thought that she had any designs on Ballard's money she would be mortified. How long had they been friends? How much had they shared? She could not bear it, if he really thought that, then he could get out of her life completely, and never come back!

She deliberately refused to take any money for herself. Admittedly she did think that it was justifiable to use the fund's money to replace necessary personal things, like clothing, and of course she needed a reasonable level of decent things to wear in order to look respectable when she gave talks. The jewellery was not real, and most of the clothes came from the nice dress shop in town, not from a department store, so that was supporting local business, wasn't it? And how dare Brian pass remarks about the amount of tropical fruit and expensive super food supplements she used in the kitchen. She had to be fuelling herself to the highest level in order to function so tirelessly, didn't she? Admittedly she was fed up with being expected to create healthy meals on demand for Julian and his friends. She was not a chef; she had so many more important skills and a genuine purpose to be fulfilling. But it was part of the deal to be available, and anyway, in practise Julian was away a lot of the time.

The phone rang, and Brian's voice interrupted her just as she was getting her head around the tricky business of the summer menu plans.

"Just because you think what I'm doing is trivial, that doesn't give you the right to mess with my life. I don't tell you what you should and shouldn't do" she said grumpily.

"That's because you don't give a shit about me, you never even ask what's going on in my life. I don't even recognise you any more Daisy." Brian sounded so very cold and distant.

"Well so be it! I haven't changed; it's you who've got jealous, and suspicious, and bitter because I've used this opportunity to try to make a difference in the world. I wanted you to be part of this with me, but you won't even come and see what I'm doing here."

"I'm not your lap dog, and I have no intention of becoming one of Ballard's bloody butlers".

"Who are you without me anyway? We'll see how useless your single voice and lone pair of hands are, without my guiding vision."

Uh oh, did that sound like she thought it sounded? This is no time for false modesty, she soothed herself, and pressed on: "I'm in this position because I have the skill set to manage things at this level. If you lack the grace to accept that, then we probably need to part company now."

Oh no, that's not what she meant to say, yet somehow she felt compelled to continue, "If you're not with me on this – it sure feels as if you're pushing as hard as you can against me these days."

Damn damn damn! Why did she have to be so plain speaking and upset everyone so? Why couldn't people hear the truth without taking it so personally? Or was it herself who couldn't listen to anyone else's truth? But no, because all of her ideas and arguments had been well thought out and could be backed up by facts – they were not mere personal opinions. Oh she was so tired of this struggle and bickering – it was all so unnecessary and time wasting. When every day mattered, every wasted moment could have been put towards the primary cause of ending suffering.

"We have to stop this, right here and right now. It's doing my head in and it feels like I'm going to burn out or make a mistake. I'm not going to spend the rest of my life regretting not giving it my best. That would be so pointless." It was as close to an apology as she could manage, but Brian's only response was to hang up the phone on her.

# Chapter 19

Daisy realised that she had not found the time to meditate, do yoga, or pray like she used to do. Even her daily dog walks were forced route marches where she could not spare the time off from thinking and planning, to just enjoy the beauty all around her. She no longer noticed the loveliness of the gardens as she stamped past them, and the joy with which she had first glimpsed the orangery was completely absent from her now. All she noticed if she went that way was the stillness of the air and the unnaturalness of the glass surrounds. Part of her wanted to tear it all down – the connotations of elitist entitlement, bought by the sweat of countless labourers to perpetuate the fossilised class system. Oh wow, in Brian's absence she had become a part of him – she had internalised his belief systems and attitudes and now they were threatening to direct her actions.

She had to take stock of herself, who she was, and where she was going, before she got any further out of kilter with who she believed herself to be, and what she truly wanted to do. But it was not as simple as just deciding to take a few days off. There was so much riding on her every day now. She began to see why people resorted to drugs in order to slow their minds down, or keep themselves going, or calm their jangling nerves. She knew well enough the warning signs and how the physical body soon enough takes over and expresses the angst if it remains unresolved. Her tell-tale lower back pain had been increasing of late, and she realised that it had been a very long time since she had burst into song.

Feeling exhausted yet incapable of resting, the mounting anger inside of her was building up. She stomped outside to talk to the horses in their stables. She didn't often go there because it upset her that they were not allowed outside in the fields, and it was completely unnatural for horses to be shut up in little boxes. Horses didn't go to sleep for 8 hours at a time like people did. Why couldn't they be allowed to live in the paddocks, with open shelters to use when they felt like it? But Julian said they were thoroughbreds, not native ponies, and had to be kept safe and warm inside. Laying her head against the warm flank of Frankincense, a beautiful bay, she thought he was begging her to take him out.

Daisy had serious misgivings about riding horses, it seemed such an imposition of human will and domination, and she hated those metal bits and nailed on shoes. She used to ride her school friend Jennifer's horses without saddle and bridle when she was younger, and she was a competent, confident rider. Perhaps she could just slip a head collar on Frankincense and go for a quick ride around the parkland. It would do them both good.

There was nobody about, and before she knew it she had led him over to a mounting block and slid her leg over his back. His ears pricked up and he was very keen to go.

"No galloping Frankie boy, just a gentle stroll" she said, trying to keep her energy down and calm. But Frankie had other ideas, and he broke into a swift canter the moment his feet touched the grassy track. When she tried to slow him down he began to skip sideways and prance, and she was in danger of falling off, so she thought that it might be better to just let him run. "OK nice and steady, and in a straight line, Frankie."

It felt wonderful, exciting and refreshing to be not exactly in control of this magnificent powerful animal, moving with such fluent speed. The rhythmic thud of his hooves on the turf was hypnotic. The flash of the sun as it sparkled through the leaves made her feel very high. The breeze in her hair and the touch of sunlight on her face was exhilarating. The delicious smell of horse, and the warmth beneath her; the way she had to concentrate on staying perfectly poised and balanced with his cadence. Everything else had disappeared, except for these immediate sensations, and she felt transported to another dimension.

They were approaching the gallops, and Frankincense quickened his pace in eager anticipation. 'Why not, it'll be safer going round the track', Daisy reasoned. But even leaning forward over his neck and grabbing tightly to his mane she still felt as if she might slide off his rump, such was his turn of speed. Yet it would have been foolish to try to pull him up whilst he had so much energy in him, and instead she imagined that she was on the ocean, glancing off the tops of the waves, skimming over the depths of the unknown. Her legs were strong from all the swimming she had been doing, and she felt him telling her that he would keep her safe, and that she was a fairy flying along with him. Oh how beautiful, to realise that she was a fairy and had wings!

Round and round the 2 mile track they went, at a flat out gallop. Then Frankincense began to slow down, but Daisy wanted to keep on flying for ever, like a child on a roundabout. She kicked him on, commanding him to keep going. She couldn't bear for it to end, and she wasn't tired yet. "You wouldn't slow down at first when I asked you to, so now you'll have to keep going because I tell you to." On and on she pushed, and willed, and drove him; kicking his sides with her heels as hard as she could. Round and round again, in a frenzy, even though she could hear the sound of his laboured breathing. She flicked the end of the rope on either side of his neck, trying to drive him on faster.

'Now I know why they wear spurs, for when the wretched horse won't do what it's told', she muttered to herself. Frankincense's ears flicked back and forth, as if asking her when he could have a break, and he almost stumbled. Even then, that ruthless part of her wanted to force him to carry on galloping. She should have brought a whip with her, that would have made him go faster.......grimly determined now, as if she was carrying a message of vital importance to king and country. It was she herself who was driven, and lashing herself on, not the animal. All of her conflicts and frustration had come to a head, and she had lost control of what she was doing. Where did she even think she was going with such relentless force?

Daisy began to come to her senses, and to realise that she was screaming and frenziedly kicking. Suddenly she was very afraid that she was falling apart, and could not see how she had even come to be this horrible crazy person. Then she felt with horror that Frankincense was sweating and trembling beneath her, his flanks heaving. Immediately allowing him to slow down to a walk, she jumped from his back and tried to apologise. The sweat was pouring off him, and she was appalled to see him breathing so desperately, nostrils all distended and head drooping almost to the ground.

"Oh my God I could have killed you, I am so sorry" she burst into tears of mortified shame. What had come over her? She could hardly believe that she had allowed herself to take out her feelings on this poor, defenceless horse. If she had seen anybody else doing that she would have been outraged. Thank God she hadn't taken a whip, that's all she could think, she was so very ashamed of herself.

Trying to gather her wits whilst leading Frankincense back to the stables, and hoping that he would cool down before she got there, Daisy made a vow to herself to never, ever sit on a horse's back again. That would be her penance, for she clearly could not be trusted. She had to punish herself; and anyway, getting on a horse and forcing it to obey could not be justified by any true animal rights person. Even using so called natural methods, bitless, bareback or with a treeless saddle, it was still a human being dominating a horse. Approaching the stables, she got a stab of fear; what if the stable girl caught her and told Julian? She might get thrown out. Then where would she go?

'Oh dear Daisy', she said to herself, 'Whatever are we going to do?' How come she felt so overwhelmed, and that she had no autonomy over her life. She reflected wryly that about the only deliberate choice she exerted in her own life was over what she ate and when, but even this was no longer true. Her usually plump cheeks and rounded curves had fallen away, and her face had taken on gauntness, her body a shrivelling dryness about it. In place of the plain fruit and vegetables, brown rice and lentils which had formerly constituted the bulk of her diet, now she was using all sorts of supplements and so called 'super foods' in the weird concoctions she read about from health gurus.

For certain she did not feel as healthy or as happy as she made out. As if she were counselling a dear friend, she tried to stand aside from herself with sufficient objectivity to make some useful comment. Feeling as panicked and powerless as she had when her mother had attempted suicide, she realised that she was sinking into depression. Life had been swallowing her up, and chewing away at her vitality bit by bit, until only a wraith remained.

Somehow she managed to get the horse safely back in his stall, rubbed down and mollified with some hay and carrots. Even though she reasoned with herself that he had been through much worse whilst out hunting all day with Julian, she could not forgive herself. She knew better, she was supposed to be an upholder of animal rights. She hated herself for what she was becoming. She couldn't trust herself, she was hurting people, so maybe she'd be better off dead. Making sure that nobody was watching, she crept into the dismally dark house and into Julian's office. She peered at herself in the mirror, and saw a pale reflection, drained of any bright colours or lifted spirits.

Spirits, spirits, it felt as if she had been drained of vital essence by something. Or someone.... out of the corner of her half closed, jaundiced eyes, she was certain that she had glimpsed the glint of a malevolent grin. Almost as if some demon had sneaked up and stolen one more little portion of her life-force and was running off with it. "Get away from me, you slimy worm!" she shouted at the mirror.
Who was she even talking to?
She was completely losing the plot!

What had happened to the Daisy who used to ramble for mile after mile, singing to the sky and communing with the trees? And people had thought her weird then. 'Now look at yourself, at what you have allowed yourself to become'........there was that mocking internal voice again – who was this part of her who took it upon themselves to split off, judge, and commentate back to her? What authority had they?
She felt like turning a blowtorch upon that babbling brook aspect in herself and boiling it all away, back to the nothing it had come

from. What was it going to take to get some peace? To force that voice to shut the heck up!

Oh no; dangerous, sharp-edged, subterranean knives were glinting now, showing themselves by the characteristic sound of their rasping. For she had slipped back into her old habit of cutting herself lately; it helped to ease the stress, and was arguably a better choice than drugs. Julian and his friends sometimes had cocaine and other stimulants around the place, and she had started using marijuana because it was, after all, a natural plant, wasn't it. It seemed to ease the pain a bit, and level out her thinking. It took her mind off wanting to really damage herself.

Through the haze of the very strong joint she had just lit up, her gaze was drawn to the pastel painting hanging above the fireplace. The one she had felt the compulsion to paint as Clara's face had seemed to appear that fateful day.

Suddenly, like a flash of lightning hitting her, a realisation came. It was Clara!

Oh my God, that was it! The ghost of Clara, or the evil spirit which had taken Clara's soul away, was now tightening its deathly grip upon Daisy's throat. Whether from her own, over active imagination, or paranoia, or for real, she sensed demons exhaling toxic fumes upon her.

Stricken with mortal terror, she fled from the office, faster than her legs knew how to carry her, in flight up the stairs to her room. Throwing the contents of her suitcases all over the floor, she sought in desperation for the bag of special things which she had brought with her to the Grange. Rummaging through it, she felt the velveteen texture of the little pouch which held her prayer beads, the ones she had been given by her aunt Agnes from the Holy Land, made from olive stones from the Garden of Gethsemane. Throwing herself on her knees she prayed fervently.

"Blessed Lady of the Light, please help me! I'm trapped, and all around the prowling, howling monsters are closing in. I don't know what I'm doing here, I've lost my way and I need your help now!"

She prayed as she used to when she was little, terrified of the darkness, and the nameless horror beneath her bed. She prayed as she had when she thought her mother was dying. She prayed like she had done when Joe was very ill with whooping cough and she felt it was her fault. Somehow, it was always her fault. 'Clara got cancer and died because of you' came a horrible thought, and no amount of effort could bring her back, or make up for that. Clutching even tighter to her rosary, saying the words of comfort she wished could be true, slowly the panic began to ease.

As she started to calm down, Daisy sensed the warm presence of the Lady she had glimpsed in hospital as a child. The sickening stench which had smothered her downstairs in the office was banished, and her breathing gradually slowed and deepened. "Thank you, oh thank you." she whispered, still not able to open her eyes in case the death face of Clara had followed her. Puny and broken as she was, she gave sincere gratitude to the Power above her which had kept her safe this far, and guided her away from many a terrible experience. Sometimes it was more than she could manage, just to stay alive, by herself. But the Lady's presence proved that she wasn't on her own, and seemed to be showing her a way to escape from her bad thoughts.

She was already feeling a thousand times better for remembering that she was not in charge of everything in her life, and for realising that it was not down to her own miserable efforts to save the world. As her racing mind and heart began to ease, she resolved not to stay in that cavernous old mansion another night. During her rambles around the estate she had explored a dilapidated, unused coach house, and thought it might be fun to move in there and do it up, so that she could invite fellow activists to stay without imposing on Julian. She needed her own space anyway, and the mountain of boxes containing leaflets and pamphlets for the stalls she took to fetes and events were becoming a trip hazard in the formerly pristine hallway.

Thankfully, Julian had been very busy when she put her head around his office door and asked him.

"Yes, yes, off you go and play in the coach house. But you'll have to do it up yourself, I have no time to help.  It's been empty and shut up since the old gardener retired and moved to Cornwall years ago."

She could go and stop there, now, tonight. Put a bit of distance between herself and what she felt was the ghost of the manor. For all she knew there was more than one of them, unhappy ancestors haunting the place. No wonder it always felt cold in spite of roaring fires and blistering radiators. Yes, that's what she would do, she'd be safe there, regardless of the damp and cobwebs.

Kettle, teapot, sleeping bag, and a bag of hastily grabbed food, those were the only essentials. A beam of light had entered her mind, and a ray of hope had entered her heart. She just needed some down time, in silence. She would take Nancye, the old mastiff bitch who had taken to following her about the place, she would be good solid company. Maybe then Brian would come and visit, now that she was out of the Grange. She had been sorely missing his company and the warmth of his touch.

# Chapter 20

The advent of the internet, and online forums, was transforming the face of activism. Daisy spent increasing amounts of time sourcing and sharing information and participating in discussions on the computer. It was so much quicker and more effective to be enabled to communicate instantaneously with like-minded others worldwide on the web. Inevitably though, the strong personalities and various approaches of the individuals who constituted so diverse a group as animal rights activists, often caused friction. There were those charities who believed that working to improve the conditions and treatment of farm animals was the best use of resources, working from where reality was, towards greater respect of the perceived needs of the animals. These were loosely termed "welfarists" and most of them were not even vegetarian.

Then there were those like Daisy, who realised only too starkly that the only way to curb the outright abuse of animals was to push for the replacement of all animal products with plant alternatives. They had witnessed the devious way in which the very powerful farming industries and animal exploiting corporations had tricked and duped sincere activists into channelling their efforts into ineffectual, single issue campaigns. Indeed in many cases, years of campaigning and work actually ended up reinforcing the exploitation of the very animals they thought they were liberating. The banning of battery cages for egg laying hens was one example. These cages had been legally replaced by massive, intensely overstocked barns, containing thousands of chickens standing not on bare wire, but crammed together in the saturated ammonia of their own excretions. Engineered and fed to grow impossibly fast, some could not support their own body weight, and failed to reach the water spouts. Hock burns and featherlessness, were one visible result, and the burgeoning use of antibiotics to reduce infection rates which was causing lethal superbugs, was another.

Because Daisy stood firmly in the 'abolitionist' camp, this cost her harsh criticism from the welfarists, who were focussing on alleviating the actual suffering of the millions of animals already in captivity. She had the long-term view, and her visionary ideals, and these were always uppermost in her actions. She tried very hard to be a peacekeeper, and to oil the friction between the various factions, pleading with them all to join together as a united force rather than squander their energy on internal squabbles which diluted both their credibility and effectiveness. She applauded any effort by anyone towards raising the profile of animal issues generally, and public consciousness of the sentience of the creatures they so thoughtlessly ate and wore every day. Humour was in short supply, and she was only too aware that most people got turned off by graphic depictions and descriptions of what went on behind the closed doors of factory farms and abattoirs. She was in awe of those brave, stalwart souls who somehow managed to infiltrate these institutions with secret cameras, and brought out actual footage of the atrocities taking place there.

Any levity which might be introduced to lift the pressure of sorrow amongst her activist comrades she grabbed with both hands. So she was excited to discover a new face on the vocal vegan scene in the form of a young American, recently converted to veganism, who was making and uploading short videos on the internet. His name was Tristan Steyning, and he exhibited a shocking level of personal disclosure and honesty. He clearly felt that it was not only possible, but in his case mandatory, to employ nudity, profanity and outrageous exhibitionism to get his point across.

Tristan divided the camp into those who either loved and applauded him, and those who hated and wished to demolish him. Coupled with his overt silliness was an astonishing lack of talent, such that the musician in Daisy would cheerfully have paid him to stop singing his abysmally tuneless songs. At the same time she recognised a kindred spirit in the capacity he had to expose himself to the ridicule which came his way. Turning inadequacy into a virtue, almost, like converting personal wounds into the sword of activism.

It was truly lamentable to witness people in the same movement resorting to attacking each other's offerings to the cause. None were ideal or perfect, and what failed to appeal to one might just get through to another of their target audience: the 99% who continued to pay for the ongoing and accelerating animal holocaust in all its guises.

"That vile Tristan has just posted a truly inappropriate video – he's really gone too far this time, the guy is making a spectacle of the vegan movement and he has to be stopped!" Brian was complaining.

"Ah leave the bloke alone – he's coming from the heart, he's passionate, and he stirs people into talking – all good in my book" Daisy responded defensively.

"What? I can't believe you'd support him, someone on here says its made them want to order a bacon buttie! I've already stopped telling people I'm vegan because of this unhinged guy. He's turning us into a laughing stock" Brian really was angry.

"If you allow me to observe, Brian, the amount of controversy the likers and detractors of Tristan is generating has got to be a good thing! All publicity is good publicity when you're seeking to raise public awareness. We used to complain that there was infighting between the welfarists and the abolitionists – and how if we could just stop arguing about the hows of animal rights and get together as a united front we would be a powerful pack. But what if, just consider, if the very colourful diversity and freedom within our movement that the array of personalities allows, is an asset. It might in fact be a strength, rather than the weakness we have been perceiving it as. I sense that we need both to lighten up massively, and simultaneously get way more serious about things: paradox, like all the best, most truthful things – no?"

Seeing his quizzical look, she went on to explain, "What I mean is, we take ourselves ridiculously seriously when it's so not important. Protecting our dignity and our egos and position; bothering about what others think of us. When there's nothing we can do about their judgements, and it's actually none of our business what they think. And then conversely we spend way too little time focussing on what really needs attention, in ourselves, in society and its structures."

Oh no, she's off on one of her rants..... thought Brian, mentally preparing to hunker down and weather the approaching storm.....

"And another thing......

"And while we're at it, isn't it about time.....

Realising from painful past experience that Daisy was a runaway train, Brian gave in.

"OK, I'll say it in my blog: 'Tristan Steyning is arguably the greatest thing ever to happen to the animal rights movement'" Brian announced, somewhat sarcastically it had to be said.

Realising that she had indeed been "off on one" again, Daisy started laughing, and gave her best friend a huge hug and a kiss, "Oh I do love you Brian my darling friend! Would I not have exploded years ago were it not for your calm dulcet voice, a veritable balm to the inflamed mind. Thank you."

And she hugged him again. It was all too rare for him to feel the warmth of her delectable body next to his, and he wrapped his arms passionately around her and inhaled her enticing scent.

Then, just as he thought he might be getting lucky, she leaped up to put the kettle on. "Always with the tea, woman, and just when I hoped you were going to be really grateful....." the intensely smouldering gaze she saw coming from him then, caused her to literally run from the room. "Whoo hoo! Go and take a cold shower boy, don't be coming at me with that piercing look, you know I'm a card carrying celibate!"

"Yeah, more's the pity, what a bloody waste!"

"Let's take all of our pent up passion and pour it into the next promotional, shall we?" Daisy said a little too brightly. She hated being reminded that somewhere beneath her baggy clothes there still lurked a sexual being. She felt she had wasted too many years and too much energy in that direction for one lifetime. Even though her highly sexed friend Jean maintained that the thing most people regretted on their death beds was not having had more sex..... Daisy could not believe it. She felt that what she would regret would be any time she had not been actively righting the wrongs and correcting the ills of society. She wanted to depart knowing that her life had made a real difference, not by counting how many orgasms she had notched up.

"We have to make extra effort to be compassionate, towards fellow activists especially, Brian. I personally am prepared to cut them humongous amounts of slack because they're coming from the right place; however that might appear to be expressed, no? If Tristan was one of the dissers, one of the trolls, and pouring that degree of energy into anti-activism we'd be in trouble, don't you think?"

"I still don't want to watch his excruciatingly bad videos or listen to his appallingly dreadful songs."

Daisy had to laugh, "Agreed they're neither skilful nor polished, but that's compensated for by the sheer volume and variety of them. You have to hand it to the guy; he makes a lot of effort, and churns out a lot of videos. How about thinking that their very awfulness, their lack of talent and cringe worthiness, is in some way part of their charm and impact? Because it is for some people. They're so bad that they're good, in that funny way some things are. I mean, nobody else could do them like he does, could they? And they definitely make me laugh and cheer me up, especially the controversial ones! I love how he doesn't take long over doing them, doesn't get all prissy and perfectionist, and just keeps churning them out, day after day. A seemingly unstoppable torrent of genuine emotion. Real 'Stream of Consciousness' stuff. And just imagine what his output could be if he linked up with really talented, committed people?"

"Uh Oh. I don't like where this is leading, Daisy. Please don't say you're thinking of inviting him over here?" Brian had grown despairing of the increasingly odd mixture of people Daisy had been inviting to stay at Bothies Grange's Coach House. Julian had given her free run of the empty coach-house on the periphery of the west side of his estate, and it seemed as if all manner of misfits and vagrants were encamped there. Daisy was so naïve that a convicted mass murderer could turn up and be invited to stay if they said the magic 'V' word.

"However did you guess? America needs a break from him, and they've had a monopoly on him for too long. Furthermore, nobody gets appreciated in their home town, even Jesus wasn't respected back home in Nazareth. Tristan needs to be spread about a bit. There are lots of nice English activists, ladies especially, who would enjoy spending time with him".

"Oh what? I can't believe you're buying into his attention seeking behaviour. He'll just get worse and more over the top. He's already making a mockery of serious activists. For crying out loud, leave the bloke in America." Besides the talentless music and tasteless videos, in which if he wasn't naked Tristan had dressed himself up in all manner of costumes, he also posted frequent forthright status updates concerning his lack of and desire for, female sexual partnership.

"His unacceptable language and behaviour is disrespectful and detrimental to real activists who get our hands dirty and our hearts bruised on the front line" Brian continued, with intensifying fervour.

"All that vulgarity and obscenity cheapens what we've been spending years working towards, Daisy" was his last appeal. But to no avail, for Daisy only countered that idea with the chilling words, "I think that if he was given some support he could be a great ambassador for us, and we'd be lucky to have him on our side of the pond. What if our old mode of activism has had its day? I mean, PETA deliberately use controversial and sexual means to get attention quite effectively. Aren't you prepared to get your kit off if it's going to save lives?"

"No actually; and by the way, I thought you couldn't bear the sight of men's willies flashing in front of your eyes."

With a barely perceptible wince, Daisy flung back: "Tristan doesn't push his penis in anyone's face, he gets naked to show his solidarity with the vulnerability of the animals. Surely you aren't feeling threatened by that?"

"The man's clearly a megalomaniac attention seeker, all that posturing and strutting about. I don't think his primary motivation is helping animals at all. I think he's after getting laid by as many women as he can –why he even says as much!"

"Brian, he's only using his assets to best effect, if he had talent and looks he'd already be a pop star with the fearless character he has. Let's face it, he's not got much going for him. You've got way better a body than his scrawny one, but you're too shy to show it."

As this was clearly the closest thing to a compliment or reassurance he was going to get, Brian decided to end the conversation by saying, "If he's using the vegan platform to gain followers, and to perform for admirers, he'll show himself up for what he is soon enough".


Tristan was indeed invited over. Daisy even paid his airfare from the Holy Cow Trust Fund coffers, reasoning that with his energy and input they could more than recoup the money in publicity. She installed him in the apple loft above the courtyard of the Grange coach house.

They were sickeningly, cloyingly absorbed in one another. Jesting and fooling around like idiots thinking they were so very funny and special. Daisy was turning every other sentence into a ridiculous song and dance routine. She even told Brian that she thought she had fallen asleep and woken up in a musical.

He had one last attempt to get through to her, but she just brushed him off saying, "Look Brian, you know how loyal I am, and that once someone's in my heart there's nothing I can do to remove them..... Of course I'm not in love with Tristan, what a ridiculous notion! I love and I pray for all our fellow activists, even though I may never meet them or have any contact it doesn't mind – love crosses all boundaries – in fact prayer recognises no boundaries cos they're all fake constructs.

Just like the lines humans draw on the globe between countries that aren't really there. Trouble is they convince one another they're real and important and then the next thing you know tribes are killing each other because of them – how crazy is that?"

Brian couldn't stomach it. She wasn't hearing him, and even if she could she wouldn't listen to him. Daisy's lady of the manor act was in full swing, and she as blithely blind, or was it indifferent, to his feelings as she had ever been. She would call him if she wanted something, he realised. So Brian decided he must bow out. He had planned to stick around in order to be on hand should things turn unpleasant for her, but this behaviour would have tried the patience of a saint. Using the offer of a stay in an ashram in Scotland with some Buddhist friends, he took his leave of her, and besides a perfunctory sad smile and a childish wave, she barely acknowledged his departure.

Daisy met up with Jean in the old village coffee shop. Jean made no pretence at disguising her shock at how unwell Daisy looked.
"If you consider yourself to be a vegan ambassador, then think about the first impression you give to others. Skinny and stressed is reinforcing the stereotype, you know. Listen, you remember my helpers Andy and Chris, well we and a couple of my Para friends are renting a villa in Italy in order to do some seriously inspired writing. I've always known you have a book in you, you have such a gift for words Daisy. You could sit down and dedicate a month to writing down all your thoughts, all the great information you put so much effort into sharing with others. Then you'd have a book you could get printed and share with millions of people. The power of the pen, Daisy, just imagine it, your name in print and your message properly out there. Then it wouldn't be down to you day after day struggling to speak to a handful of people. It would be beyond the one person at a time, painstaking conversion you're so good at. More bang for your buck!"
Daisy's face wore a sceptical expression.
"It would be both/and, don't you see? Another string to your activist bow." Jean pressed on.

"No Jean, it's tempting, and I've always wanted to go to Italy. But I have commitments here."

"How about just going for part of the time then? Or going at the start and if you're really not flowing you could leave?"

"I know you care about me, Jean, and I appreciate the idea, but I can't just drop everything and disappear."

"Sweetie, when I had my accident I had no choice but to drop everything. You know, life has a way of forcing us to slow down or change direction if we don't do it voluntarily. You really are entrenched here, aren't you? I never would have thought you would struggle so long for your freedom just to stick your head into someone else's yoke."

"That's harsh and unfair, Jean. I don't want to fall out with you over it, but I'm not going to have you push me off a cliff like this. I'm living in a gorgeous place other people only dream of; I'm saving lives and caring for animals, why would I want to leave?"

"Because it's a trap, that's why. However gilded and ornate, a cage is still a cage."

Aha! Jean had clearly hit a major button there. Daisy's face clouded over, her lips narrowed to a thin pursed line, and she took in a long slow breath as if preparing to flame Jean with a fiery exhalation.

Instead she closed herself up like a book, stood up with a dismissive head shake, and finished the matter by saying, "It's been nice seeing you Jean, but I've got an appointment at three so must dash. Let's do this again sometime."

And with that, Daisy placed a kiss on top of Jean's head, grabbed her bag and exited as fast as she could.

Gilded cage indeed! All the way back, driving way too fast, Daisy became more and more angry with Jean. 'I shouldn't have let her speak to me like that. Just because she's in a wheelchair she thinks she can get away with saying whatever comes into her head. It's a known thing that these counsellors screw people up. I'm so cross with Jean for being so rude and pushy. In fact I'm beginning to wonder if she's a good therapist after all. The way she got me to write down all my secrets, telling me it would exorcise the demons and liberate my inner child. Well all it did was open up a terrible trauma and make me relive it again. I haven't got over it, and in fact I'm worse since she did that to me. At least before I was in a relationship, even if it was a horrible one with Neil. I've never been able to get involved with anyone since then.

Why are all my friends turning on me? They're obviously jealous. Idiots, when I wanted to share everything I've achieved with them. But no, they have to go off and have their own pitiful lives. And then have the cheek to come back and criticise my work. Who do they think they are? They've got no right to come poking around in my life. And with me being so busy and stressed as well. That's the last time I'm going to let them wind me up. That's it from now on. If they ring me I'll be permanently engaged. That Jean can take her unsolicited advice and give it to one of her boyfriends. And Brian has been hanging off my apron strings all these years, well I'm glad he's finally got himself a life, good luck to him. They can all go to hell'.

Daisy's ego was rearing and brewing up for a major tempest. Next to her in the passenger seat of the canary yellow two-seater sports car, Nancye the mastiff tried to appease the wrath of Daisy by licking her hand. Daisy yelled at her, "For God's sake Nancye, can't you see I'm driving, you stupid dog? I shan't bring you with me again, you can stay at home with the others." Daisy's foot pressed even harder on the accelerator, pushing herself to career round the upcoming hairpin bend faster than she ever had. The rear of the car slithered and skipped a little in protest, and she snatched aggressively at the steering wheel in response, causing one wheel to mount the kerb. She would dominate this infernal machine, in the same way as she had tried to enforce her control over Julian's horse, Frankincense, when she had ridden him. And cars didn't have feelings, so she wouldn't have to feel guilty about it.

Grimly attempting to power the car through the steep bend with maximum throttle power, rather than easing back, she felt herself approaching a threshold of power over force. The next moment the whole back end of the car had whipped round sideways, whilst the front wheels left the ground and in an instant she was ploughing backwards into a ditch. Nancye leaped from the car as the passenger door sprang open, and darted to the safety of some bushes. In fury Daisy screamed at her, "Cowardly dog! So you're deserting me now, well bugger off then you ungrateful creature!"

Then Daisy began to cry, tipped backwards there, looking and feeling ridiculous. She felt her hands begin to shake, and suddenly thought how close she might have come to killing herself. How very embarrassing, and Julian would not be at all pleased that his rare sports car had been damaged. Maybe it would have been easier if the ground had swallowed her up completely, then she wouldn't have to face everyone, wouldn't need to keep driving herself literally round the bend.

Blast it, she knew she shouldn't have taken the keys to the car that morning. She'd had a strong warning premonition about it, but stubbornly took it anyway. It was a lovingly restored, 1969 Porsche 911 in pristine condition, and she knew it was one of Julian's favourites. She didn't know how to deal with this. On the one hand she felt angry and resentful that a chunk of metal could have the power to reduce her to tears. And on the other she felt that Julian cared way too much about his possessions, and was greedy and avaricious because he had too much. Still, she reasoned that the way this accident was presented to him might cause some unfortunate backlash on her and her plans, and so would need diplomatic and sensitive handling. Definitely not her forte.

Taking her mobile out of her bag, she dialled her best friend. "Brian...." she wheedled, "I've been an overbearing bitch, haven't I? I'm sorry."

From the other end of the phone, Brian did not speak, but his outrush of breath was an affirmative.

"Well you didn't have to agree with me!" she pouted.

"What can I do for you?" Hearing his familiar caring voice, Daisy felt her bottom lip trembling against her will..... She hated crying in front of anyone, but she just couldn't help it. She felt so vulnerable, and hard done by, and misunderstood, and unsupported. And angry, and afraid. He hadn't even asked if she was hurt!

Driving too fast was the one thing that made her feel better, as if she was pushing back at the crushing forces opposing her. Exceeding the boundaries of safety made her feel in control of at least something in her life. Did that make sense? Brian said that he had taken up smoking because it helped him to feel in control of his death, which certainly didn't make sense, at least to Daisy.

"What does it matter which bloody car I pranged, Brian?" she had said, in answer to his question, just before he had agreed to come to her rescue. Mercifully he had arrived before the recovery vehicle appeared. Thank God he knew how to organise these things, for she was a jibbering mess. They sat close together in his old campervan.

Seeing her looking so thin and pale, he had to raise a smile from her. "It would be his favourite Porsche now wouldn't it, no half measures!" he chided gently.

"We're a screwed up pair of weirdo's aren't we, Daze" he said softly, daring to reach over and put his arm around her shoulder. She looked even more beautiful to him when she was being meek and sorrowful, than all ablaze and flashing her ruthless green eyes at him. Her customary spikey suit of armour, which normally kept him at arm's length at least physically, had fallen off. He was very tempted to take advantage of this and initiate intimacy between them, even though whenever this had happened before she had flamed him. It was as if she felt compelled to punish both herself and him for the forbidden lovemaking.

Whilst he was tousling between his conscience and desires, Daisy snuggled into his shoulder and began hugging him ever more insistently, like a small creature desperate to be held safe.

All of his protective instincts were fired up; he might have lost her forever in that car accident!

"You're coming back with me, we can sort out breaking the news to Julian in the morning" he said commandingly. This might be his last opportunity to express his love for her, to close the agonising gap between them which caused him so much pain. Maybe if he could reach through her fears and blocks with the strength and force of his adoration, he could heal her, by proving that he loved her so utterly and completely.

The tow truck was ready to leave, and Brian dealt with them, handing over the keys to the Porsche. Brian took full charge of Daisy for the first time in their association. He wanted her so desperately that it was excruciating to him, and he thought he was going to burst. Right there and then, everything came to this one point of intensity, and should it cost him his very life it would surely be worth it. And Daisy was responding to his gentle stroking hands, like a flower unfurling from a tightly shut bud. Her breathing became audible and deeper, like the sighing of the sea, as her body lost its rigidity, becoming sinuous and lithe. Her eyes were tightly shut, her mouth open, and she arched her back and wrapped her legs reflexively around him in a pinioning grip of passion. Bending to kiss her lips, his own eyes closed involuntarily, as the delicious scent coming from her engulfed his senses, and a dance of delight blurred away the line between them. He could not have held himself back now for anything; and she needed him, she wanted him, she demanded and commanded him to assert himself. The ecstasy of restraint, the responsiveness of his muscular body to her voluptuousness so exquisitely revealed and offering itself up, overwhelmed him. In the cadence of rising and falling, the cascade of crescendo and piercing sweetness, was their simultaneous, expansive vastness, and single-poised vanishing point. There was no separation, no agonising chasm holding them apart, there was only the perfection of oneness in joy filled flight.

Hours must have passed in a honeyed embrace, yet with a dreadful inevitability Daisy came to her senses, feeling a sickening remorse and embarrassment. Just before she reclaimed her personal territory, and re-exerted control over herself, Brian's beloved Jezebel held his gaze and whispered her love and gratitude to him. When she returned from her pee break outside in the dark roadside, it was the old familiar Daisy who came in, and coldly dismissed him with the words, "I've got to go, I never share my sleep space, you know that".

"You're not leaving now, it's late and you've had an awful shock. Please stay here and I promise not to come near you till the morning. Now get some sleep".

Poor Daisy, so tortured and torn within herself. So desperately sad that she had to hate whomever had the effrontery to breach her defences. He retreated to the driving seat, closed the curtains, and carefully, lovingly wrapped every precious moment of their lovemaking into an indelible tableaux that exceeded in beauty and splendour every work of art ever created. What a tragedy that she could never see herself through his eyes. How was it possible that she thought herself ugly, and fat, and unacceptable when she was quite simply the most perfect and gorgeous thing he had ever seen? What a cruel reversal of the truth, caused by her damaged past's cursing her life. Cursing his life too, for regardless of the cost to him he knew beyond any shadow of doubt that he was committed to her for ever, in so unconditional and un-severable a bond that it would stretch even beyond death.

The next morning as he awoke, Brian took some comfort from the fact that Daisy must love him really, because she never yelled at him for taking advantage of her vulnerability. As well she might, for he had come to her aid with the intention of getting his hands on her. It was as if she could only permit her guard to drop when she was in a bad way.

He tip toed in and placed a mug of black English breakfast tea next to her, retreating discreetly. Declining to shower, he determined to hold her scent upon his skin and her taste in his mouth as long as possible. Daisy, by contrast, could not wait to begin the process of expunging all evidence of their communion from herself. She scrubbed and splashed, scoured and scalded her poor mutinous body relentlessly in the tiny shower cubicle. Her ablutions continued for a very long time, before she emerged looking very pink and speechless. She was clearly needing to leave the crime scene rapidly, eschewing both eye contact and food. Even though every fibre of his being longed to touch her and hold her tenderly, to profess his undying devotion, to offer her whatever token of love it was in his power to give, he had learned from bitter past experience to leave her be. Determined to seal the bond between them before she scurried away, he did make some effort to engage her in conversation.

"How about allowing yourself a break, just for a while, from all of the activism? You could come back refreshed and renewed. With a new perspective, instead of being so strung out, stressed and exhausted, like you've been getting." Pressing his advantage he added, "We could go on a road trip somewhere, like we used to."

Daisy replied in a muted voice, "It sounds so very tempting to imagine that it's not all down to me to save everyone, that if I bowed out for a day or two the world wouldn't end. I do get that I've taken way too much upon myself for certain, yet perhaps because of this I feel pressurised to push on all the harder. I feel I'm barely moving as it is, and that if I let go I might lose my reins so to speak, or drop the whole bunch of sticks I've so painstakingly gathered into my fists..... I realise I'd be advising anyone else exactly what you're saying, but it's not easy counselling yourself, is it?" And at last for a brief moment she allowed her eyes to meet his.

"I don't want to see you get burned out Daisy..... you'll be no good to the animals then, will you?"

"Well, who can say? I might be better but in an entirely different way – we none of us know what's down the road, so we all just keep going the best we know how. And I do really appreciate your saying these things, just like I'm glad you're around for me; I don't know what I'd do if it wasn't for your support."

"That's OK, just remember, I am here for you, yes. But that doesn't necessarily mean I'll be able to go all the way with this Grange thing, it's far reaching, it has consequences, you know?"

Brian could tell that Daisy had already drifted off and away from listening to him, as she so often and so infuriatingly did. Starting the camper up, he drove his beloved cargo carefully back to where she wanted to go. Away from him.

Daisy thought that she should try to disconnect for a little while, meditate or something, because Brian wasn't wrong. Brian was never wrong, even though she couldn't admit it. Why can't I even make myself do some yoga, or just some stretches? Her body felt so alive and vibrantly glowing following the hastily denied, illicit night's adventures. I know it would help, so what's this wall of resistance I've got? But she had fallen into the classic trap of trying to think her way out of her thought prison by thinking all the harder about it. A similar bind to the time pressure one: no time to stop, and indeed the mere mention of time put the squeeze on even more. If it was anyone but herself Daisy would have said 'Deselect time pressure' in her familiar cheery way, but her nose was by now too well and truly up against the window of her own issues.

As they do, circumstances overtook her reverie, and the glum confrontation awaiting her with Julian over his damaged car. At least he had not yet objected to her having installed the ebullient Tristan in the apple loft above the stable block at the Coach House. Presumably his business interests prevented him from bothering to watch the recordings which were being made in his studio. Maybe he felt that Daisy and Tristan were welcome presences to at least partially plug the aching gap in his life which his daughter Clara would never again fill. Daisy could only imagine the pain of the loss of one's only child.

She was genuinely sorry for inconveniencing him, even though with his level of wealth surely the impact of her damaging one of his fleet of cars, all well insured, could not match the cost to a less financially buffered, poorer person. Tristan rationalised that such little accidents were actually positive, because they allowed some working person to have a paid task sorting them out. In his estimation, the only good thing about rich people was that they provided jobs for the rest of society. But he harboured a deep resentment of acquired wealth, second only to his disgust at inherited wealth. To him, all resources should be equally shared, and property was theft. So he justified their using the premises and facilities Julian generously provided by saying that to serve a revolutionary cause was the only rightful purpose of such things. Daisy thought this was taking advantage, and resented Tristan's suggestion that she make herself indispensable and further infiltrate herself into Julian's life.

Frankly, Tristan was becoming overbearing and lazy, and she had been wondering how to get him to move out. She never could handle confrontations, and it was her habit to watch out for a convenient event that she could take advantage of in order to bring about change. That way it wouldn't be her fault, or her doing, so she wouldn't have to feel guilty. Because guilt required punishment, and she knew what a dark alley that always led her down.

# CHAPTER 21

Jean had left innumerable messages for her, and Daisy was feeling extremely irked by the intrusiveness and tone of them. Jean had taken to simply appearing at the Lodge House and expecting to be entertained. Daisy was determined to put Jean in her place once and for all. She had made far too many allowances for her already, and frankly she was tired of being called on so frequently. If only she could think of a reason to have a terminal argument with her, as the excuse to get rid of her. Jean knew way too much personal information about her, and it was high time she was removed from the position where she felt she could just impose.

Maybe she could use Julian as the reason in some way? Why should she have to put up with seeing that annoying blue van, arriving unannounced? Might she get the self-opening gates changed so that she couldn't just drive in? She should never have given her a pass key! She would have to pretend to be so offended or upset that she asked for it back. That might work. In that case she'd better meet her one last time, and get it over with.

Daisy walked into the coffee shop to see Jean looking decidedly edgy. I'm not a hypocrite, so I won't give her a hug and kiss, she had already decided. Feigning exhaustion, she stopped short of the table and collapsed onto a chair. Before she could say anything, Jean blurted out, "Daisy I can tell that you aren't too happy to see me, and I want to apologise if you think I overstepped the mark by sleeping with Tristan."

"You WHAT? You really are an alley cat aren't you, just can't leave men alone!"

"That's a bit harsh isn't it? Sorry if he didn't tell you. He was only too happy to have sex with me, and you said yourself he was outrageously erotic. You're not jealous by any chance are you?"

"Me, jealous of you? Hardly..." and Daisy made a very unpleasant gesture of disdainful contempt.

But Jean had further ammunition with her, "It's not my fault that you're frigid. Neil never told you that he had been abused by his aunt when he was a boy, did he? But he told me. That's why he couldn't get any satisfaction when you were together. I thought you should know, it wasn't his fault he was like that."

A dangerous red mist of pure rage had risen up in Daisy, and she sprang to her feet and shouted, "I told you to never speak of him again! I warned you. I only ever gave you one rule and you've just broken it. That's it, you've stepped over the line and there's no trusting you. Give me back the gate key, you're not welcome at the Lodge ever again!"

Daisy held out her hand imperiously.

Driving home, Daisy felt deeply satisfied and relieved at how Jean had provided the perfect excuse to get rid of herself. Well that was surprisingly easy, she congratulated herself gloatingly. And I didn't resort to swearing or telling her what I really think of her, how controlled was that?

Stifling the little regret which was trying to speak, she thought to herself of all the new contacts she now had, and was going to make, and the new direction her life could take.

So, Tristan had been a naughty boy had he?

Well he'd be the next to be ousted.

She'd make sure of that.

# THE END

37213883R00132

Made in the USA
Charleston, SC
30 December 2014